TRA

Guy Woods

This paperback edition is published by:

Q Tank Press
64 Upper Mulgrave Road
Sutton, Surrey SM2 7AJ

Copyright © 2023
Guy Woods

Second edition

ISBN: 978-1-0684047-2-6

This novel is entirely a work of fiction. The names, characters and incidents portrayed in it are the work of the author's imagination. Any resemblance to actual persons, living or dead, events or localities is entirely coincidental.

Guy Woods asserts the moral right to be identified as the author of this work.

In loving memory of
Bob & Dorothy

Acknowledgements

I am grateful to many people who all, so kindly, took the time and trouble to read my drafts and provide me with invaluable feedback.

However, before I thank them by name, I must first thank Miss A2RW 80/3/. She knows who she is - though sadly I still don't, albeit not for want of trying to identify her. I moved into a house in 1990 and whilst unpacking belongings, I fell across a 1941 Collins Midget Gem Diary belonging to Miss A2RW 80/3/, which had self-evidently been lost in darkness and back of a high-up bedroom cupboard. It was my attempt to repatriate the diary with the owner or her surviving family that caused me to look through the diary carefully for clues to her identity. In the process the lives of some of those living in rural Shropshire in 1941 came alive and my curiosity was piqued regarding what was actually happening in the county during that difficult period of history. It was only once I decided to write this yarn, decades later, that it seemed entirely appropriate to base my story in her county during the period of time that she lived there.

As to those of us living in the 21st Century, I must express my considerable gratitude to a multitude of supporters, including Jane, Sheila, Philip, Gary, Claire, Simone, Lynne, Kate, Wendy, Giulia and Frank. Thank you for all your comments and recommendations. I hope that I have done them justice.

Chapter 1

Day One (Monday)   12th May 1941

It was only as she had cycled past the barn in Tibberton, at that moment, at that time of day, that she was fleetingly aware of a dim yellow light touching her right-side peripheral vision.

In surprise she had stopped so quickly that she had nearly catapulted herself over the handlebars. And then nearly fallen off the bike she straddled as she had quickly heaved and bounced the front wheel back around the way she had come and shuffled forward to crane her neck to peer again.

Four dim flashes every fifteen seconds. Surely not! And yet, there again, another four flashes, seven seconds of darkness and then four more flashes ... repeating ... four flashes every fifteen seconds.

All she needed was a watch and a ticket and she'd be transported back in time and place to Strumble Head near Fishguard, near where she grew up. But she did not need a timepiece, as the

Strumble Head lighthouse pattern was indelibly stamped and etched in her memory. Always demanding attention, dependable, ever comforting, ever watchful, Strumble Head's unique illuminations were woven into the fabric of her life. The lighthouse had been, from early childhood, her Protector: from storms; from anxieties of what her future might hold; from fears of annihilation. It had been her unquestioning and unquestionable closest friend, in whom she had confided and shared everything.

In truth she had almost missed the flashes – as usual, miles away in idle thought as she had cycled through the Shropshire countryside, where she now, a young woman in her early twenties, lived with her parents.

To begin with she wasn't sure what had caused the light, as its source was patently weak. Indeed, she wasn't sure if she had not simply seen a reflection of the rising sun on a mirrored surface of farm equipment. It also didn't help that it was quite a misty morning and that once the ground fog had burnt off it would turn into another bright sunny spring day.

But there had been just enough of the remnants of night to allow her to notice things before full daylight swamped all her senses.

However, it was definitely there, and it was generating that, so familiar, pattern of flashes, each quartet entreating her to anticipate, with slightly bated breath, the next, as she had so often done as a child.

Gradually she became increasingly certain that it came from artificial lighting: possibly from a lantern or from a torch? But why, as this was inland Shropshire, not coastal Pembrokeshire? And this was in almost daylight and a weekday!

Alice then happened to glance down at her watch and suddenly realised the time. She cussed herself aloud. 'Oh, botheration, just look at the time Alice Peters, Old Strumble will get you into trouble again if you don't get a shift on and get in to work. Those aircrew mouths won't feed themselves and you won't be able to buy that bloody lipstick you want for next week's dance if the canteen docks your pay for being late'.

Work at the local RAF airfield was her escape where she could feel normal – and unusual. It nourished her self-esteem and craving for independence and nurtured her sense of community at a time of crisis. Work was her route to expressing herself and how she wanted to be seen – not as an invalid surrounded by fit contemporaries all doing vital war work, or as a person who was unable to even be a Land Girl, but rather as someone noticed, appreciated, and valued in her own right and for her own modest contribution to the world that she inhabited. Well, that was her dream anyhow. The reality was that she prepared food, cleaned the canteen tables, and made gallons of tea every shift – but it helped to pay the bills and buy personal items, like cosmetics.

As she pumped her legs ever harder and hurtled around the bends of the narrow single-track, high-hedged, country road towards the RAF station at High Ercall, all she could think about was a clock and Margaret, the Canteen Manager, tetchily drumming her fingers on the tea urn. Alice was annoyed that she had overslept that morning and castigated herself that she had stayed up far too late the previous evening after going alone to the picture house to watch Henry Fonda in Wings of the Morning.

Eventually she reached the guard post at the main entrance to the air station. More just a wooden shack bolted onto which was a weighted barrier that could be raised or lowered by hand by sentries, it nevertheless served well as a control point and deterrent, discouraging unauthorised access.

Alice showed her pass to a lanky young lad on barrier duty that morning. She knew he was called Private Harris, that he was often on duty and that he never seemed to properly to fit his slightly over-sized, albeit well-pressed, uniform, What she also knew, much to her chagrin, was that he clearly had an eye for her and, tiresomely, repeatedly made a point of finding excuses to delay her passage onto the base so that he could either peacock and attempt to exert power over her, or secure almost any excuse to speak to her. Consequently, over the past few months Alice had had to develop ways to deal with his incessantly uninvited overtures.

This morning was to be no different to any of the other mornings whenever he was on duty.

He began moves to oblige her to dismount and sign the Visitors Book that he had earlier, deliberately, and inconveniently, placed on a trestle table right at the back of the Guard Room hut.

Unfortunately for him on this particular morning, because she was nearly an hour late for work, Alice was primed, ready for battle and quite unwilling to play his ridiculous games.

Acting as well as any film star, she gushed her apologies, saying that she couldn't stay to chat, claiming, with theatrical aplomb and considerable fiction, that there was a bit of a flap on and that she urgently needed to get to Hut Mike. She desperately hoped he would expedite her access and gambled on him being impressed that she was security cleared to visit Hut Mike, recognised by everyone serving on the air station as the most mysterious and secretive building of all of them with its own protective sandbags, guards, barbed wire and antennae. That Alice didn't actually know anything about Hut Mike was not the point – all she needed was for Private Harris to wave her through security as quickly as possible.

For good measure and playing on him being a bit soft on her, Alice flashed the soldier her brightest, warmest, of smiles, while cocking her head on one side allowing her long locks of fair hair to cascade over her shoulder, in certain knowledge that doing so would knock him off balance.

She was right! Confronted all at once by beauty, mystery, and war duty, he capitulated.

'OK Miss,' he conspiratorially replied, 'but you make sure, mind, that you're here tomorrow by 0730 promptly. New access procedures now. It's gonna take longer to sign in from tomorrow, you understand because of the extra security procedures. And because of yer, well, you know what ...' His voice tailed off and he nodded his head towards the ground around her feet.

Alice tried not to roll her eyes in exasperation. In her head she asked the Good Lord for salvation. She knew full well what he was referring to but just did not have the patience that morning to humour him. So instead, she elected to fight fire with fire, even though she was running late.

'And what exactly do you mean by *"because of yer, well, you know what..."*, Private Harris? Are you, by any chance referring to the fact that I have one short leg and one weak leg and a general lack of physical fitness from viral lung damage contracted from polio in childhood – and so I don't have the same mobility that you are blessed with? Is that your point Private Harris? Though I cannot imagine for a moment what my physical disabilities have to do with signing into the darn air station tomorrow morning?'

Alice could see immediately that the hapless guard realised that he had put if foot in it. He just stood to attention before her, his mouth silently opening and closing with no noise emerging, like a goldfish wanting food. Fleetingly she felt a bit guilty duping him, but not long enough either to capitulate or reveal her compassion – she simply had to get to work, and she intended that nothing would get in the way.

She decided not to wait for a reply when it was evident from the guard's face rouging, and from his complete inability to form words, that she would not get further sense from him. With the clock still ticking, she quickly got back onto the saddle of her bike, glowered at him one final last time, and made a play of showing him the security pass that was hanging around her neck. She then gingerly walked and nudged the front wheel of her bike forward until she could duck under the half-raised barrier. Instantly she set off, peddling furiously towards the Canteen, avoiding people, lorries, and cars until she was able to screech to halt and throw her bike at the outside of the Canteen's wall and barge into the storeroom by its side door.

Propelling herself forward with such urgency, she almost fell into the building, initially, noisily, crashing into a mop and bucket that had been carelessly left out, blocking the narrow passageway. She then had to sidestep a pile of sack potatoes that appeared to be gradually collapsing uncontrollably into the passageway under its own weight, and then twist left to press her back against the wall and breath in as she shuffled with small crab-like steps towards the main hall so as to avoid two sets of poorly stacked boxes of dry food that had also encroached onto the floor of the side door access route.

Eventually she emerged from the side passage into a poorly lit lobby edged variously with metal cupboards, clothing pegs, and metal shelving, crammed from floor to ceiling with boxes of assorted colours and shapes.

In a single sweeping motion, she threw off her coat, grabbed her apron from one of the pegs, barged through the nearest door and landed, body and soul, in the main hall of the Canteen, just behind the tea urn, already smiling for the customers.

Alice's lungs were scorched with the exertions of the morning, and it took all her concentration to control her breathing and not reveal to anyone that she felt exceptionally de-oxygenated.

For five minutes, at least until her body calmed, she prayed that nobody in the room wanted much more from her at that exact moment than a 'Good Morning' or a fixed smile.

Chapter 2

And so began yet another day in the NAAFI Canteen of RAF High Ercall, a small airfield in rural Shropshire, that for the previous three years had concerned itself with maintaining aircraft – but which was now the home of Fighter Command.

To avoid Margaret's withering look when she finally caught her manager's eye, Alice busied herself, as she did every shift, preparing refreshments, serving them, keeping the Canteen stocked and clean while also taking turns in a small NAAFI kiosk selling tobacco and confectionery and other such rare pleasures. She knew only graft and penance would save her skin and her modest £1 14s 6d weekly pay packet from being docked, given that it hadn't been the first time she had been late to work.

Helen, one of the other girls on the shift who had joined the Canteen staff around the same time as Alice was her usual suggestive and friendly self, as they stocked the servery with sandwiches.

'Well, whoever you went to the flicks with last night must have been worth it Al. Come on, I want names, places, and details. It wasn't one of those Young Farmers, was it? What's his name, Gerald? Cor, what I wouldn't give for an hour on the back row under the projectionist's loom with that specimen, heh heh heh'.

Helen's accompanying suggestive actions with her arms and body and pushed out chest tipped both women into fits of giggles.

Margaret growled from the other side of the servery. 'Don't encourage her Helen, Alice is on borrowed time, I remind you two ladies, ever since the base was reconfigured for fighters, that night operations have increased – as have aircrew and ground staff numbers, all wanting tea and snacks, all the time, including in the middle of the night. If you want your shifts to be night shifts the whole time then I can easily fix that,' she warned.

Previously a quiet station, now it was Blenheims, Beaufighters, Hurricanes and Havocs filling the skies above the base in response to the night-time raids by the Luftwaffe over London and the concern that the Blitz bombing, which had been crippling the city and other urban and industrialised locations, would only increase and geographically expand.

As a result, the Canteen staff had to work far harder to keep filling the servery shelves and stomachs of the hordes of aircrew, engineers and ground teams who constantly poured through their doors for sustenance and down time.

'You wouldn't change the shifts to do that Margaret .... would you?' Alice hesitantly asked, hoping that she was only joking.

The Canteen Manager bent down and peered at both Helen and Alice through the carvery's shelving, 'Try me, if you dare! You girls had it far too easy before the airfield reconfiguration with your NAAFI shifts always ending at sundown. I can tell you it is quite a struggle now for me to cover the clock, even having divided you all into four shifts to cover every 24-hour period. Just remember, duty aircrew are now on just 30-minutes notice to fly and so we, like them, must respond to the operational needs of the base.'

Helen and Alice grimaced in unison. They both knew the Canteen was short-staffed, particularly in the dark hours when most of the cleaning and re-stocking from stores needed to be done while the operational crews were airborne and while the Canteen itself was, at least in theory, a little quieter.

Helen mumbled to Alice out of Margaret's earshot, 'Gosh Al, the boss almost sounds serious. Nights are exhausting enough without adding extra night shifts to our rotas. I don't know about you, but I actually find this job emotionally exhausting enough on top of the physical graft that we have to put in – particularly in the night hours. And I, for one, certainly don't want extra nights.'

Alice glanced across to check that the Canteen Manager had disappeared from the servery and that their conversation would remain private. 'I agree. I know it's not exactly a difficult job, but it's

11

demanding of time and of emotional energy. Don't we always have to show our best side to the crews? Always presenting a cheerful and respectful face, especially when some aircrew never return?'

'Yup, that gets through to me too,' Helen concurred, 'Just when we all that hot swords have been plunged through each of our hearts. I know it's not all the time or every returning sortie, but it is often enough – and it's primarily the night shift staff who have to deal with the men when they return before dawn.'

Alice agreed again, 'I confess Helen I get quite anxious whenever I am about to go on the night shift. I desperately will the nights to pass quickly and without incident … if they can …'

Her words tailed off as memories of miserable shifts flooded her mind, and she recalled sad nights when some sorties had resulted in multiple aircraft losses and forlorn and exhausted airmen slumped over teacups deep in their own thoughts.

Helen stopped what she was doing, turned, and touched Alice's hand without speaking, simply nodding and grimacing in agreement with what Alice had just said, both women holding back tears, each recalling faces and characters who would never be seen again.

To stop herself crying, Alice busied herself for the next hour sorting out what stocks she needed to order for the NAAFI shop and helped to prepare some of the food for the next shift, in between checking levels of the water in the tea urns. However, her mind was just not fully on the job that morning for some inexplicable reason.

She initially put her agitation down to the fact she had been late for work. Or had it been her fractious exchange with Private Harris that that had caused her to feel distracted, or even had it been the shared confessions with Helen?

But, as the morning progressed, that early sense of fluster did not diminish, and so next she wondered if her monthly cycle had arrived early, or that she had, worryingly, picked up a chest infection – which would be another blow to her efforts not to let her polio define her.

She nipped into the staff toilet and squeezed past all the cleaning buckets and draped coats and took her temperature with a thermometer that she always carried with her. She also checked her pulse. All her vital signs were entirely normal.

So, still perplexed, she went back out into main hall and then, just as she reached the servery counters to check again what needed filling, it suddenly hit her that her edgy feeling had actually been caused by the completely unexpected recollection of the Strumble Head light pattern earlier in the morning – and that it had been this that had been gnawing away at her subconscious.

The very thought of the lighthouse brought Alice an unexpected evocation of warm memories of Pembrokeshire, of a stable family life and happy youth, of the small and busy coastal town of Fishguard and recollections of the calming Llys-y-Fran reservoir, its local community of people and unpronounceable names.

She mused that her blessed childhood and life back then was in stark contrast to the life that she now led and the jeopardy that she now suffered in

Shropshire – under constant threat of being bombed to death while being surrounded by people who caused and endured death daily.

All of a sudden, she woke from her Welsh reverie – and very much to her own surprise, because not only was it out of character for her to seek public notice but she also hadn't been planning to speak – Alice Peters found herself blurting out a question for anyone in the Canteen to answer.

'Excuse me gents, but does anyone know what four flashes mean?'

The whole of the cavernous room went silent and every face turned towards her. Immediately Alice flushed, feeling hot with embarrassment. For a moment she did not fully understand why everyone was looking at her, and then realised, in utter shock, what she had just done … and suddenly craved for the ground to swallow her up.

Two men, one civilian and the other in army uniform, seated a couple of tables away, stopped talking together in hushed tones and swivelled in their seats to face Alice. Two air crew who had been standing chatting to a seated crewman on a table at the far end of Canteen straightened up, looked at her with bemusement and then each shrugged their shoulders and pointed to their ears to indicate they were foreign and did not understand what she was saying. A couple of junior RAF maintenance engineers piling sandwiches onto their plates at the servery glanced up, quietly exchanged, presumably salacious, words between themselves and then

14

burst into hysterical laughter before earnestly resuming their foraging mission.

Alice knew her face must be puce with her sudden and inappropriate public verbal outburst. She now desperately hoped that someone would respond and castigated herself for not staying silent.

The army officer seated at the closest occupied table replied for the room. 'Before anyone rotten asks you in what language, or makes any suggestive comment concerning your question ...' he pointedly eye-balled the two RAF engineers who in turn dipped their heads in embarrassment and shuffled off as fast as they could to the till to pay for their food with, '... may we ...' he nodded meaning himself and, to his right, his civilian companion too '... know what you mean by your question? What is flashing?'

Alice was immensely relieved that someone had responded. 'A light, sir,' she replied simply.

This time it was the turn of the civilian acquaintance of the army officer to speak. 'What sort of light? In the air, or at ground level?'

Alice's attention was immediately drawn to the civilian's sparkling eyes, his wry smile and his beautifully rich Welsh-timbred, accent. Momentarily breathless and praying that he had not noticed, she quickly composed herself.

'Ground and I suppose, presumably, a lantern or a torch maybe?' she hopefully intoned.

'Rapid flashes?' asked the civilian.

'Steady flashing rate. Flash, flash, and so on and then darkness.' Alice used her right hand to simulate the flashes, cutting the air with her hand as she spoke. She, however, elected not to share that there was a pattern of flashes and darkness because she now felt very exposed with everyone looking at her and listening in on the conversation.

'H.'

'Sorry?' Alice replied, bemused.

The civilian drew a deep breath and spoke at machine-gun speed. 'It's the letter H in Morse Code. Four short flashes. If it is Morse Code that is. It cannot be four long flashes because such a grouping does not exist in Morse for either letters or numbers. Why are you asking?' he demanded.

'Just keeping your Morse Code skills up to speed, sir,' she cheekily flung out in quick, panicky, retort instead. 'Lesson Two next shift.'

Then, immediately, Alice lost her confidence realising that she would look a complete idiot trying to explain in public why she wanted to know – and what any of it had to do with lighthouses. Inside her head she dived for cover under a blanket ... while staying, just a little bit, intrigued by the civilian's self-evident knowledge of Morse Code.

The civilian stifled a smirk and briefly cocked his head on one side to acknowledge her while the army officer shrugged his shoulders and indicated to his table companion that they needed to get back to what they had been talking about before being interrupted. Which they then did.

However, the eyes of the civilian only left Alice when she finally decided to take fright and grab a calming breather outside the Canteen in the fresh air.

Chapter 3

Both Helen and Alice stayed out of Margaret's way for most of the remainder of their shift, knuckling down to their work, interspersing it whenever they could with humorous anecdotes, laughter, and almost constant friendly chatter.

When the shift ended, they set off together on their bikes for The Plough pub in Crudgington, a short distance away and the closest pub to the airfield, where the monthly pub social and skittle evening for all off duty Canteen staff was taking place.

'Did you go to the last one Al, I can't remember?' Helen asked as they cycled side by side along the lane.

'Yes, I was there, don't you recall, I accidentally poured a pint of cider all over the Group Captain's new driver when he made the mistake of trying to wiggle past me for the toilets just at the very moment I swung round from the bar with a full tray of drinks? Er, he wasn't too impressed that his highly polished shoes took a shower. I am not sure he has yet forgiven me, although in my defence I would say it wasn't my fault because my arm was jogged by someone standing at the bar.'

'That's your story, is it?' Helen asked sceptically and in jest.

'Oh Helen, you're a wicked stirrer." Alice replied in kind. They both laughed.

'Talking of wicked, what's with you and that good-looking bloke you were chatting up in the Canteen this morning? All that talk of flashing and such forth, you old dark horse you!'

'Helen, you really are wicked! You're so naughty!' Alice shrieked in delight and embarrassment in equal measures.

Helen laughed. 'Well, there's not much else going on around here, so we need to get our entertainment whenever we can!'

'Oh goodness I suppose I deserve a ragging. Actually, I wish I hadn't said anything now,' Alice confided. 'The thing is I came across a strange thing this morning. On my way into work.'

Helen sensed that Alice wanted to say more and so encouraged her to do so. 'So ... what happened?'

Alice hesitated, momentarily not knowing where to start her explanation. 'You know I grew up in deepest Wales, don't you?'

'Well, I know you have mentioned in the past living near Fishguard. Plus, you have a funny Welsh accent!'

Alice stuck her tongue out at her friend, who smirked in response.

'Well, I grew up near the Llys-y-Fran reservoir in a tiny hamlet called New Moat, near a town called Haverfordwest. You've probably not heard of any of these names before, unless, of course, you have been there. They are all in the south-western corner of the country.'

'I've heard of one of the names, but I confess I don't know much about the geography of the area. What's the relevance?'

Alice pondered how she would explain away the Strumble Head connection with any clarity.

'What you don't know is that school had been in Haverfordwest while my formative teenage years had been spent on buses and bicycles to places like Fishguard and St Davids on the coast. The point is that, for years, I have watched the ferries leaving Fishguard for Ireland always with an intense envy and longing to finish school so that I could start my life to escape rural boredom. I guess like all kids I simply wanted to begin to taste and enjoy the mysteries of what lay beyond the horizon.'

'You, me and thousands of others at the same age Al,' Helen sighed, in a matter-of-fact way, 'but I still don't see what any of this has got to do with something that happened this morning on your way into work.' She sensed that Alice still had more to say and so nudged her to keep her talking.

'This is all going to sound very silly,' Alice retorted.

'I'm sure it won't ……. when you finally get around to explaining things!' she said pointedly.

Alice glanced sideways at Helen who circled her hand to invite Alice to continue.

'OK then ……' Alice took a deep breath, '…. but don't laugh or think me weird.'

19

Helen put her head on one side and sighed in slight exasperation, 'I won't Al, I promise.'

Alice briefly hesitated again before plucking up courage to finish her story.

'So, growing up in the area had been glorious fun, but in truth the rides on the bike or in buses to chase my horizons were usually ridden alone. And it was my trips to Fishguard that first introduced me – and then caused me to fall in love with the Tresiwen and Trefasser coastline there – and particularly to fall in love with the Strumble Head lighthouse, as strange as that sounds.'

'It does sound strange for sure.' Helen acknowledged, under her breath.

Alice continued. 'If you don't know it, Strumble Head is a pretty imposing structure standing on St Michael's Island just to the west of Fishguard. It's separated from the mainland by a very narrow gap through which the sea boils and froths in stormy conditions. I haven't ever told many people this, but I used to stand for hours looking past the lighthouse, out to sea, musing how many ships had struck rocks there before it was constructed – and since. Cumulatively I have probably spent months of my life marvelling at the unfettered power of the sea, driving up the rock and up the face of the lighthouse and up behind it through the narrow channel to its rear. It's probably the inner engineer in me but I have always been thrilled and quite inspired by the fact that humans were taming this unstoppable force with simple pullies and weights. I am sure you don't know, but every twelve hours a huge weight has to be re-wound to the top of the lighthouse so it can drop to the bottom and keep the light's turntable rotating – helping seafarers to navigate the treacherous coastline as they transit south-west towards South Bishop, or north-east up the Irish Sea towards Scotland and the North Channel separating Ireland from the Scottish mainland. It's amazing!'

Helen raised her eyebrows, surprised by Alice's detail and passion, 'Wow, so you're in love with a phallus! Tell me something about a good looking twenty something woman that I am not able to guess!'

'No Helen!' Alice shrieked and leaned over and gently slapped her friend on the arm, 'I am not in love with a ... well, you know what .... but with the sense of comfort and familiarity that I have grown up with at Strumble Head.'

'And your point is...?' Helen asked, her voice trailing off, still not clear why her friend's mention of a particular lighthouse was either important or relevant.

'This morning I encountered something making a light pattern that exactly matched the light pattern of the lighthouse that I am awfully familiar with. The point is that if I hadn't been so familiar with that light pattern, I am sure that I would never have noticed the lights this morning at all. It was the familiar pattern that triggered recognition in me.'

'You said lights.' Helen corrected.

'Well probably light, singular ... probably ...well, what I mean is that there was a pattern of lights from one light ... and that pattern I recognised and recalled from my youth. And

21

that's what I was asking about in the Canteen don't you see,' Alice urged, 'as I don't have a clue about signalling patterns or Morse Code or any of that stuff that military people all seem to know about.'

By this time Helen and Alice had reached the pub. They both dismounted their bikes without speaking and leaned them against the wall.

Helen was nodding clearly in deep thought processing what Alice had just told her, while Alice held her breath waiting for a response. 'Seems to me Al, that you're doing the right thing asking around as you are, but it will probably end up being something inconsequential in the end. But I agree, I suppose, that there's no harm in asking about.'

She didn't sound too convinced though Alice felt.

'But there's far more immediate and important fish to fry this evening old girl. Like let's get this skittles match on the road ...' and with theatrical point of her right hand towards the pub, Helen propelled her body forward to shove open the pub's door with both hands and enter it, closely following by Alice, more scuttling than striding.

Chapter 4

The moment Alice and Helen walked through the entrance of The Plough, the civilian's eyes were back on Alice.

Unaware that she was being scrutinised, Alice nudged her way through a cheerful throng of Hawker Hurricane pilots from No. 247 Squadron who had just arrived at the airfield and were starting to work with the Blenheims of No. 68 Squadron to deliver coordinated night patrols against the growing threat of the Luftwaffe night bombing raids.

She spotted another of her colleagues, Dorothy, waved at her and then attempted to navigate a route through the bodies to reach her, saying sorry to everyone she encountered who was in her way. In her line of sight, she suddenly spotted the civilian staring straight back at her. He grinned and waved. Alice immediately blushed. Twice in one day!

She sidled up to him and apologising, Mea cupla, but I was actually waving to my friend Dorothy.'

'In which case I'm offended,' the civilian replied.

'What?' Alice queried, bringing herself up short because she did not understand what the man was saying.

'Well, given that we already know each other...' he expressed himself with an assured Welsh tone.

'—But I don't, we don't—' Alice was about to protest. He cut in, clearly keen to engage her.

'My name is Ray by the way, Ray Thomas. I am a linguist and interpreter. I assist the Czech aircrews flying out of Ercall.' He held out his hand for her to shake gently, which she did.

'Nice to meet you Ray. I am Alice Peters from the Canteen. And for the record, in my experience the Czech aircrew don't need any assistance whatsoever!'

Ray laughed. Her comment had tickled him. 'Nice to meet you too, Alice-Peters-from-the-Canteen.'

Alice decided to take charge of the situation. 'While it's nice to bump into to you, I actually need to get over to Dorothy over there who seems to be waiting for me, rather impatiently I think.' She pointed towards Dorothy.

Ray looked over his shoulder to see Alice's colleague beckoning her, although her friend wore a huge smile and had raised eyebrows and was giving Alice a very knowing look.

'Please don't let me keep you Alice-Peters-from-the-Canteen – for now at least. Perhaps we could arrange our own drink another day, that is, of course, only if you would like to?'

Alice put her hands on her hips and took a step back to look at Ray, initially overtly and theatrically to size him up, but also, in a manner she had never ever done before, boldly and without inhibition to display herself to him, like a creature in the animal kingdom performing the first moves in a mating ritual.

Slowly, thoughtfully, and gently she answered him, 'Yes, I would like that.'

Their eyes locked.

She did not know why, but she continued to stand her ground and stare him out. 'And it was a repeating pattern of four, by the way, like Strumble Head.'

Ray, imperceptibly, juddered slightly and hunched forward to speak quietly in Alice's ear. Her gossamer hairs rioted the instant they detected his warm breath.

'Really?' he, equally slowly, responded in a contemplative way. 'In which case we need to be guided by our Welsh lighthouse, don't you ... tomorrow after work?'

She stepped back a pace and held his gaze again, pretending to decide.' I can't do tomorrow, or the day after. Sorry. But I was planning to meet some friends in here at 5 pm on Thursday for a drink. You would be more than welcome to join us, that's, of course, only if you would like to,' she parroted.

He smiled. 'So, Thursday evening you say?'

Alice had fully stopped breathing.

'That sounds simply perfect,' he lied.

Alice started breathing again, all the while the two of them locked in on each other's faces, taking each other in.

She then excused herself and joined Dorothy. Just as she entered the skittle alley she glanced over her shoulder, only to see Ray fast disappearing out of the pub entrance. Alice shrugged her shoulders slightly and turned towards the bowling alley for an evening of fun.

Chapter 5

Alice didn't stay at The Plough for long.

Her unexpected encounter with Ray had distracted, intrigued, and excited her in equal measure.

She felt her axis had been rocked seeing him there and almost immediately felt an inexplicable urge, nay urgency, to find out more – anything she could – about the man before meeting him again.

This meant that she was not the greatest company during the evening, more going through the motions and pretence of enjoying herself than having the good time that she normally did at the social evenings.

When she wasn't taking her turn at the bowling alley bowling at the pins, she found herself in quite a distant and distracted space, feeling that she was a spectator listening in to everyone's conversations through a thick wall rather than being a social participant in the room.

And her mind was flitting, flooded with ten thousand questions. She found herself totally absorbed thinking about Ray and visualising his facial features. She wondered what had brought him to the air station – and how long he might now be around. She audited the day and her two encounters with him, asking herself whether, perhaps, she had misinterpreted their conversations. Repeatedly she tried, unsuccessfully, to work out why she felt so, discombobulated. She wanted to know if it had been coincidence that he had been at the pub – and how long he had been there before she arrived. She wanted to know if he knew she would be there. She wondered who he had gone to the pub with. She wanted to know why he had picked The Plough in particular. She also wondered why he had left so immediately after she had spoken to him. She even wondered why he hadn't bumptiously attempted to muscle in on the Canteen social in the bowling alley, like most males she knew would have done once they had got beer inside them and sensed a date was on the cards.

About three quarters of the way through the evening Alice made her polite excuses, thanking Margaret for the event and privately intimating to Helen and Dorothy that her monthly cycle was to blame for not being up to par and needing to get off home reasonably early.

As she'd cycled back to her lodgings trying to work out how she could learn more about Ray, she hit upon a way to identify him, but which could only be achieved if she was willing to allow young Private Harris on the Main Gate to chat her up again – if he ever had the gall to do so again. Although the prospect of having to suffer Private

Harris' attention was unattractive, to put it mildly, the prospect of digging up information on Ray Thomas felt thrilling and far easier to justify hardship – and so she vowed to go into work early again the following morning and to bite her lip to give herself time to find out what she wanted to know. There was now a new visitor registration regime in place she recalled Private Harris mentioning to her earlier in the day – and she was determined to make it work for her!

Further along the road to her family's lodgings she also attempted to analyse why, exactly, Ray's appearance on the scene had so affected her.

She conceded that ever since she had first shown signs of physical frailty, which was later was declared a disability and diagnosed as polio, she had been forced into the background and treated differently – all too frequently, less equitably than her able-bodied friends. It had been like that at school in Wales growing up and was not largely different now as a young woman yearning to carve out her own future. She especially recalled painful memories of life as a child, enviously watching the bodies and characters of her schoolfriends strengthen and blossom while she herself was obliged to engage her world from the side-lines – more commonly or not from a chair or via hospital treatment rooms.

Bizarrely, she pondered whether the enjoyment she had got from visiting Fishguard, loving the sea, and watching people start journeys to unknown horizons all those years ago, had possibly even been a perverse form of jealousy, even though she never thought herself to be a jealous person. Ever since he spoke to them when she was a young girl, the words of her much-loved Uncle Frank echoed in her mind and resonated with her daily – that at sea there are neither roads nor signposts but an almost unlimited number of ways of getting from one place to another. And that navigation begins with knowing where you are starting from. His words had always stuck with her – kindling hope deep inside and nourishing her ambitions.

She stopped just short of her house and breathed in the early night-time air, marvelling, as she always did, at the display of majestic stars twinkling in the skies above. Her ride back home had been cathartic and liberating and just what she had needed.

It was all clear to her now.

Convention meant that most people didn't notice people like her with disabilities, as ability was all too often predicated upon someone's physical prowess, on their body shape, or on having an ability to climb a rope or run a distance in a particular time interval. It did not occur, let alone matter, to many people that those carrying a disability had other skills too – and frequently considerably greater insight and resilience that many of their able-bodied contemporaries.

But Ray did. He didn't care about her disability, that's if he had even noticed it. He didn't care that she was a Canteen Assistant. He had clearly spotted something in her to spark an interest, which Alice sensed was far more than merely trying to gather information on a mystery light pattern. Plus, he was Welsh and somewhat good looking!

And it dawned on Alice that her mind and body had, subliminally, already processed all this, and decided that she should have no inhibitions or anxieties in his company.

As she unlocked the front door to her house she smiled – proud of herself and, for the first time in a long while, very contented and unshackled.

Chapter 6

Day Two (Tuesday)   13th May 1941

Shadows caused by sunlight hitting the four radio masts cut through the early morning spring fog to create sharp grey lines at ground level reaching off into the distance. As the sun rose higher in the sky so the shadow lines slowly began to rotate anticlockwise and shorten until the mist was burnt off completely and the shadows had all but disappeared. The masts were each approximately 30 feet tall and arranged to mark out the corners of a square approximately 20 feet x 20 feet, each mast topped with a small crown of 8 metal prongs orientated parallel to the ground.

What passers-by could not see was that the four masts were linked together with cabling chamfered into the ground that snaked back through a rear access point to back room of a large classic red-brick Edwin Lutyens residence set in magnificently designed grounds, to an airless and humid back room in which was installed an oscilloscope and seated at which was an operator with headphones on.

The squirrels running along the branches of trees in the garden and the moles burrowing under the lawn gave passers-by a very false picture of calm that morning. It had been a long night for everyone at the Whitchurch signals intelligence Y-station, one of approximately 50 in Britain and some 600 worldwide.

Overnight there had been three separate waves of Luftwaffe bombers and support fighters entering British airspace. The pressure had been relentless throughout the dark hours with the Y-station staff having to identify individual aircraft crossing the North Sea coast attacking Birmingham targets: listening to the pilots talking; working out the compass bearing of each aircraft using a clever analysis of signal strength; and then tracking their bearing movements so information could then be passed to Fighter Command for its use in helping, in as near real time as possible, to triangulate their actual positions and vector in its air defence counter-attacks.

The Station Manager, a long-served Foreign Office official, was weary. His radio operators were weary. His technicians were weary. And the support staff and secretaries who had spent the night relaying data to Arkley View in Barnet for collation and onward dispatch to the Government Code and Cypher School at Bletchley Park were also exhausted. Everyone knew that daybreak offered some respite because the number of air raids were less in daylight than at night.

It was currently 0543. Satisfied that everyone had pulled together overnight and excellent service had been given both to Fighter Command and to Bletchley Park, the Station Manager had just done a set of rounds to check that everyone was OK in all the departments on the site – a location with thirty technical, operational, and non-technical staff. He had decided to wait for the watch change at 0600 before returning to his nearby digs for a much-needed sleep. He had only just settled in his office chair with a steaming brew of tea when his telephone rang.

'Tug Parsons here Sir, can you please come to the huff-duff at once. We have just picked Yankee Four Six One transmitting again.' He had used the familiar name for the high frequency radio intercept and direction-finding equipment.

The Station Manager leapt up knocking over his mug of tea onto the floor and was already heading for his office door still holding the handset to his ear.

'Are you sure? Same frequency, same azimuth bearing?' he asked.

'Same, same.' Tug replied.

The Station Manager let the handset drop towards the floor without replacing it, only for it to be saved from hitting the wooden floorboards by its fixed cable length. He then ran fast along a corridor and through two small rooms housing other electronic equipment into the Intercept Room and straight up to a position behind the operator, alongside Tug.

Three faces now stared intently at the oscilloscope. But there was nothing showing by the time he had arrived.

'It's another burst transmission. Lasted ...' Tug looked down at the operator's notes that he was pointing to with his pencil, '... 12 seconds this time. As usual Morse, not voice. Started at 0545 on the nose. The transmission frequency was, again, 5.72 MHz. Best bearing, again, south-east of here between 152 and 170 degrees. But unfortunately, there wasn't enough transmission time to detect it and refine the bearing. Signal strength was Four.'

Tug look up apologetically to the Station Manager.

'Same time as before? What about the signal strength – same too?'

Tug walked over to consult a logbook on a table in the corner of the small room. 'No, not exactly the same time, though, looking at its transmission history, we do seem to be seeing most transmissions from Yankee Four Six One before 9 o'clock on the days it transmits. And they all seem to come from that compass sector, every time. The signal strength seems to oscillate between Four and Seven – never less than Four and never more than Seven.'

The Station Manager was pensive.

'Can you please contact the Y-stations at Newbold Revel near Rugby, east-south-east of us, and Stockland Bristol, south-south-west of us down in Bridgewater, to see if either establishment caught a sniff of this morning's transmission. If they did and managed to capture their own huff-duff bearings, we might stand a chance of triangulating this bloody radio and stand a better chance of understanding if it is transmitting from a fixed location or if it's moving about. Oh, and get details from them of any previous huff-duff records of it over time since we first detected it to see if we can narrow down the intercept bearings.'

With that instruction the Station Manager marched out of the Intercept Room back to his office.

Once there, he quickly surveyed the carnage of the tea and telephone wreckage he had caused only moments beforehand and went to the staff kitchen to clear up the spilt liquid, replacing the heavy black Bakelite handset back in its cradle.

Immediately he picked up the phone again and asked the operator to put him through to a Welshpool telephone number. He drummed his fingers on his desk while he was being connected and looked out of the window to check the state of the weather outside. He was not meteorologist but reckoned it was going to be lovely day once the mist burnt off, which annoyed him a bit because he knew he would have first to sleep off the night's labour and miss much of the day's sunshine.

Eventually he was through to Welshpool on the line.

'Is that Ray? Hello Ray, good morning to you too. Yes, it's Clive here. You were busy last night too with the three raids I presume … yes … it was full on, wasn't it.'

The Station Manager wished that he still had tea in his mug that he could supp. 'Look old fruit, I have called you because we have again intercepted another burst transmission from Yankee Four Six One ... yes ... the same bearing sector and signal strength. Did you chaps pick it up at 0545 this morning too ... you did, excellent ... and captured the full morse message ... perfect.'

On the other end of the line Ray Thomas was gingerly perched on the edge of his desk in his small office located on the Criggion Hills. He too was checking the weather looking through a single, small, barred, window in front of him. He had only been passing his office when the telephone had rung, and so he was now leaned over talking on the handset plumbed into a telephone situated on the far side of the desk, almost lying upon various piles of paper and reports strewn across the desktop.

Ray liked Clive Bridgeman who he thought was a good leader with decent peripheral vision and a healthy considered approach to most things, 'It's OK Clive, we will flag up to Station X the need to prioritise for analysis our capture of transmissions between 0540 and 0550 and let it sort the wheat from the chaff in terms of the analysis of the encrypted content. As for localisation, well, as you know, your Major Burton and I have been discussing a plan to use his vehicle-based intercept aerials and equipment and move the kit around our region at the times we predict that transmissions will be taking place in order to provide a better cross-fix on the bearings identified from the fixed Y-stations, such as from your own Whitchurch site.'

'Are those plans progressing well?' the Station Manager enquired.

'Yes actually,' Ray responded trying to stifle yawn as he stretched to get more air into his tired body, 'The Major and I met up at the air base yesterday and agreed a plan over the next 5 days for regular intercept cross-fixings along a bearing line heading almost due south from your location. If you map all the Y-station intercepts to date of Yankee Four Six One and factor in all the bearing errors of the hardware – and make an intelligent assumption that the primary target area is to the south-east of Whitchurch, the Major and I both think this is as good a potential triangulation method as any. Obviously, we will have egg on our faces if Yankee Four Six One doesn't transmit during the hours we know it has transmitted previously – but that won't mean that our plan is necessarily defective.'

Clive Bridgeman was quietly impressed – and pleased – that one of his team had already been working with Criggion on identifying other Y-station intercepts. And that it sounded that a coherent plan to locate the mysterious radio source had been agreed. But he was also privately a little embarrassed that only that morning he had thought of blending intercept information from other Y-stations. There again, he rationalised to himself, this was why people like Ray Thomas and the Major were the future of signals intelligence and intelligence analysis, while he himself was just an old-fashioned engineer with a competent set of hands. He could live with that acceptance of role and rationalised that pride had no place in the war when those with technical proficiencies or exceptional skills should always be encouraged to push boundaries.

'I like the sound of your plans Ray. In fact, only this morning I asked my Night Watch Leader to chase down whether either the Newbold or Stockland stations had picked up anything so that we could try to refine the transit location. But it seems you have beaten me to it!'

Ray responded to this diplomatically, not sharing that he was already aware of the information request that had been made of Newbold Revel minutes previously. 'Well, it's good that we are all thinking along the same lines – and the same bearing line. I am sure the faster we can pool and validate the technical information, then the sooner we will be able to deploy the cross-fixing platform with more accuracy.'

They finished their conversation cordially.

* * *

At Criggion, Ray replaced the handset in his own telephone's cradle. He stretched again and yawned, once more glancing through the window to check the weather, as it often changed quickly in the hills. He still had a lot to do before he could leave the radio station and head back to RAF High Ercall with verbatim transcripts of the overnight cockpit chatter between attacking German aircraft. Time was also tight because an early

39

morning briefing had been called by the airfield's Commanding Officer.

He reflected on the night's work. He had a good team of German linguists working for him listening for voices on the HF channels that were identified by the Huff-Duffs of the Y-Station network and sweeping other HF channels for voice or Morse Code transmissions. They were all young graduates and undergraduates from the universities – and as keen as mustard. It had taken time to get them up to speed and to generate fast, accurate, transcripts but they had all responded well to training and were like sponges with a thirst for new information on dialects, acronyms, or operating procedures. What none of them were told was why they were capturing this information.

Ray chuckled to himself. If only his parents could see him now – a Watcher and a Manager! His much-loved mother always accused him in jest of spending 'far too much time watching and not enough doing young Raymond' and that the 'world will pass you by if you're not careful.' Well, he pondered – and chuckled a little more – she got that wrong, didn't she? He sighed and spoke quietly into the small room so nobody else could hear, 'Look at me now Mam, a proper spy with my own department.'

An hour later he had collected, read, and written a covering report for Bletchley Park on all the transcripts of the night's interceptions and arranged for his paperwork to accompany the magnetic tape recordings that were required to be couriered down to Buckinghamshire daily.

Wearily he drove out of the radio station and set off for RAF High Ercall and the morning briefing.

Chapter 7

Alice awoke exceedingly early on the Tuesday morning tired but still single-minded. She washed and dressed swiftly and set off on her bike again back to the airfield. As she passed Home Farm and its barns in Tibberton she glanced around to see if she could spot the light sets again, but nothing was apparent. So, she peddled on, cycling steadily, until eventually the RAF station came into view.

She stopped short of the entrance for a moment to compose herself, catch her breath and to fluff up her clothing and hair in preparation for her dawn assault on airfield's guard post, hoping that Private Harris was again on duty, not really knowing how she would deal with things if he was not there.

She fleetingly felt a tinge of guilt knowing that she intended to take advantage of the young soldier: but then, almost as swiftly, expunged any notion of compassion towards him, recollecting the number of times he had unjustifiably, and often uncomfortably, impeded her passage on and off the air station.

She need not have worried that he had a stand-in. Private Harris was there and had spotted her a long way off. He had also recouped his power of speech.

'Did you have a puncture, Miss? I saw you stopped down the road there and wondered if I was going to have to get on my white charger to come and rescue you.'

'And good morning to you too, Private Harris. How nice to see you this drab morning. And how kind you are to concern yourself and worry about my tyre pressures today.'

Private Harris chuckled. 'All part of the service, Miss, if you know what I mean.'

'Once again, I am sure I don't know what you mean, Private Harris. And I also think that we ought to keep to bland banter and move things forward for me to be able to get onto the base so that I can do my job. Here is my identity pass.'

Alice showed her pass to the young guard. He did not bother to scrutinise it at all.

'As I told you yesterday, there's new access procedures from this morning Miss, I am afraid. I know who you are, and if it were down to me, I would let you in on a nod. But I am sorry to say the big RAF boss does not know you – and it is the big boss who wants to know about visitor movements on and off the airbase from now on, so you will need to sign out when you leave the airfield, as well as sign in when you arrive. And on every occasion from now onwards. So, could you now please park your bike and pop into the Guard

Room to the complete the Visitor's Log open on the table in there. My colleague, inside, can help you. And Miss, before you go, I really apologise if how I spoke yesterday morning sounded bad. I didn't mean it to: it just came out of my gob all wrong. My girl says my mouth will be the death of me.'

Alice stopped moving and faced the young soldier. 'That's kind of you to say that Private Harris. I admit I was a bit taken aback at the time, but I accept your meaningful apology and won't dwell upon the incident a moment longer. Consider the matter closed.' The poor tortured soul looked so relieved on hearing her words that Alice nearly laughed – but she knew to do so would have been as equally insulting.

Alice then went on to agree that the new security measures were tiresome but sensible, while privately agitated that she would not now get to see the old-style Visitors Book making her early start potentially pointless.

She wheeled her bike to the side of the Guard Room and leaned it against its wall and then mounted the three shallow steps and entered the small Guard Room.

An unsmiling army corporal, whose face she had not seen before, awaited her arrival and bid her good morning as he took her ID card. Using the card he completed the left-hand page of the Visitors Log, timed her entry, and then asked her to complete the remainder of the information needed on the right-hand page, which she did in silence and without catching the NCO's eye.

Alice could see that her visit was the 6th entry on the second double spread page of the newly opened book and realised that the previous pair of pages would be the starting pages. Checking the rest of the Guard Room for the familiar India-tagged manila folder that had been the previous visitors book and not seeing it anywhere, Alice's only hope to find out who Ray Thomas might be, was to sneak a peek in the new logbook to check if he was on the base and had already signed in. So, she took a gamble.

'Oh, I do so love the smell of new stationery Corporal, don't you?' she mused. 'It's that blend of freshness and unsullied paper that for me, at least, makes using new stationery a joy. Do you agree?'

With that verbal flourish she made a theatrical play of lifting the pages of the register near the end of the book and bending down and drawing in a deep breath through her nose, and then repeating the same action having turned the register to the first pair of pages. As she started to bend forward to smell the front pages, she scanned the entries with her eyes knowing she only had an instant to do so.

Two names leapt out at her. One was for "THOMAS, Raymond" who had written under the 'Unit' column "War Office, London". The other, roughly a dozen lines below Ray's, was "SIMPSON, Pearl" of "Cruddy Theatre", one of her best friends.

She was delighted that she had been so successful given that she had only had the briefest of moments for intelligence gathering.

45

She thanked the bemused Corporal for his assistance and almost danced out of the Guard Room. Then, collecting her bicycle and avoiding further contact with Private Harris, who was now standing by the window of a car driver who had just arrived at the road barrier, Alice wheeled her bike towards the Canteen.

So, Ray was not only already on the base – clearly doing important war work for the War Office, whatever that meant – but Alice's good friend Pearl was also on the airfield at this ridiculously early hour, which seemed more than beyond the call of duty for a mere theatre seamstress. Alice resolved to find out more from Pearl later, because she wanted to ask her a favour in any case.

Privately Alice envied Pearl. She had recently secured the position of seamstress and general administrator with the local Crudgington Theatre Company. A matter of a few months earlier the theatre company had been formed by a couple of theatrical entrepreneurs who had arrived from Cornwall and who had bought a local semi-derelict school from the local council to create a bijoux 80-seat theatre for arts and cinema showings – in what locals felt was a much-needed boost to their cultural and emotional needs during what all sensed was an increasingly dark moment of history.

As far as Alice was concerned Pearl was now working in a glorious fantasy land where anything was possible with a bit of cloth, a pot of paint, a few ropes and rack of lights. Meanwhile, between concerts and occasional visits from travelling theatre companies and famous actors like Sybil Thorndike entrancing the audience with magnificent Shakespearean renditions, everyone piled into the theatre to watch all the latest films like Chaplin's The Great Dictator, Geronimo, and numerous others that both educated and enchanted its audiences.

Alice stepped light steps towards the Canteen, amused and buoyed by the success of her undercover casework.

Chapter 8

Alice did not have long to wait for the opportunity to speak to Pearl Simpson.

She had only been in the Canteen for five minutes, and had only just changed into her work coverall, when she went into the main hall to wipe down the serveries – only to find Pearl and three men there chatting and looking up at the ceiling halfway down the cavernous room.

She sauntered over. Pearl shrieked with joy on seeing her. The two women hugged and kissed each other cheeks.

'Hello, Pearl! What an earth are you doing up so early? I thought you thespian types slept in until noon.'

Pearl beamed at her friend.

'Hello Al. I thought I might see you here. No such luck darling I am afraid. We are here at this godforsaken hour to avoid the crowds. It's all a bit hush hush really – but only to give people a pleasant surprise. We are going to be putting on a musical and comedy revue here in the hall in a few weeks with some guest acts all the way from

London. My Theatre Manager here, Mr Bernard Miller ...' she indicated the taller of the three men, '... and his Technical Manager here, Mr Lawrie Sumner ...' she indicated the shorter of the three men, '... wanted to come to the base to see what the facilities are like – the main aim being to work out what equipment we will need to supply so that we can put the show on.'

Bernard Miller smiled and nodded at Alice in polite acknowledgement but did not say anything. The other man just raised his left hand in a wave, he too without speaking, but also without bothering to look at her. Behind a smiling façade, Alice bristled a little at his rudeness. Bizarrely she could have sworn detecting a fleeting sense that the man was making a theatrical pretence of earnestly looking at the roof space stanchions for fixing points but scanning the faces of those seated and relaxing with refreshments in the room while his face was turned away from the group.

'And the Chaplain here, who is the Station's Entertainment Officer ...' Pearl indicated him too with her arms with Alice moving forward to shake his hand '... very kindly made himself available to give us an early morning establishment tour before the day gets busy and the Canteen is topped up with flight crews.'

'How very exciting – nothing normally happens here!' said Alice. 'Can I possibly make anyone a tea or anything to charge the spirit at this time of day?'

Pearl checked the faces of the three men before replying having appeared to get no response, 'Um.

that's sweet of you but no thanks, we still have a lot to cover on the visit and so must get on.'

'OK that's fine, just let me know if you change your mind. I will either be doing something around the servery, or I will be in the kitchen behind prepping things for today. Oh, and Pearl, dear, may I please call on you later this afternoon as I need a big girlie favour?'

'Sure, no problem. How about around 4 pm this afternoon? But it will have to be at the theatre. I will be there until quite late today, so you will have to visit me if you want to see me. I will reciprocate with a pot of tea offer!'

'Fabulous, thanks, I will see you then – if not before, should you need anything while you are still here on the base. Bye.'

Alice left the four of them to continue their tour and discussions and got on with her own chores in the kitchen.

She was thrilled to have discovered that something different was going to take place on the air station. She had got to know many people on the base since first arriving there and had come across many hilarious comedians or great closet singers. She had also seen notices on the base about the new Gang Shows and knew well that there was a rich seam of extrovert musical and comedic talent on the airfield that would just relish an opportunity for exposure.

Alice even started singing to herself as she cut up vegetables, for the first time in a long while feeling extremely satisfied with her lot.

Chapter 9

It had rained overnight. Succulent green leaves charged with water captured high up in the trees now released their liquid loads quietly as a warm light breeze gently stirred branches enough to cause them, haphazardly, to disgorge their multiple reservoirs of fluids.

Keeping his body stock-still, the Field Office craned his neck to look up through the tree canopy towards the sky to assess whether the water now flowing down his neck came from yet more rain clouds or would likely to stop soon once the wind had dropped and the branches and leaves had again settled.

Dressed in a muddy dark green waxed jacket that matched the hue of the earth around him and seated cross-legged on the ground, cradling in his hands a Browning pistol, he was looking forward to shifting his posture and getting circulation back into his feet and lower limbs. He smiled to himself that if he had to move suddenly, he would more than likely fall over, due either to poor circulation or a problem with his blood pressure as he had been seated as he was, completely motionless and concealed in the undergrowth, for the past fifty minutes.

He thought he had turned his collar enough to stop the rain, but as anyone in the field can tell you, water has an uncanny ability to find you out if you haven't taken adequate protective precautions first.

The Field Officer slowly turned his head, first to the left and then to the right, to look along the edge of the tree line on either side of him, as he had repeatedly done over the preceding hour. There was still no sign of the person he was expecting to see. He was now almost overdue at the rendezvous position. The Field Officer decided to give him another 30 minutes grace, after which he decided he would pull plugs on the handover and vacate the drop area. Full daylight was just beginning to take control and the workday in the fields around him would soon recommence. He didn't want to show out to any of the local farm workers.

'Bloody Italians,' he quietly mouthed to himself. 'All they do is jeopardise us – and for what in return? It isn't as if we don't have enough to do without them!'

He was frustrated. Only three weeks earlier their newly established *Abwehrstelle* had received radioed instructions unexpectedly to establish, support and serve a POW extraction route in its area. On top of all its other responsibilities this felt a task too far and risked their limited resources becoming far too thinly spread.

A few days later they had set up the first rendezvous location for what the intelligence unit had been told was a "high value POW" who had to be extracted and repatriated with "utmost expediency". When the POW had finally arrived at the rendezvous point, he had been so late and had complied with almost none of the instructions that he had been given, that he very nearly compromised the operation. The final straw had been that nobody could communicate adequately: a pure-spoken Italian being instructed by an English-speaking German who did not know a word of Italian proved to be a recipe for disaster.

Hoping that handling POWs had been a one-off event, the Field Officer had been dismayed when, with almost no warning just three days previously, his unit had been instructed to support another POW camp escapee that morning.

'And here we are again,' the Field Officer whispered venomously. 'Does Berlin even know how an *Abwehrstelle* functions, or what it does? Pah!'

He shook his head slowly in resignation.

'And what of this morning's priority tasking signal, I ask you Berlin?' he continued to talk to himself in whispered tones.

'You now instruct all British *Abwehrstelles* to prioritise the location and the extraction of Reichsminister Rudolf Hess back to the Fatherland?! Seriously? The Deputy Führer is in Britain? And needs our protection? Really? This does not make sense!'

The Field Officer had been shocked to decode Berlin's message that he had received a little after 5 am that morning, just before he had set off for the pre-arranged POW rendezvous. He could not stop himself wondering why Hess might now be a POW if he was in Britain on an official diplomatic mission. And if he wasn't, but was in fact escaping the Reich or trying to go behind the Führer's back, then why hadn't the instruction simply been to terminate him? Naturally, The Führer would want to know what had happened to him – ideally from the man himself – but the possibility of being able to locate, release and extract him back to Germany was almost zero. Surely they knew that? And attempting to do so would also place dozens of people along the repatriation network at significant personal risk and potentially jeopardise all of Germany's effort and investments in developing its intelligence network in Britain.

He sighed, a thousand questions swirling around in his mind.

'Or has he in fact been on a mission to secure the support of senior British sympathisers? But if so, why hasn't the Abwehr been tasked to secure those relationships and support rather than the Reich dispatching its deputy leader in person?'

Another thought came to him, 'Or has the Reichsminister in fact been working on an appeasement plan that The Führer would never contemplate?'

He shrugged his shoulders, knowing there was nothing at that point in time he could do to get any of his questions answered.

'Orders are orders,' he acknowledged, realising that there was a great deal of research and planning ahead of him.

Meanwhile, he told himself, there were far more immediate responsibilities and that the new orders would have to take a back seat, at least for the next few hours while he waited to meet up with this bloody Italian.

And with that his eyes re-scanned the edge of the woodland and once again he leaned forward slowly, half turning his head to the left and right to listen for the noise of anyone moving through undergrowth. Sill nothing.

The Field Office was long served in the Abwehr. In his opinion it was one thing to gather foreign intelligence and flush out anything of intelligence interest about Anglo-American military affairs or on technical, military or economic matters, but it was something else for the same deep cover unit to be expected additionally to feed, clothe, house and support a repatriation route that moved and extracted POWs from the region, propelling them towards freedom and a route back to the Fatherland via Ireland. However, he also knew that Admiral Canaris, who was his boss and Head of German Intelligence, was locked in a power struggle with Himmler and Heydrich – and that sourcing Italian speakers for Libya formed a key part of the Admiral's strategy to consolidate his position at the top of the Abwehr. And so, like it or not, the Admiral's battles were now also their local *Abwehrstelle's* battles, obliging them to expend valuable resources and effort receiving Italian

POWs for extraction who, eventually, as the quid pro quo for being freed, would be inserted into North Africa, where they would then covertly serve the Third Reich.

The Field Officer was about to give up on the rendezvous when to his right he heard the crack of a foot on a branch on the ground. His fingers curled around the handle of the Browning pistol. He imperceptibly leaned forward so as not to break up his camouflaged profile in the undergrowth and turned his head slightly to look in the direction of the noise. Sure enough, he could see a small man moving along the tree line, moving slowly and cautiously, never leaving the cover of the woodland. He was certain that he was no farm hand from his olive skin and Neapolitan look.

When they were fifty yards apart the Field Officer tensed his body and gingerly got to his feet, conscious that he would not immediately be able to either walk or run until the blood supply to his legs and feet had fully re-established itself. The POW still hadn't seen him and continued to move along the tree line. By the time the Field Officer felt confident enough to move and step out into the path of the POW brandishing his pistol they were a matter of feet apart. The POW nearly had a heart attack in surprise and stopped in his tracks.

The Field Officer lowered his pistol and leaned forward to shake the POW's hand. They shook hands warmly and smiled at each other, neither speaking.

The Field Officer then bent down pick up a large parcel of clothing, food and maps wrapped in brown paper and string that had been laying alongside where he had been secreted away in the undergrowth.

The POW nodded his thanks then looked confused 'Where, London?' he asked.

The Field Officer sighed and pointed to the parcel, because he knew all the necessary information and instructions were contained in it. But the POW held his hand at his side palms open indicating he did not know which way to move from the woodland. 'Where London?' he intoned again.

The Field Officer pointed to the parcel for a second time – and then decided to get his local map out of his jacket and point the Italian in the right direction towards Shrewsbury railway station. After a minute of hand signals, pointing to places on his map and at the land around, the POW then understood where he needed to head. He bobbed his head to the German in gratitude – and then quickly turned on his heels and set off at right angles to the way he had arrived, into the distance, towards the north.

The Field Officer himself immediately set off back towards his car. He couldn't deny to himself that he was nervous: the delayed rendezvous had resulted in the quality of daylight being far better than he would have liked it to have been, and which, in turn, meant that there was now a much greater chance of encountering – and even worse, being recognised by – early morning risers out walking dogs or heading off to work along the country lanes.

He felt very exposed and cussed Berlin for insisting that his intelligence cell be established in the local area. And for the second time that morning he asked Berlin a question aloud. 'I ask again, do you really know how an *Abwehrstelle* functions and what it does? I honestly think you do not!'

Reaching his car, he got in and then set off, remonstrating with the Abwehr in his mind as he drove away. He was frustrated that the Abwehr had been so slow in getting funding together for his unit, in the process losing an opportunity to establish the cell in the more populous urban London location of Hornsey, where its agents and visitors could far more easily blend in with the local community and find it much easier to disappear from view whenever necessary. Furthermore, he felt the Abwehr had been unrealistic expecting to be able to establish a fully live and productive *Abwehrstelle* in a matter of weeks, just as British evenings were getting longer, and it was becoming ever harder to move around and explore the region under cover of darkness. He despaired that the unit had to be based in a deeply rural location, in the process complicating organisation and making it hugely difficult for his *Abwehrstelle* staff covertly to move its radio around the region to take advantage of different reception and transmission sites in order to avoid counter-detection.

'Do we have amateurs in charge now?' he asked himself, aloud once more.

Chapter 10

Early that same morning, Dougie Newton, a farmhand, was working on Home Farm and was driving a small herd of cattle to the Upper Field.

Normally he would have taken a direct route, but because it had rained in the last week and the ground was still waterlogged in places, he had to drive them on a more circuitous route between a couple of major coppices the local landowner was cultivating.

The most northern coppice was exceedingly difficult to reach with tools – locationally out of the way and too far away from the nearest track to allow any heavy equipment to be used there – but it was also going to be the best of the two coppices, with oak, sycamore and willow trees being nurtured there, competing with the hazel and sweet chestnut tress being cultivated in the southern coppice, a few hundred yards away to the south of it.

Dougie loved the land and approved of any work to preserve and develop the natural environment. Employed on the farm under the

Reserve Occupation Scheme, he knew he was lucky and privileged to be able to spend his war working on land that he knew well, having been born only a couple of miles away.

He saw the Pathé newsreels of course and just could not imagine himself in mud and trenches fighting hand to hand with the Germans. But that was not to say that his life was easy either – his income was marginal, his living conditions on the farm involved a cold cottage with a wood-fired range, and most days working from around 4 am until, often, midnight, was exhausting. But when all was said and done, he relished the freedom he had to work on the fields planting and harvesting crops and building up the farm's herd of Hereford beef cattle.

That morning he was, as ever, enjoying the early morning dew. The fresh smell of spring and the noise from the morning chorus was just starting to ebb away. He had set out with the herd before sunrise because he needed to get some tractor work done mid-morning and so wanted to get the cattle into Upper Field before he got too distracted with other farm matters.

The herd were in front of him sauntering randomly as they always do, in no hurry. He did not need the dogs this morning because the route to Upper Field involved field channels – and if he were behind the herd, he could nudge it slowly forward where he wanted it to go. Between the north and south coppices there was a rise of land before the ground then dipped right towards Upper Field's gate, leaving the northern coppice to the left of Upper Field on the higher ground and the southern coppice to the right of it on the slightly lower ground.

The dawning sun was already bright, though still not warm, but nevertheless it coloured the rears of the cattle walking forward, making them all glow auburn.

Dougie was just thinking about what he would have for breakfast once he returned to the farm complex to sustain him for the tractor work when his attention was taken by the glint of something metallic in the northern coppice catching the early morning sun. As he was the only person working on the coppice, he knew there was nothing metal there, so he was not even sure that he had seen anything.

His immediate worry was of armed poachers, so he ducked down a little to keep the coppice in his line of sight while trying to keep his own profile below a horizon of cattle rears that were bobbing about. Then, using the cattle herd as cover, he moved into a position that he could check the northern coppice out without, he hoped, being seen.

As the cattle gradually moved up and over the crest of the hill and before their descent right between the two dense woodland enclaves towards Upper Field, the detail of the northern coppice to his left became increasingly clearer. He had not been mistaken – there were two people in the coppice at its edge and further glinting of the sun on something confirmed that something metallic was being handled by one of them.

They both appeared to be men. One was tall the other smaller and slimmer. They each approached the other cautiously at first and then shook hands when they finally came together. The tall man then handed over to the shorter man what looked like a soft-wrapped package, perhaps a soft bag. He also took out from an inside coat pocket a piece of paper that they both consulted. The tall man then proceeded to point in various directions with the smaller man nodding, making Dougie presume that they were looking at a map. Finally, the tall man handed the glinting object to the smaller man – which Dougie was sure looked like a handgun.

They parted as quickly as they had come together, the small man setting off to the north along the northerly tree line of the northern coppice, while the taller man set off east towards Newport. Their encounter had lasted no more than two minutes.

Dougie, wise for his years, having had to deal with many gypsies and poachers, opted to stay ducked down low behind the Herefords to keep himself out of sight. He knew it was dangerous to challenge anyone in the open without support – especially someone armed. The gate to Upper Field was not that far away and so for the next fifteen minutes he stayed so low he almost crawled. Eventually he was able to nudge the herd into the field and close the gate.

Once he was satisfied that he could not see either of the men any more he ran as fast as he could back to the farm, resolving on the way back to ask around in the pub to see if anyone in the locality had had poacher or traveller problems over the past few days.

He had had enough trouble with the law in the past not to want to immediately raise a flag. And the last thing he wanted were the local bobbies infesting the farm and finding his gin still or flushing out the farm's black market egg business.

Chapter 11

Alice clock-watched all day in suppressed excited anticipation of visiting the theatre and, although Pearl did not yet know it, co-opting her to make a dress for her for a Red Cross Charity Ball taking place in a few days at the nearby agricultural college.

She had decided a few weeks earlier that she needed to get her life back on track and in control, now that she and her school and college cohort had moved on into adult life. She simply did not want to feel or to be viewed as a victim of anything and, therefore, vowed, albeit privately and nervously, to seize any opportunity presented to her. Alice knew things needed to change in her life otherwise her existence on the Earth would go unnoticed, that is if the explosive ordnance failed to erase the record of her presence on its surface first.

In her head, the charity hop offered her a perfect opportunity to cast off the cloak of invisibility that had largely characterised her adult life to date. What was more, she did not mind that she herself would not be able to dance as elegantly as her able-bodied contemporaries: just being part of it all was what she craved. And, naturally enough, she wanted to look nice while accepting that she had a miniscule budget to work with on her low wages. So, for Alice, Pearl Simpson was central to her rehabilitation plan.

Shortly before 4 pm she propped her bicycle against the outside of the new theatre.

The building had originally been an infant school, but over time had fallen into disrepair and had been of limited maintenance interest to the local Council. Consequently, when a couple of affable Cornishmen had suddenly arrived in the area, about six months earlier, and offered to buy the premises to set up a combined local theatre company and picture house, the Council had been extremely keen to take their money and divest itself of what had become an unwanted public asset.

Since being converted from a school, she had already visited it and seen Nine Till Six, a stage adaptation of an early 1930s film in which a couple of women of different social class find themselves working together. More recently she had gone to watch an excellent murder mystery play called Ladies in Retirement, which had only recently been on the stage on Broadway in New York.

For Alice, the theatre and all that it did, from costume hire, putting on plays and screening films, to hosting visiting theatre companies or taking the magic of theatre and comedy into the community and onto military bases, provided her with a chance to take herself out of her reality and envisage a peaceful future and dream currently impossible dreams. In fact in an idle moment, earlier in the day, she had dared to visualise the noise and laughter of the Gang Show on the airfield, and had even allowed her mind briefly to wander fancifully into imagining herself performing a play on a stage in front of an enthusiastic audience in a London theatre and then being feted by a phalanx of photographers and journalists afterwards.

Alice knew her way to Pearl's small workroom and quickly moved around stage props and half-maintained lamps to a small suite of rooms on a corridor to the side of the stage and its sumptuous deep red audience seats.

'Knock, knock?' Alice proffered as she poked her head around Pearl's door.

'Gawd Al, is it that time already? I mean, hello dear,' Pearl was hardly visible under a large blue dress and appeared to be sewing on sequins. She bobbed her head pretending to air kiss Alice's cheeks.

'I am so behind with my adjustments I can't tell you. Of course, no darn thanks having to spend such a long time this morning at the airfield. God, men do go on interminably about the most boring of technical things – so many questions about the squadrons, the aircrew, their aircraft and what they do – even the Chaplain was flagging by the end! And even after the visit so little is still known about how we are physically going to put a Gang Show on and recruit a pool of players to entertain and amuse people enough that they will not start throwing rotten eggs at the performers five minutes after the show starts! I don't know, we are going to have to re-visit, I am sure. Thankfully, the Chaplain is setting up unrestricted access passes for Lawrie and Bernard to the air station which means I won't have to go and trail around behind them.'

'Do you know what?' she went on, 'I am so stressed at the moment. Look here—' she stretched behind her to pick up a naval military jacket from the table behind her and showed it to Alice '—this is a naval officer's jacket that we are using for one of the touring Gang Shows. I was so tired the other day that I sewed on the arm braid rank the wrong way round. You see, here, this is the gold braid for a Lieutenant. The braid of the upper rank with the ring on it should start from the inner arm side and end up sweeping over to the outer arm side. But in a rush of tiredness, I sewed the braid to the wrong arm – in fact, I did it twice because I didn't realise I had done it, even when it came to sew the second rank incorrectly onto the other sleeve.'

Alice could see what Pearl meant peering closely at her handiwork – the rank insignia was indeed the wrong way around on both sleeves.

'So, what happens now with it?' she asked sympathetically.

'Well, I don't have a choice other than to unpick everything, switch the rank over and start again. Which is not what I need when I have all this other work to do ... plus, I need to try to get that red paint mark off the bottom of the rear air vent of the jacket too. Someone must have sat on a prop while the paint was drying. Oh gawd, work, work, work –'

Alice could see what Pearl meant. The bottom inch of the central vent of the jacket was almost all vermillion in colour.

'Oh dear, you do sound to be going through the mill.' She commiserated.

Pearl put down her sewing and squared up to Alice looking her straight in the eyes.

'That, Al, is an understatement. Do you know what too, Bernard, the Theatre Manager, has just decided to increase the local RAF station touring Gang Shows from two to six performances this year. I just don't know how we are going to cope with the production load. Plus, I just get this constant sensation that I am fighting an uphill battle as the costumier. I keep adjusting mounds of clothing which gets sent to various establishments under our costume hire programme, but I never see the costumes again because they are all sold on. If only I could build a comprehensive costume wardrobe here, then I could save myself so much time and not feel that I am more a tailor than a costumier now.'

Alice never liked to see her friend in distress and let out a quiet sigh and mumbled, 'Oh.'

Pearl recovered her composure and sat up with her back ramrod straight. 'Come on Al, so what do you mean by "Oh" Tell Auntie Pearl,' Pearl could see Alice appeared crestfallen and adopted a voice of a nanny.

'Well as you are so busy ... never mind ... no, I shouldn't have asked to pop in ...' Alice mumbled.

'Al?' Pearl quizzed. 'What's on your chest? Come on girl, tell me. Let it out.'

Alice now felt embarrassed asking Pearl for help given what she had just complained about, but then thought, why ever not.

'The big favour I wanted to ask you, but I can see that it is now not feasible ...' he hesitatingly started to say.

'Al—?' Pearl implored Alice to express herself.

Alice took a deep breath and just blurted out what she wanted. 'Well, the big favour I wanted to ask you is could you possibly make me a dress for a dance? There. I have said it! I do not have very much money for it, but you are welcome to have whatever I have ... and I think I have lost my heart to a Welshman ... and the ball is at Harper Adams Agricultural College in two weeks ... and I do not know if the linguist is going to the ball ... and I am so excited that you are putting on a show in the Canteen ... and how I wish I had your skill with a needle and thread ... and I am meeting Ray again in a couple of days ... but I have arranged to do it as part of a group drink and I do not know if I should have arranged to see him alone first ...and what is more, I am petrified because I believe, deep down, we already know each other ... and—'

'—whoa Al, slow down, you already know him?' Pearl had a big grin on her face.

'Well not actually know him, but know him, you know, a connection, a frisson ...' Alice tried to explain.

Cocking her head Peal winked. 'Sweetie, I have dreamt since a small girl of finding one of those, I can tell you – '

'Oh Pearl, trust you to lower the tone!' Alice castigated, 'Not that way. A nice man. A bright man – and, amazingly, someone in whom I am actually interested.'

Pearl held up her hand to stop any further talk. 'OK, let us see if I have got things right. First, you need a dress for a charity dance at Harpers in a fortnight. Second, there is a man who has come on the scene who you like and who you think may be interested in you? Third, you have not a partner yet for the dance and haven't yet plucked up courage to ask him out to it? Fourth, everything else is unimportant? Correct?'

Alice had been nodding throughout, finally drawing a breath and blinked. Both women then dissolved into fits of laughter.

Suddenly, into Pearl's workroom swept Pearl's manager, a perfectly timed entrance from stage left. He burst into the office space, barged past Alice, and shoved some material aside on the table behind her so that he could then turn and perch on it to face Pearl's guest.

'So, who is this fine lady, Pearl, to whom you are complaining about how hard I am working you?'

Alice and Pearl snatched a quick glance at each other without saying a word and then acted as if nothing had been noticed, though both were wondering if he had been listening in on their conversation all along.

'Bernard, this is my friend who you met this briefly morning when we were in the air station Canteen earlier this morning. You may remember her? Alice Peters? Do you recall I introduced her to you and Lawrie when we were with the Chaplain? Alice, do you remember Mr Miller from this morning?'

Bernard Miller made an act of peering at Alice. 'Hmmm, yes possibly I do now, although you are now in civvies.'

'It's genuinely nice to meet you again, Mr Miller. Of course I do. It is wonderful that you have started a theatre company here and opened a theatre for us locally. It is such a treat for us all,' Alice responded graciously.

'Yes, well,' Miller retorted strangely and gruffly. 'So, do you spend your time fraternising with aircrew then Miss Peters? I gather there are a fair number of foreign pilots on the station these days. The Chaplain said there were many were Czechs flying out of the air base. Got any names for me by any chance?' Alice was sure he briefly hesitated and quickly swallowed to cover and suppress a blush, '– um, so that I can invite them to take part in the Gang Show.'

'Oh, there are many of them who would be stars given half a chance, if their singing skills over Victoria sponges are anything to go by, but I wouldn't know what their names were,' she lied, feeling irrationally protective towards the Czechs, though could not fathom why. 'But I would be happy to give the Canteen Manager a poster if you want to invite any of them to contact you. It's just that I am not sure what the procedure is for posting notices in the Canteen.'

Alice's answer frustrated Bernard Miller. 'Hmmm, well I may just do that. Yes. Good idea. But if you know the name of anyone then do please let Pearl know and she and I can then interview the man.'

On hearing that she would be involved in auditioning, Pearl's eyebrows shot up and her eyes widened in surprise – this was all news to her. Alice picked up her non-verbal message which, fortuitously, Bernard Miller could not see because he was seated behind Pearl.

A moment later, Miller leapt up and launched himself at the doorway listening like a fox, holding onto the door jambs and cocking his head a little to hear.

Pearl and Alice said nothing but briefly caught each other's eyes again. Increasing in volume they could both hear two male voices talking. The voices had, self-evidently, just come into the building. Bernard Miller suddenly dematerialised without excusing himself.

As the two arrivals moved up the corridor and neared Pearl's workroom the women understood that they were in an animated conversation about voltages and signal strength. And as they passed Pearl's workshop door one of them glanced in and appeared startled to see someone still in the room, let alone someone chatting to another woman. It was Lawrie Sumner, the theatre's Technical Manager. Pearl did not speak but just waved at him and then turned back to face Alice. In an automatic response he half-waved back, also without speaking, so as not to interrupt the verbal flow of his companion. Alice recognised Sumner from the morning encounter in the Canteen – as much from seeing his insincere wave again as from recognition of his facial features.

As the two men started to move away from her door, their conversation got quieter with each disappearing step. From what they could overhear, Pearl and Alice discovered that the conversation had something to do with what Lawrie Sumner called "the theatre's solitary microphone without which all the productions are stuffed". The conversation appeared to involve the companion then saying that he was sure he could fix it, but only if he had his equipment with him. The problem was that he needed an oscilloscope to check input and output voltage signal strengths, and that his measuring equipment was, unfortunately, currently on an aircraft, so it would be a few days before he could test it. Sumner therefore suggested they meet for a drink in the Sutherland Arms that Saturday lunchtime at noon so the broken microphone could be returned repaired. Sumner added that he had not known that he was aircrew. His companion retorted that he was not but that he did "do a bit of this and that from time to time in the air on new equipment fits", which Sumner said he found fascinating and looked forward to having many more conversations with him about electronics and bandwidths.

Gradually their voices began to diminish until they were merely unintelligible low frequency background noise.

Neither Alice nor Pearl had spoken since Bernard Miller had been in the workroom.

Alice leaned forward a little and frowned, speaking in hushed tones that only Pearl could hear. 'I know that man who was talking to your

Technical Manager. I have seen him at the air station. He is some sort of senior engineer from one of the technical units. He's not military. He spends much of his time playing with aircraft electronics. I know this because he often brings bits of his kit with him when he comes into the Canteen. Every time he apologises for doing so saying "it wouldn't do leaving things laying around while I enjoy a tea break".' She mimicked his voice.

Pearl also frowned. 'And *I* did not know that any of the microphones are broken – plural not singular, as we have three in the theatre. In fact, I heard Lawrie testing each of them in turn after we got back from the air station earlier this afternoon. They all sounded to be working absolutely fine to me.'

The two women looked at each other, both frowned incomprehension and then shrugged their shoulders in unison. Pearl spoke next.

'Well, that will teach us to pick up fag ends wouldn't you say? All interesting I am sure, but I really must get on dear, otherwise I will still be here at midnight. By the way, what exactly is the actual time, Al?'

Alice checked her watch.' Oh goodness it's getting on ten to five. I had quite forgotten the time. I really must be away myself. I promised my parents that I wouldn't be delayed this evening after rolling home late from the skittles yesterday. Particularly as you and I are meeting Emma in the pub on Thursday night, which I'm sure won't be an early finish.'

It was Pearl's turn to be pensive. She looked at Alice quizzically. 'And I thought you said to Bernard you didn't know the names of any of the Czechs? I know you do from what you have told me in the past.'

'Well, I must have sort of lied then Pearl! 'Alice said quietly conspiratorially and winked. 'Mainly because I cannot pronounce, let alone spell, their bloody family names! Far too many consonants for an English rose like me to handle.'

They both shrieked with laughter again and embraced. And with that Alice flew out of Pearl's workroom, headed for her bicycle, and set off for Kynnersley.

Chapter 12

The radio operator spoke first.

'Yes, the message is authentic. The codes and call signs are valid. Headquarters has signalled to a limited group: to our call sign and to two other call signs. I presume there are two at least other *Abwehrstelles* operating here in Britain?'

The Field Officer nodded, 'Yes, it would seem at least two, but I don't know where they are, of course, or if there are more than two.'

'And we don't know what the messages have been to each of them as they have their own crypto codes. We can only decode our own signal.'

'It's a strange signal though, isn't it ... I mean ... drop what you are doing ... we have lost a Reichsminister, last known heading over to Britain ...'

'How careless can you be to lose a Reichsminister,' the junior observed drily, chuckling to himself, 'But it's also unhelpful.'

'What do you mean unhelpful? What's unhelpful, the signal?' the Field Officer enquired.

'Well, the signal wants us to initiate a search for the Deputy Führer, who could be anywhere in Britain right this moment, and it doesn't allow us to coordinate our work with any other *Abwehrstelles* to help us all efficiently sweep the ground. To me this risks duplication and showing out. What if we know the same people that other *Abwehrstelles* know?'

The Field Officer briefly considered the point his radio operator was making. 'In theory, yes, I agree, there is a risk of exposure from duplicated activity. I also agree that we should be working with other networks for greatest efficiency. But unfortunately, that is not a luxury or reality that is being afforded to us. We keep or networks separate to prevent wholesale exposure should someone be compromised. And what did the signal actually indicate? That it was known that the Reichsminister flew to Britain on Saturday 10th May, only three days ago?'

He drew breath and continued, 'So, my reading of the situation is that Headquarters probably didn't know he had disappeared for at least 24 hours, possibly even 48 hours, and perhaps only yesterday, Monday, worked out that he had flown over to this country. While Headquarters would never indicate that it is panicking, I sense it probably is panicking. And so my guess is that the broadcast that we received earlier this morning, alerting us to the Reichsminister's disappearance, was purely a call out to all units to file immediate reports of any unusual activities that might potentially involve the movement, incarceration, or interrogation of a high value German High Command asset.'

The radio operator nodded his agreement with his senior officer's assessment of the situation.

The Field Officer continued, 'So we need to ask ourselves two critical and immediate questions. Firstly, are we aware of anything going on in our area that locals say are abnormal? And secondly, who can we approach who might know someone who knows where the Reichsminister is currently located?'

Both looked at each other without speaking as each contemplated their responses.

The radio operator spoke first, again.

'Well, I have picked up that at RAF High Ercall there is a building, separated from all the other buildings on the airfield, which is very secure and surrounded by its own security protection – with sandbags, wire, and armed guards. You can just see it from the perimeter road if you clamber up the bank on the north-eastern side of the airfield. It's quiet and out of sight there.'

'So, you've already had a look at it have you?' the Field Officer asked.

'Yes, yesterday in fact. But the point is that over the weekend I heard chatter in the pub that the airfield has just changed is access security procedures and that, yesterday, two lorries filled with armed soldiers arrived late afternoon. I understand that they have been told that are not allowed off the base and are being accommodated on the airfield, in the middle of it, and not in the usual camp accommodation – none of which has gone down well, as you can imagine.'

The Field Office shuffled himself to the front of his seat facing the radio operator, clearly animated by what he was being told.

'So, the suggestion is that this building in the middle of the airfield is, what, possibly a bunker that houses people, rather than a building housing ordnance or whatever else you might normally expect to be on an air station located well away from the crowd?'

The radio operator nodded, 'That seems to be the suggestion.'

'Do we know how extensive this bunker is underground, or what else is going on down there? An interrogation centre? Secure accommodation for visiting Reichsministers perhaps? Do we know why the airfield should suddenly need to have its security reinforced?'

The radio operator gestured ignorance, shrugging his shoulders, thinking to himself that his senior officer really needed to do more listening than talking, while wondering why he hadn't noticed this intelligence himself before now.

'OK, we obviously need to draw up a signal on that. And we need to take a closer look at what's going on there,' the Field Officer concluded. 'Meanwhile, what about the second question: who can we approach who might know someone who knows where the Reichsminister is currently located?'

The radio operator interrupted him. 'Sir, before you change topic, there is something else abnormal going on in the area.'

The Field Officer never liked to be silenced but had no choice on this occasion.

'What?' he curtly asked.

'Again, from visiting the local pubs, I have gathered that there are now gypsies and black marketeers working the area. I haven't seen any yet, but it seems to me only prudent for us to keep a careful eye open from them when we are meeting the POWs – and only act upon the agreed signals. If we don't get the right response signal, we must immediately terminate the handovers and vacate the rendezvous locations.'

The Field Officer ignored his radio operator's reasonably expressed caution with a dismissive wave of his hand. 'I can't imagine that we will be affected by travellers and spivs, do you?'

For his part, the radio operator looked icily at his boss, and not for the first time considered him a naïve, stupid, fool.

The Field Officer pressed on. 'So, what about the second question: who can we approach who might know someone who knows where the Reichsminister is currently located?

'That's your part of ship, Sir, not mine. Who might *you* approach who might know someone who knows where the Reichsminister is currently located?' the radio operator retorted, unwilling to offer anything constructive any more.

The Field Officer briefly lost his flow. He blinked, not sure if the radio operator had been insubordinate, and equally not certain what then do if he had been.

'Um, well, I am having dinner with the wife and Commanding Officer of RAF High Ercall next

Thursday since you ask. Meanwhile I am scheduled to play tennis at Lilleshall House with the Duke of Sutherland and a small tennis party a week today I have been given to understand that the Duke makes military equipment, including small arms. I gather they are made in his foundries on his Donnington estate. I am hoping I may also get a sense of what else is going on regionally that might interest our Masters. As regards the vanishing Reichsminister, well, I can't imagine that the Duke wouldn't know something of him. So, I am optimistic I will pick up a trail then.' He stretched and yawned as it had been a long day already. 'But unfortunately, all that will have to wait for next week – I cannot expedite the diaries of these men.'

He then picked a fleck of cotton from his sleeve. 'But there are things that you can do in parallel.'

The radio operator was wary. 'What have you in mind?'

'Find out all you can about how this cluster of bodies physically arrived at the air station. I'm thinking transport methods. What routing? Where from? When? How many people? What's their skills mix? Confirm they sleep underground? How do they eat? What do they eat? What is going on underground there? Why the sudden increase in airfield security?'

The Field Officer briefly considered his plan.

'If it takes a few days to piece together a picture for Berlin, then that's what it takes. Better we give them accurate information than half-cooked information that might be misleading.

When we send the signal to Headquarters, in a moment, we need to tell them that they have no choice other than to be patient. They won't like it, but who cares. We can't move faster than we can with limited resources if we are to stay embedded and camouflaged.'

The radio operator nodded, relieved that the Field Officer was finally being pragmatic.

Chapter 13

In the moments and quiet that followed Alice's departure, Pearl drew a very deep breath and then started to sew more sequins onto the blue dress that still lay over her lap.

Ten minutes later Bernard re-appeared at her door.

'Has she gone?' he quizzed.

'Yes, she has Bernard, family commitments.' she explained.

'You going to be here long?' Pearl always felt Bernard had quite a brusque military air about him with little small talk.

'I hope not Bernard,' Pearl replied in her most exasperated voice, trying to concentrate on her work and also let Bernard know from the way she spoke that he was interrupting her, 'I just have a couple of more things to finish off this evening and then I am off for a bath and a sleep after this morning's early start.'

'Good,' he replied, 'I am away myself now for the evening. Lawrie has now left for the day too. So, you are the last man – err woman – standing.

Can you please lock up and I will see you tomorrow morning?'

'Yes, no problem Bernard. As I say, hopefully I won't be too long.' Bernard departed. She heard the front door close behind him.

Pearl was now all alone in the theatre. Quickly finishing off the sequins and leaving the tedious unpicking of the military uniform braid for the following day, she stood up and stretched and then switched off her workroom light, forgetting that there were no other lights on in the building and that it would soon be sunset and blackout time.

She could not be bothered with setting all the blackout curtains and so was quite content to move about in semi-darkness. She then decided she had a craving for a cigarette before heading home.

She couldn't smoke in the theatre as Bernard would smell the stale smoke in the morning. Nor could she smoke at home without her mother complaining. So, she decided there was nothing for it but to have a crafty fag behind the theatre by the rubbish bins before calling it a day and setting off home.

Grabbing what Bernard called his 'Theatre Manager's torch' from a leather satchel that hung behind his office door, she started to make her way outside. She had first seen him using his torch a few weeks earlier during an evening dress rehearsal and had been quietly impressed with it. Compact enough to be handled and operated in one hand – a distinct size and weight improvement on many torches she had used –

what was particularly brilliant about it was that it had a main beam and an alternative low light setting if you wanted to use the torch for what Bernard called its 'theatre prompt' mode. She thought it was extremely effective for the long distance pointing of a narrow light beam onto the stage from the auditorium when Bernard wanted to explain something to an actor and point to a stage position but did not want to get out of his seat. And it was just as effective when being used to read scripts in the dark for stage prompts while performances were taking place.

Selecting the low light mode of the torch and switching it on she navigated her way to the rear door of the theatre. Unlocking it and pushing it open caused her instantly to be immersed in a waft of early Spring warmth and that first smell of succulent growth and sense of what the summer would bring.

She stood there for a moment pleasurably sucking in the fresh air and then made her way to the dustbins. She switched the torch off, pocketed it and took the cigarettes and some matches out of her other pocket. She then extracted a cigarette, lit it, and paused motionless momentarily to allow the first tobacco hit of the day to caress her senses, making her slightly light-headed.

When the cigarette was at its end and while cogitating nothing in particular, she delved for the torch and switched it on, double-checking it was still in its suppressed light mode. She then lifted the dustbin lid, took the cigarette stub from her mouth, bent over and then carefully stepped on its lit end to snuff out any last remaining tobacco embers. Picking it up and tossing it into the dustbin, she leaned over the bin and shone the torch into it just to check that the stub had fallen into a crevasse and disappeared, keeping her tobacco vice secret.

To her surprise it had landed on a small piece of orange paper that looked burnt around the edges. Curious to know what was burnt in the bin, she moved the torch closer to read what was printed on the paper and could see that the paper remnant appeared to have two columns of hieroglyphics printed on it.

Her curiosity well and truly piqued, Pearl flicked off the cigarette butt so that it vanished from view and then gingerly picked up the burnt remnant between her thumb and first finger and examined it with the torch in her other hand. At first it just looked like a child's drawing until she turned it around clockwise to discover that the paper had what appeared to be Morse Code printed on it. The left-hand column looked like it was showing the Morse Code for the letters g, h and i and the right-hand column appeared to be showing the Morse Code symbols for t, u, v and w.

Pearl suddenly felt very exposed. She quickly replaced the dustbin lid, ran through the back door, locked it behind her and then ran to her workroom to pick up her bag. She then found a used envelope in her bin and carefully placed the burnt remnant into it, stuffing the envelope into her bag.

She next ran to the front door and was about to leave when she realised that she still had

Bernard's theatre torch in her hand. So, she returned to his office, switched the torch off and put it back it in the satchel and used her hands carefully to feel and touch her way back to the main door in the dark as a blind person might.

Once outside she locked the front door, briefly stopping to listen if there was anyone out there and then, satisfied that she was alone and unseen, ran as hard as she could all the way home, with a million questions in her head.

Chapter 14

Day Three (Wednesday)   14th May 1941

Alice slept well overnight. Both Monday and Tuesday had been long days. She had relished having a lie in and the prospect of a day off work so that she and her mother could take the train over to Shrewsbury to go shopping.

Her mother tapped on her bedroom door just as it was starting to get light.

'Good morning darling,' she said as she put two mugs of tea down on Alice's bedside stable and leaned over to kiss her on her forehead.

She then perched herself on the edge of Alice's bed and bent across her to pick up and sip her steaming brew, holding it in both hands and blowing across the surface of the liquid to cool it a little.

Alice wriggled up the bed until she was in a seated position and gingerly turned to get hold of her own mug without knocking over a bedside lamp and a tall pile of books by her side on the bedside table that were all in various states of being read. Alice always had at least four books on the go at any one time so she could select one or other of them to read as her mood dictated.

'Dad's just left for work. And it doesn't look as if it is going to rain today,' she announced to the room as statements rather than topics for dialogue.

Both women then happened to take slurps of tea at exactly at the same time.

Alice's mother, face still in her mug, glanced at her daughter and made a silly face. Alice reciprocated, catching her mother's look over the top of her own mug. They both then nodded to each other and at simultaneously took huge noisy slurps of tea, dissolving into fits of laughter.

Alice's mother coughed and spluttered with mirth with her tea going down the wrong way and everywhere down her front as she tried to control herself, only just managing to put her mug down in time before coughing again between shrieks of laughter. To regain control, she threw her whole body back, so she lay facing the ceiling on her back on Alice's blankets, still coughing, still giggling, and panting hard to control her breath.

Alice touched her mother's shoulder affectionately. 'Mummy dear, you'll do yourself – or me – in if you do that again.' They both were grinning broadly, both mother and daughter savouring the bond and love they had for each other.

Neither moved nor spoke for the next couple of minutes. It was heaven. The dawn chorus was just about audible, and it was this that they were both silently listening to and enjoying. Daylight was starting to force itself around the edges of Alice's blackout curtains.

Her mother heaved herself up and stood to turn up the blackouts to let more light into the room. Suddenly shards of sunlight lit up the wooden floorboards, highlighting the amount of dust in the air as constantly moving, swirling, dust particles were themselves illuminated by the beams of light and the sun's warmth.

'So, what's the plan darling?' Alice's mother asked. 'Do you still want to pop into Shrewsbury for the material for dance dress?'

'Rather Mummy. If you don't mind helping me choose. I just don't have enough knowledge of what material is suitable for it, let alone have the confidence alone to choose the right colour.'

'Oh, I'm sure you do really, darling. It's more perhaps just having a bit of experience and practical knowledge of dressmaking.' Alice's mother always sought positively to counter her daughter's constant worry that she was not good enough or could never match up to her more able-bodied friends.

'I'm not so sure about that,' Alice bemoaned, 'I think it's also a lot to do with self-belief, and as you know my relationship with that particular human characteristic is somewhat inconsistent at times.'

He mother understood what lay behind Alice's comment. 'But surely, we all like to dress up from time-to-time Alice darling? Surely, we don't do it only to attract flies, do we? Isn't it important to feel part of a group that has common styles, likes and dislikes – so that you blend in with your friends and their surroundings? Surely more so than simply to dress up to invite peacocks round for tea?'

Alice giggled,' Mum you use such gloriously evocative language!'

Alice looked hard into her mother's eyes. 'I know what you are saying. But why, exactly, am I tarting myself up and so anxious about getting the material type and colours right? Is it because all that seems left now is to attract flies, as you so bluntly say?'

He mother touched her hand on Alice's arm. 'Is that what you think, darling? That, aged only 21, there's nothing left other than to try to find a mate?'

'Well, in truth Mummy, sometimes I think that.'

'Oh' was all her mother could say in shocked reply.

'I know you never like me to compare what all my friends are doing with what I am doing, but I just can't ignore the fact that contracting polio has affected my life and has not affected theirs, at all. You suggest that we all ought to dress up to be part of group with common styles, likes and dislikes and not dress up purely to attract the opposite sex, but just take a moment to consider what that means in relation to who and what I currently am compared to who and what my lovely friends are.'

Her mother could see that Alice was starting to get agitated, but she didn't want to interrupt her opening up and saying what she really felt about things.

'Just remember that polio prevented me from signing up as a naval communicator, as Emma – Colonel Parry's daughter from down the road – was able to do. As you and Dad well know, I felt really crushed by that because I had always wanted to join the Royal Navy. I suppose I must be quite shallow – but I had always had a vision of being posted to exotic climes in a smart naval uniform.'

Alice's mother was taken aback at the strength of Alice's feelings. She wondered what might have prompted it but didn't get the opportunity to ask at that moment because Alice was now in full flow.

'Meanwhile, Tom, my lovely Tom and first love is now working on secret work somewhere near Oxford. He is now even engaged to a girl he met there from nearby Summertown. And Phil Tasker? Ever the reliable and a doe-eyed hopeful for my affections for years at school? Well, he went to sea in the merchant naval service – but is now lost and presumed drowned following a torpedo attack on his convoy. And do you remember Tina Brown? Another schoolfriend from Haverfordwest, well she now works as a Land Girl in Lancashire tending sheep.'

Alice was starting to list people close to her. 'Uncle George was in the Army and is currently posted somewhere abroad in Africa. Chas Large, the noisiest of my Haverfordwest school friends, is now a quiet and pensive soul working as design engineer mechanic in the RAF. Catriona Williams works for the new Ministry of Information in some secret capacity that I presume involves propaganda production or propaganda monitoring or something like that. Gareth Jones, another Haverfordwest schoolfriend, is now a Royal Engineer on deployment, having spent his childhood working on agricultural equipment on his parent's smallholding by the reservoir. Even Bethany Curzon who you will recollect was my partner in childhood larks and quite the funniest person I have ever encountered, is now working in some central government role to do with transport and planning supporting foreign military deployments.'

Alice's mother didn't speak as she was now herself distressed and unsure how to respond.

'Mummy, the point is that all my friends and contemporaries are – or were – active and engaged in serving this country. But for me, my ambition – to have responsibilities and serve too – are dying a daily death as job applications are continually terminated the moment I must reveal my medical affliction. I am so browned off with all this at times I want to scream in frustration. So, am I dressing up to blend in with long-standing friends … who have moved on in their lives … or am I simply doing it to find a mate? And if the latter, what happens to my aspirations and ambitions, what happens to my life, why did I ever bother getting educated? I know I am not pointless, but some days, Mummy, waves of despair drown me. Forgive me for speaking like this.'

Alice then burst into tears. Her mother sat back down on the bed and held Alice to her as tight as she could. Alice buried her head in her mother's loving embrace and sobbed and sobbed and shook until she had no more tears to give.

The two women were motionless for a full five minutes, both still firmly linked, the mind of each swirling and unfocussed not really knowing what would happen next or what should now be said. But it was Alice's mother who the walls of the room heard next, albeit tentatively and sensitively.

She cleared her throat but didn't move her head or relax her embrace. 'Alice, darling, can I please ask you a question? You don't have to answer it if you would rather not.'

Alice stifled a snivel and squeak quietly to indicate her consent.

Her mother cleared her throat for a second time. This time she pulled her head back to gaze over the back of her daughter's head and cascading locks, her daughter's face still pressed hard into her chest and shoulder. She stroked her daughter's hair a couple of times with her right hand and then went back to holding her close to her. 'Has something bad happened to you?' she nervously asked.

Alice didn't speak but shook her head quickly in a way that her mother could feel it and understand her reply.

"OK darling–,' she went on, gingerly,'– because if something bad has happened, you know you can tell me without fear of anything ... whatever the problem is, we can sort it out you know ...' her voice tailed off as she felt Alice shake her head quickly again.

Both stayed motionless for a short time more, then it was Alice who lifted her head up, eyes puffy from her crying and hair slight matted across her cheeks where tears and hair had started to dry.

She looked deeply into her mother's eyes. She could see that her mother's face was ashen and worried.

'Something has happened this week–'

'–Oh.' Her mother immediately took a sharp intake of breath and tried to stifle any speech.

Alice now turned fully to face her mother. Now it was she who took turn to stroke her mother's hair. '– but not in a bad way.' She carried on stroking her mother's hair while in deep thought. 'No, not in a bad way at all, actually' she mused aloud, picking a fallen hair from her mother's shoulder, and then letting it drop to the floor.

Alice shivered from her reverie and re-focused her eyes back on her mother's familiar face. 'I can't explain yet explain Mummy, how or why. In all honesty I don't think I yet understand either myself. But I feel that a light has just been switched on for me this week. For some reason I can now see what I couldn't before. Some of what I see pleases me and some of it doesn't – but what is different from last week is that I feel that I'm now in a much better position to make choices that serve me rather than oblige me to have to accept cards that others have decided to deal me.'

Alice's mother was relieved to know that her daughter wasn't injured or hurt, but equally she didn't really understand what Alice had said or what had caused her change in perspective.

So, she chose a middle ground when she next spoke. 'So that's good? And you are happy?' she nervously explored.

Alice nodded and thought for a moment before answering. 'Yes Mummy, it's a good thing, I know it is. Or, at least, I know it will be.'

Her mother hugged Alice again. 'Well darling, although I genuinely don't have a clue what you are wittering on about, I trust your judgement. I have *always* trusted your judgement, Alice.'

Alice beamed. She kissed her mother's forehead and leaned back a little to look at her again. 'Thank you for being you, Mummy. I cannot tell you how important those particular words are to me right now.'

'So, are you still keen to get the train into Shrewsbury ...' he mother haltingly asked.

'Of course I am, Mummy. You know I love dances and cannot imagine preparing for it without your advice and assistance. So, let's get up and get going, just the two of us!'.

Alice and her mother left the house after breakfast and then strolled arm-in-arm chattering animatedly all the way to the local station.

Although the distance they had to travel by train was 15 miles, the two were so engrossed in their conversation that neither noticed anything of the journey and were both quite surprised when their train eventually pulled into Shrewsbury General station, a Victorian-era construction with an unusual imitation Tudor façade.

It was busy at that time of day, the station's connections with Wales, Birmingham and London

96

being the primary reason. There were goods being moved, people in colourful clothing, uniformed military personnel with their kit bags on their backs, steam from the engines, the aroma of coal and steam filling the air and a general sense of urgency and determination all around.

While Alice and her mother were getting their tickets clipped as they waited to leave their platform, Alice looked around and noticed someone in naval uniform at the front of their queue. The figure looked like a good-looking woman, a role model for how her friend Emma Parry might be dressed as a naval communicator. Then, briefly embarrassed by her error, Alice realised it was in fact a good-looking man with slightly olive-skinned –who also seemed to be a little lost and was having directions towards the platform for the London train connection explained to him by the ticket inspector.

Then she noticed something else that no one else appeared to have noticed. His naval rank was on the wrong arms. And when he drifted away Alice saw a red flash bordering the bottom of the central vent of his jacket. She immediately knew that she had seen that uniform before and committed herself to mentioning what she had seen to Pearl the moment that she got back home.

Alice elected not to share her platform observation with her mother, deciding instead that it would have been far too complicated to narrate the whole story.

The two women emerged into the daylight outside the station and looked around. Alice grabbing a surreptitious look at her watch to ensure that they would get back to Kynnersley in good time.

'Shall we grab a cup to tea first?' she suggested, hoping that they would then be able to go back to the station from the shops and not introduce a risk of their trip back being unduly delayed over refreshments.

Alice's mother hadn't noticed that she had an agenda and timetable. 'That sounds perfect darling. We can then decide which shops to attack, and I can also look at my list to see what your poor father has asked for. We also need to think about your cousin's birthday coming up and I need to get something for my sister too as Edith and Charlotte have their birthdays that are on the same day annually.'

After a couple of minutes, they found a tea shop and settled themselves into their seats.

'What does Edith do these days?' Alice enquired. 'And what about Charlotte? I know Charlie is about to finish school. I suppose they will all stay in Wales on the farm there. Seems like as good a place as any to see this war out'

Her mother replied. 'Well, I think the Ministry has now mandated that they must remain ... or at least Geoffrey and Edith remain ... to fulfil milk production quotas, but as for what Charlotte will do after she has done her school exams, I am none too sure. I know from correspondence from Auntie Edith that she is worried that Charlotte will move away to somewhere at far greater risk from night raids, but I suppose that's almost inevitable if she moves anywhere away from that tiny corner of Wales and the countryside. But she also many not do that quite yet. Edith mentioned in her last letter that they are thinking of making a couple of the farm buildings into dormitories and hosting evacuees there from the cities – I understand there is a huge need to find places out of harm's way for the kids being evacuated. And I gather Charlotte sounds quite up for being the local youth leader to help them settle in and act as a child minder.'

'Goodness, who would have thought of Charlie being responsible for a troupe of kids! If only the government knew that she is such a tomboy and anarchist!' Alice laughed, picturing her cousin in her mind, and recalling the antics they both used to get up to.

'I hope you mean that in a nice way Alice, as in wants to challenge the status quo and push the boundaries, rather than have an interest in causing problems for the sake of doing so? Because we really don't really need to have to deal with that kind of behaviour at this tough time. The authorities have quite enough on their plate at the moment.'

'Yes of course I mean in it a nice way, Mummy! Charlotte is a sweet person – but a little like I was saying earlier with my yearning to participate in the war effort, she too wants to contribute and start her life ... and doesn't feel she can in that Welsh backwater.'

Her mother grimaced. 'I know what you are saying and understand where you are coming from. But I personally think Charlotte should be slightly careful what she wishes for when it comes to this war. I know living in a

Pembrokeshire hamlet is life limiting in so many respects, but it could be a lot worse ... and life limiting ... if she ended up somewhere busy, industrialised and highly populated. But isn't giving safety and a life to dozens of children meaningful and fulfilling enough? I can tell you that if and when it happens, she will find her hands full before she knows what's hit her. And she might also enjoy it. She has the character to do a splendid job there. And it is vital war work. As important as fighting Germans in the minds of many parents who have now found themselves in the line of fire in some way.'

Alice nodded. 'You're right of course, but the yearning doesn't diminish. Well, with me it doesn't diminish.'

Her mother leaned over a squeezed Alice's hand.' I know darling. It's hard being as patient as you are.'

Alice lifted her head and looked straight into her mother's eyes. 'It's harder still being a darn patient, I can assure you.'

He mother looked away knowing that she needed to change the subject. 'Well, I think we should order and then get off shopping.'

Alice managed another surreptitious look at her watch. Then, shortly after they had eaten and drunk a particularly fragrant pot of tea between them, they set off for the shops and for the remainder of the morning in Shrewsbury they both achieved what they needed to achieve.

Material bought, plus a few small personal items requested by her father, the two of them returned to the station early afternoon and headed back via Newport to Kynnersley.

* * *

As soon as she was back Alice grabbed her bike and cycled back to the Crudgington Theatre, desperately hoping that Pearl was still there.

Happily, she was – though she was surprised to see Alice again.

Alice used the excuse for suddenly re-appearing of bringing her the new material for the dress. As they chatted Alice quietly snuck a look behind Pearl to see what was on the table behind her. The naval uniform that had been there the previous day looked to be missing.

Once the two women had discussed dress patterns and looked at the material that Alice had bought, and over which Pearl had swooned she decided to raise the subject of the uniform.

'Gosh, you were a busy bee yesterday after I left you,' Alice sympathised.

Pearl became suddenly and unexpectedly defensive. 'What do you mean?'

'What do you mean by 'what do you mean?' Yesterday afternoon, you had a mountain of work on your plate – I recall a blue dress onto which you were sewing sequins, you needed to unpick a uniform and re-sew the rank the right way around, you also had some tasks to start preparing costumes for the next swathe of shows the theatre company will be putting on. That's why I felt so bad asking if you had any time to make a dress for me ...'

Alice's words trailed off in slight protestation that Pearl was asking her to explain herself.

'Oh yes, sorry, I am a bit discombobulated today for some reason – must be my time of the month.'

Alice knew immediately that Pearl was deflecting. 'Well, I wouldn't be in your shoes with the amount you have to get through. I mean,' she fished, 'for example, how long did it take to deal with the naval uniform – there was a massive amount to work needed for that. It must have taken you until the wee small hours to unpick all that braid and then re-sew it.'

Pearl looked surprised with what Alice was talking about and turned in her seat to look at the uniform 'But I haven't done it yet Al – 'she lifted other bits of material and patterns on the table and then looked under it and around it. 'Where is it?'

Alice could see that Pearl was now quite agitated. 'Where is it, Al?' Pearl again asked, this time in more a whisper.

Alice went round Pearl's workbench and looked all around as well to satisfy herself that the uniform definitely was not there.

'Um, could you have mended it this morning first thing perhaps and forgotten that you had done so? Or did you, possibly, put it somewhere yesterday to do – or even take it home with you to deal with while listening to the wireless after dinner last night?'

Pearl was not really listening. 'No, no I didn't ... Bernard!' she shouted from her seat. 'Oh Bernard' she sang in a two-tone pitch, just like a dog owner calling a recalcitrant hound to heel.

A minute later he appeared at her door.

'Did you call me? Sorry, I was in the auditorium with Lawrie, err ... um, mounting the stage light sets.'

He then spotted Alice and suddenly displayed inexplicable hostility towards her. 'Oh, it's you again,' he said and then tried to check himself to cover his rudeness. 'How lovely to see you once again. I hope you are not delaying Pearl from her vital war work.'

Alice responded politely, but for her coolly, 'It's fine Mr Miller, I am just dropping off some material that Pearl has kindly agreed to make into a dress for me ... in her own time of course. I will be off in two seconds.'

'Ah, OK.' he replied satisfied to know why she was back at the theatre and with Pearl again.

He turned to face Pearl 'You called?'

'Bernard?'

'Yes Pearl?'

'I don't *think* I am losing my marbles *yet* Bernard, and no Mother's Ruin has passed my lips for days, but ...'

Alice could tell that Pearl was obviously plucking up courage to ask Bernard Miller the key question.

'But, what, Pearl?' he replied starting to sound impatient.

'But what has happened to the Lieutenant's uniform that I needed to repair, and which was on the table here only yesterday afternoon? It was there – I picked it up yesterday afternoon. And I haven't moved it or worked on it.'

'Are you sure Pearl?' he asked.

'Most definitely Bernard' she asserted.

His eyes darted between Alice and Pearl. 'Ah, of course, I know what's happened Pearl. I'll have a word with Lawrie in a moment when he has finished dealing with the light sets in the theatre. I bet you he has taken it to RAF Rednal for their Gang Show, not knowing it needed some running repairs. Yes, that's certainly it. Let me talk to him to confirm that.'

Pearl was now quite cautious in how she spoke. Like Alice, she had noticed Bernard's strange response.

'Well, if it is only Lawrie and a Gang Show than that's fine. But it ought to give the military audience a good few laughs though.'

'Why do you say that Pearl?' he asked curiously, realising that he suddenly needed to feel his way.

'Well, it's just that the rank on the uniform is the wrong way round and is bleeding obvious to any military person worth his salt. Very noticeable, but not a problem if you are only using it in a comedy sketch.'

Bernard coughed and immediately turned to leave, 'Hmmm, well I will talk to Lawrie right away – but I am sure that will solve the mystery.' He then set off for the auditorium at pace.

'Thank you, Bernard.' Pearl called after him, purely for politeness' sake and without meaning or emotion.

Alice moved to stand right in front of Pearl. Loudly so Bernard Miller could hear Alice bid her farewell – if he was still listening. However, with one hand she held a finger up to her lips instructing Pearl to be quiet while she urgently beckoned Pearl to come closer. 'I'll be off now Pearl – mother and I are baking later. Thank you again for so very kindly helping with the dress. I am so glad you like the material too,' she said at the top of her voice for the benefit of the theatre manager.

She then leaned into Pearl's ear 'Are you still on for tomorrow in The Plough? 5 pm? We need to talk – I saw the Lieutenant's uniform being worn in Shrewsbury earlier today. Someone was passing themselves off as a naval officer – acting.'

Pearl's eyes enlarged and her mouth gaped in shock. She whispered back very quietly, 'I need to tell you things too, Al. Important things. No ... particularly important things.'

They held hands for an instant without saying a further word, both nodding.

Alice was then gone from the theatre and peddling home.

Chapter 15

Day Four (Thursday)   15ᵗʰ May 1941

Thursday morning arrived and was one of those dismal rainy days that did not encourage too many outside activities. Inside buildings clothes steamed as they dried out, while windows fogged up.

Getting to work by foot or on bicycle had not been enjoyable as people battled their way through sheet rain and gusty winds.

Everyone elected to move between points only when necessary and then only with the least amount of communication or interest in their surroundings. Meanwhile driving cars, or avoiding them, had been a hazardous occupation.

Alice's Canteen shift was already hectic.

Overnight the air station had been busy and had flown multiple sorties, which it was increasingly having to do when the weather was bad. However, although she did not know how or why, that morning she had picked up possibly good news snippets from banter between two aircrew suggesting that the crews were now 'finally getting an edge' over the Luftwaffe with the help of some 'new kit,' Whatever it was, she just hoped and prayed that it kept the crews as safe as possible.

By 9am the remnant ground crews and aircrews exhausted from their overnight exertions started to slope off to their quarters for sleep and a well-earned rest. Not long after, the Canteen started to fill again and see its usual trickle – and then flood – of base engineering and secretarial staff grabbing timeout in it to refresh their souls and feed their stomachs.

It always fascinated Alice to see how ritualistic people became where relaxation was concerned, some eating the exact same foods day in and day out, others always ate their meals in a particular choice of seat, while others always read books to actively discourage social contact. Alice recognised the latter trait especially – as she herself often took a novel into a tea house to immerse herself in a book without interruption.

Just before noon she emerged from the kitchen with a tureen of her immensely popular hot vegetable soup. She put it down behind the servery and ferreted in a low cupboard for some clean bowls. Stacking them to one side of the tureen she looked up at the faces patiently waiting in the queue before then ladling the liquid into each of the bowls, smiling and handing them over. Having worked in the Canteen for months she knew most people by sight and a few, even, by their first name or nickname.

Enjoying the happy chatter with her grateful customers as she served them, she suddenly became distracted when, through the queue clamouring to be fed at the servery, she noticed the man who she had last seen speaking to the theatre's Technical Manager sit down at his usual table half-way down the hall to one side.

She ladled the next soup straight onto her foot, instantly making her squeak and jump back in surprise and nearly causing her to knock the whole soup tureen onto the floor. Blushing and apologising profusely to the surprised faces in the queue she set about cleaning her shoe and floor around it with a cloth that she had to hand and with a mop and bucket that she had had to dive into the storeroom to retrieve. She then rinsed her hands and once again took up her serving position, apologising for her carelessness, while giving assurances that soup would not have had a chance to get cold.

It was only when she felt she had regained her composure – and when there was a reduction in the queue – perhaps only 5 minutes after the soup spill and after yet another top up of the soup tureen in the kitchen – that Alice dared to sneak another look in the direction of the engineer's table ... which was now vacant.

Chapter 16

Ray Thomas had an equally busy morning.

After an early morning drive over to the Criggion radio station he settled into his office chair and read the overnight reports on the station's HF and LF voice intercepts of the Luftwaffe and German naval forces.

Ray liked being based at Criggion. Nestled under the western escarpment of the Briedden Hills close to the River Severn, when he had first arrived there, it had had almost no radio interception capability, instead mainly employing engineers setting up HF transmitter and aerial systems.

The year before, in 1940, The Admiralty had realised that the battle to defend and keep Britain's Atlantic re-supply lanes open relied upon effective communications. Anxious that the increasing attacks on Birmingham and Coventry by the Luftwaffe could result in damage to its primary HF, LF and VLF radio station at Rugby, Criggion had, therefore, been designated a key alternative HF and LF transmission site that would also, shortly, broadcast VLF radio signals.

That suited Ray because while the emphasis had been on the site eventually becoming an important location for transmissions, he and his team were left completely alone to get quietly on with their work of intercepting radio traffic. From an initial staff of only three in August 1940, he now had a team of fifteen split into three shifts, each shift running four linguists and one administration manager. Even in the fleeting time they had operated they had collected a wealth of intelligence listening in to HF ship-to-shore voice communications and HF voice chatter between Luftwaffe aircrews and between their aircraft and their bases.

While everyone knew that the best intelligence would come from decoding encoded traffic, it was, nevertheless, acknowledged that in the heat of battle, comments voiced between radio operators frequently and inadvertently revealed super valuable intelligence. And it was currently his team's prime responsibility to listen in to the Luftwaffe's HF voice network to provide RAF High Ercall's Commanding Officer with a daily field feedback on the success or not of the introduction of the RAF's new RDF-2A equipment and air defence tactics.

Using a new miniaturised RDF-2A radio direction-finding equipment that was being installed by Telecommunications Research Establishment engineers on all the Blenheims and Beaufort's at the air station, the RAF's aim was to be able to vector accompanying Hurricane fighters onto the enemy bombers delivering for Britain an all-weather and all-light-condition national air defence capability.

That morning it didn't take Ray long to get a clear view of what had gone on over the previous twelve hours once he had clarified one or two things with the Duty Watch Leader. He made a few adjustments to his draft Daily Lessons Learned briefing document and then set off for RAF High Ercall. A little less than an hour later he arrived at the air station's gate, completed the new security formalities, and then drove onto the airfield.

He drove between, on one side, two rows of six single-story moss-green painted corrugated iron-roofed huts and, on the other, a row of four earth-coloured nissan huts. The road then took him between two large brick and corrugated iron hangars, the main doors of both facing the runway apron.

Eventually he arrived at a car park situated in front of a two-story brick Command Building, which itself was attached onto the front of the Officers' Mess and beyond which was the air station's tall brick water tower. He parked up in one of the bays opposite the Command Building and prepared himself to brief the Commanding Officer. He checked his papers and reminded himself of some of the detail of the German language exchanges that had taken place over the previous night and then, out of habit rather than for any other reason, glanced at himself in the rear-view mirror to smooth his hair down and look vaguely presentable for the Group Captain.

As he was doing this, he noticed Jakub Novák, the ebullient and most senior of the Czech aircrew on the base, emerging from the sandbagged and sentry-protected entrance to the building.

Always pleased to see Jakub, Ray opened his door and clambered out of his road-weary Wolseley 14/60 and waved and called out to catch Jakub's attention.

'Morning Jakub, how are you this fine dank day? Were you airborne last night? I gather it was quite a busy night.'

'Ah Mister Ray, this is a delightful surprise. I want you anyway. No, I was no flying but one of us crews was yes. One Hurricane boom over Cardiff but I just heard that pilot bailed out OK time but break ankle when he lands. Hugh Archer, you know? Pilot Officer.'

Ray Thomas smiled. 'One of *our* crews Jakub,' he emphasised the word. 'One day I will understand what you say in English! '

'Ha, ja, and one day you will speak proper Czech too!!'

'And why, Jakub, would I ever want to speak Czech when all I need to do is to speak German?' Ray retorted impishly, joking that the Czechs were only Germans in disguise following the invasion of the country two years previously.

Jakub winced and laughed, simulating being struck by a spear and dying. The two of them had an excellent rapport.

'But I am pleased to hear everyone about got back unharmed – in fact, that's what I have come to see the CO about now. I think the new RDF-2A kit onboard is hurting them – and I am sure he will share what I have to tell him with you at your next flight briefing.'

'That good the know Ray. Special to know, you would not believe,' Jakub slapped Ray on the back so hard he almost felt over. 'I plus, um, plus as I talking want to ask you question – why I want see you. OK to ask now?'

'If it is quick. The CO can wait a few minutes – I will just say the traffic was busy.'

They both laughed at that because the traffic was never busy in Shropshire.

'OK I do speak now. Strange. Want to ask you – a language man.'

'So, go on.' replied Ray.

'You know Miroslav, our Batman, yes?'

Ray nodded knowing he was referring to the Czech officers' mess steward.

'Yesterday after lunch time at 1430, Miroslav walking to NAAFI getting supplies. Stopped in road by civvie man with the Chaplain. Asked him if interested in a funny show, like funny theatre, on the station soon? Miroslav is a fun guy, right, so he say yes. Man say "Tell him funny story of being Czech in England now" So, Miroslav tell funny story which end with, how you say, hit—'

'—Punch line?' Ray guesses.

'Yes, ja, good, punch line. In German tongue he give the punch. Man laughs and tells Miroslav better end for same story ... in different German, you would not believe.'

Ray still was not entirely sure what Jakub was being so animated about.

'Sorry Jakub, I am still a little unclear. Apart from Miroslav being stopped on the way to the

113

NAAFI by the Chaplain and this man, and this man being able to speak German, which many people can by the way. What is your point Jakub? What do you mean by "different German"?'

Ray was starting to think he really need to get going to see the CO.

'Point Mister Ray is man speak in perfect Sorbian– only we Czechs and Poles understand Sorbian talk in the Lausitz region – east of Dresden … like town like Bautzen or Pulsnitz … only two kilometres from Czech border. Point Two Ray is also man saw family name of Miroslav on uniform – and Miroslav now fear his family at home from German occupiers now if this is bad man and knows his family now.'

'Miroslav thinks this man is bad, or German? Why?'

'Cannot say, only feeling in boots, simple fact, Miroslav know he not speak general school German you all English speak, but special old German that only German from Oberlausitz talk. And he talk is perfect speak. Perfect speak. How he know Sorbian? Many German people not know Sorbian. Strange, ja? How he know talk Sorbian to Czech and not general German to Czech? Not to believe.'

'It sounds a bit strange, yes … and interesting. Would you like me to raise it with the CO when I see him in a minute? Meanwhile I can certainly speak to the Chaplain and ask who he was hosting yesterday afternoon – or I might even check the Visitors Log myself.'

And then Ray added as an afterthought, 'One thing Jakub, did Miroslav indicate to the civilian visitor that he had spotted something unusual in the man's German accent?'

'No, Miroslav tell me he not show man he saw his Sorbian. No speak to Group Captain please now. I will ask Miroslav questions. We speak again. I try to understand more. As this serious. Possible.'

'OK Jakub, that's a plan. Let us keep this between us for the moment, yes? And tell Miroslav not to discuss this matter with anyone else – only you.' Jakub nodded his agreement.

'I will do some digging and let us try to talk tomorrow. If that's OK?' Jakub nodded again. 'Well, I really had better get going and see the CO now. Good to catch you Jakub. See you tomorrow.'

Ray then headed in to see the Commanding Officer, but afterwards he recalled that he did not remember too much about his conversation about the new direction-finding equipment, as his thoughts were very much swirling elsewhere.

Chapter 17

Had Alice seen Pearl earlier in the day, she would have found a young woman trying to concentrate on her work, but someone also stopping and looking up with anxiety at every sound she could hear from her workroom.

Both Lawrie and Bernard were out again, which they had been a great deal over the past few days, Pearl mused.

She knew Lawrie had been out visiting a few local air stations to assess the technical requirements of hosting the Gang Shows on them. She also knew that Bernard had been involved in this process, as they all had at RAF High Ercall the earlier in the week.

However, she suspected that, having suggested to her a few weeks ago that he was an avowed bachelor, Bernard might well now have a fancy woman somewhere, because he had now taken to going out for 2 hours – blocking out his diary – first thing in the morning.

Finding the Morse Code ember in the dustbin had really spooked her.

She repeatedly asked herself why someone would, first, need a Morse Code decoder, second take the trouble to burn it when Morse Code was a well know communications method and, third, dump it behind the theatre in its dustbin.

She had rationalised to herself that the theatre's dustbin was out of the way off the road and so it would then, quite probably, be a candidate where someone doing something nefarious wanted to ditch something, even if the dumping had been carelessly executed and resulted in things being found.

But this in turn then made her worry even more, that the rear of the theatre was being watched by someone – and that was unnerving.

It also concerned her that, for some unknown reason, she had not yet felt that she wanted to share her discovery with either Bernard or Lawrie – not that they should not know, but that she had not processed things yet and wanted first to chat to Alice and Emma Parry, who she knew was home on a 72-hour leave pass from her Portsmouth-based work.

She decided that Emma, ever the leader of their trio, would know what to do and so felt easier in wanting her fresh mind to pass an opinion on her worries. Yes, that is what she would do, as she herself was far too close to events – and in any case she had a mountain of Singer work to do and did not have time to think.

Not having mentioned anything to Bernard or Lawrie yet, nevertheless, felt uncomfortable.

Pearl eventually switched her desk lamp off at half past four, locked up the building and started walking to the pub.

Chapter 18

Emma Parry was looking forward to a night out with her friends. More importantly, she was particularly curious to know if the man who was, according to Pearl, interested in Alice, was going to cut the mustard.

She knew she herself was blessed with having come from quite a wealthy background and having lived in the same house since birth on the outskirts of Newport. But she had never really managed to imagine what it must have been like for Alice and her family having to relocate to lodgings in an area of the country they did not know chasing work, and with all the problems and privations that emigrating from somewhere familiar involves. And that was not even considering Alice's difficult physical and medical position.

All she knew was that she was desperately keen for Alice to find a soul mate and have some fun.

Meanwhile in confidential truth, although she knew she herself was presentable, educated well, fully mobile, and able to chase any desire she had, she was in awe of Alice who bore her disability with fortitude and refused to allow it to get in the way of anything she wanted to do. She admired Alice's inner strength.

She had been with Alice on many nights after Alice had been rejected for war work on grounds of her physical disability, made all the harder one evening when she had to break the news to Alice that she had been accepted into the Royal Navy's Communication Branch and would be soon leaving for the south coast. Like Alice she despaired that so much store was placed on physical ability, with mental agility – which Alice had in spades, being by far and away the brightest and fastest of the three of them – coming a poor second in the selection assessments that they had all variously been asked to perform from time to time.

She herself was enjoying life now, even under wartime conditions – or perhaps because of wartime conditions, though the regular bombing of the south coast was one of its less attractive aspects. She was a terrible flirt, even if she said so herself. She scrubbed up quite well too in her navy-blue WRNS Number Ones and so had managed to build up a good social life in Portsmouth, not committing to anything or anyone, just working and playing hard and seeing how things evolved.

Perhaps it was partly because she felt guilty of her freedoms that she had agreed to meet for a drink in The Plough. She, Emma, had the world at her feet aged 22, but Alice did not or could not, at least not yet. They had both attended their WRNS interview together and had imagined their future lives in navy blue uniform, not for a moment suspecting that one of them would later be rejected on grounds of physical disability. Emma knew how hard receiving the Admiralty's rejection letter had been for Alice – and how much she remained wounded.

Emma picked up her keys and told her mother and father that she would be late and then set off for the pub on her rickety old bicycle.

Chapter 19

An hour or so earlier Ray had nearly rung the pub to make his apologies.

After seeing the Group Captain in the Command Building towards the end of the morning, Ray had taken himself to the Main Gate only to discover that the new access control procedures, now guarded over and controlled by an RAF Police NCO, had made it impossible for him surreptitiously to check the new Visitors Log to find out who the Chaplain had hosted.

So, he then decanted to the RAF Police Office and, using a pretext, spoke to the Flight Lieutenant in charge – hoping the registration details from the previous days log entries had been extracted for general intelligence sharing and analysis.

Fortunately, under the new security regime visitor information was now being captured daily and so he could see that the Chaplain had the previous day signed in and escorted a Mr L Sumner from the local theatre and that Sumner and two others had been on site, again escorted by the Chaplain, two days previously.

Later, with a bit more digging on the air station, Ray was able to establish that the Chaplain doubled-up as the establishment's Entertainments Officer – and so any slight concerns that he had initially had that the Chaplain had more than just a passing connection with the visitors were allayed.

Meanwhile Ray's thoughts were turning to seeing Alice again.

In all honesty he felt a bit conflicted – and was entirely not sure how he was going to strike the fine line between finding more out about the Morse Code that she had seen and wanting to get to know her better socially.

He was no Casanova. He knew only too well. He had never had a proper girlfriend. Yes, there were some nervous teenage fumbles at school dances up in the Welsh valleys near in the Merthyr Tydfil, but none resulted in girlfriend material.

But in his early teens he had been interested in radio and had marvelled at being able to hear obscure languages from all over the world – all talking at once. Wanting to find out what they were all saying excited him unbelievably and so learning languages and then listening for them and discovering what they were saying became his whole teenage existence. As an adolescent, at least, girls simply did not feature in his mind, or in his plans.

So, he had nearly, but not quite, rung the pub to bow out of the evening, initially arguing to himself that he was too busy with serious responsibilities that demanded his immediate attention

But he had soon laughed at himself and at the self-important pomposity of denying himself an evening out with a woman whom he could not deny had stopped him in his tracks and connected with him in a way that no female had ever done before. Plus, she had noticed something locally that had piqued his interest – and he wanted to get to the bottom of whatever it was that she said she saw.

Ray stood in front of a mirror in his digs. He leaned into it so that his face filled the reflection. He stared hard at the image staring back at him.

'Are you scared Ray Thomas? If so, what of? Revealing too much about yourself? Mixing work and pleasure – never a clever idea? Being rejected again? Guilt? That you might start to enjoy a normal life at this messed up time?'

The face looked back at him impassively.

'What have you done to me Alice, because I am now under your spell.'

Chapter 20

If Alice had seen the air engineer again that day, she would have tried to make an excuse to find out who he was. However, although she kept an eye on everyone who came in the Canteen during the remainder of her shift, she hadn't spotted him again.

When she finally took off her work smock at the end of the day, she took herself to the female shower block for a freshen up and change into clothes that she had brought with her for the evening.

She allowed the block's tepid water to beat down on her shower cap and flow down her back. But she rationalised that tepid was better that cold – and just leaning, both hands against the wall, feeling the sensation of cascading water over her, was soul enhancing and reviving.

She knew she had to explain to Ray more about the light pattern incident but then wondered how, or whether, she should raise with him anything to do with the other things that had been noticed over the past few days.

In turn this then called into question whether she had been right to classify Ray as a probable soul mate the way her own body had encouraged her to do earlier in the week when she did not know him at all.

By the time the shower water had begun to turn from tepid to cold she decided that she was over-thinking things and that she should just allow the evening to unfold in the way it wanted to, using the same philosophy she used herself to treat each day as it came, one day at a time.

She then dried herself, dressed and applied some makeup and, when ready, set off for the pub on her bike.

Chapter 21

The clock on the St Mary's Church in Crudgington struck five times to mark the hour.

Emma arrived at the pub shorty after it had struck. Seeing the pub sign and knowing there would be a roaring fire even at this early hour on a dank cold Spring evening filled her with warmth and familiarity after weeks of having been away on the south coast.

She opened the door and found an empty table in an alcove that she reckoned would be enough to accommodate their group. Making herself comfortable on one end of a wooden settle, she plucked off her gloves and unwrapped her scarf as she surveyed the rest of the room to see if there was anyone there she knew. It was still early, so there were few people in the pub – and nobody she recognised.

Next to arrive was Alice – Emma thought her to be quite flustered as she limped her way into the already cigarette smoke-filled room, quickly spotting Emma and waving, then moving over to her table.

'Wow, Ems, you look a million dollars. That sea air is doing you a load of good!'

They embraced and held each other tightly as two great friends always do.

'And I can see that good old Salop cow pooh air is giving you energy in your tank too Al. Is there nothing that ever stops you?'

'I wish ... though,' and with an impish grin, 'I am working on that!' The two women burst into laughter. 'Can I get you a drink Ems?'

'No thanks, I am OK at the moment,' Emma replied, 'Let's wait until everyone is here. I've literally just arrived myself. I was just reflecting on the good times we have all had in this place – all those pounds and shillings spent here, all those beery snogs and singing. Great memories that last.'

'Won't they just!' Alice agreed. 'I know I was late to the area from Wee Welsh Wales – do you remember Old Frank who used to prop up the bar all day and night describe it as that – but you all made me so welcome, and it became a home from home from home.'

'God, I remember Old Frank alright – he stank.' Pearl contributed. Neither woman had noticed her arrival. 'I was never sure if it was the pigs or his body odour!' she added.

They hugged each other, happy to be in each other's company once again. Emma was the first to break from the scrum.

'I think we are going to have good evening, ladies – I feel it in my bones! Here, Pearl, come around this side of the table and sit with Al and me and then we can watch all the talent coming and going and nobody need crick their neck.'

The three women launched into fits of laughter again as they each took off their coats, folded them and then stuffed them in a corner out of the way. Suddenly Alice whispered from the side of her mouth to the other two as she deliberately kept her head facing forward. 'Batten down the hatches, girls, here we go, wish me luck ...'

Pearl and Emma stopped chattering and faced back forward to see an extremely good-looking man tentatively approach the table from the doorway. 'Um ... am I disturbing something?' It was Ray. Alice had momentarily lost her voice seeing him again. Then, for some reason, she stood up and leaned across the table and held her hand out, which he shook, not saying anything, just grinning at her.

'Oh God, that's so formal isn't it, Ray! Whatever made me do that?' Alice shrieked in shock at her behaviour.

He continued to smile. 'Well, it does it for me!' He then addressed everyone. 'I think it's probably a drink all round yes, what would people like?'

Alice offered to help him bring the drinks from the bar and worked her way around the table, following him up to where he stood ordering drinks. They chatted and laughed about nothing in particular until the drinks were all poured by the publican and then relayed them to their table and sat down. Ray sat with his back to the pub facing the three girls. Alice then got up and moved into the seat alongside Ray with her back to the pub too to balance the table.

For the next hour they talked and told jokes and stories of their distant and more recent pasts, everyone studiously avoiding any talk of work or of anything consequential. It was relaxed and convivial and time flew for all four of them.

Eventually Emma piped up. 'So how did you two meet?'

Ray gestured to Alice that he was happy for her to reply.

'Well, it was purely by chance actually,' Alice replied, glancing at Ray to check is he was still happy for her to continue, which he confirmed with a slight nod.

'I know this is all going to sound very weird, but I was cycling to work on Monday morning incredibly early and was just going past Home Farm, you know Ems, the big farm with all the barns on the outskirts of Tibberton?'

'I know it well. Owned by the Garth-Williams family. Hector and Francine parents, a beautiful French lady – or at least they were the parents. Now passed. Sons, who I think still own it: Bentley and Austen ... we all used to feel so sorry for Austen being the far cheaper vehicle – the teachers even used to call them the Car Brothers at primary school ...'

Everyone laughed. Alice picked up the story again. 'Well, as I was passing the barns I noticed something or someone flashing a light – it was quite misty that morning, so I am not 100% certain I wasn't seeing a reflection off one of the barn sides – but it was definitely a pattern of lights ... of four flashes, then darkness and then four more so the pattern went on ... probably for about a couple of minutes. The silly reason I noticed it is that the pattern was the same as Strumble Head lighthouse near Fishguard in Wales where I grew up. Four flashes every 15 seconds. If it hadn't been such a familiar light pattern to me, I don't think I would have noticed it.'

Emma whistled pensively. 'H in Morse.'

'Yes, that's what Ray told me when, later in the morning, I asked around the Canteen what the flashes meant, as I haven't a clue about Morse Code. It was in fact Ray replying that was our very first conversation.'

Ray was thoughtful. 'Roughly what time of day were the flashes?'

'Around half past six in the morning. I was cycling into work'

'And did you see an actual light source, or just a loom of a light?'

'As I said, I can't really be sure, probably just a loom though it was bright – and I really don't know if I saw the light reflected off some of the farm equipment or buildings, or whether I was seeing them direct.'

'Could it have been someone switching lights on and off in the barns?'

'No, it was definitely from a lamp or torch or something of much lower power outside, even given the time of day and the fact that it was around sunrise time.'

Ray was now quiet and looking across the faces of all three women. It was Pearl who was next to speak, doing so very hesitantly and nervously at first.

'Well, since we are all talking about Morse Code, I also have a question about it. I haven't been sure what to do about finding ... this ... in the dustbin.'

Pearl had grabbed her over-shoulder bag and extracted an envelope from it. Then, from the envelope she gingerly plucked out the burnt orange remnant of the Morse Code table and placed it in middle of the table between everyone. The three others leaned forward and each in turn, picked it up, examined it and then put it back down onto the table.

Ray picked it up and turned it clockwise in his fingers. 'What dustbin Pearl? And how come?'

Pearl let it all spill out. 'I was working at the theatre on Tuesday afternoon, as you know Al.'

Ray briefly turned towards Alice, who was nodding, to absorb her response. He then he looked back at Pearl.

'Alice came to see me you see, um, to ask, um –'

She suddenly couldn't remember if Alice's request for a dress was secret or not. '– to ask me something about clothing. And after she had gone and after I had had a natter with Bernard, the Theatre Manager, I carried on working. Later I decided I needed a fag before going home. So, I grabbed the Pertrix from the back of Bernard's office door – because it's good in blackouts – and went out the back for a cigarette. When I had finished the fag, I stubbed it out and put it in the bin. It was when I put the fag butt in the bin that I saw this scrap of paper.' She pointed to the burnt remnant.

During her monologue Alice noticed that Ray had suddenly looked as if 20,000 volts had gone through him. He had gradually sat forward with the straightest of back, like an animal coiled for action.

'Hold on Pearl!' Ray exclaimed, 'Could you just wind back a moment please. You said Pertrix? How and why do you know the name Pertrix?'

'Because the torch has Pertrix No. 679L is stamped on it,' said Pearl as if nothing was unusual. 'It's just the name of some hand torch that Bernard has. About 4-5 inches in length, roughly 3 inches wide and a couple of inches deep with a big cyclops eye about 2 inches in diameter? He uses it in the theatre to point with the main beam to stage positions when he is in the auditorium watching rehearsals and wants actors to move to slightly different positions. And, as I said, it also has a low light setting – a side lever changes it from main to low light very easily. He uses the low light setting for the props and prompts so that he can view the scripts and stage directions in the dark wings – well that's how Bernard describes his use of it, though I have never actually seen him using it. But I have used it several times for a sneaky ciggie break.'

'Was there anything else remaining of the rest of the orange label in the bin?' he pressed. 'Anything, perhaps, with a little cartoon sailor boy struggling to shine a lamp in front of him?'

'Is the word D-A-I-M-O-N, by chance, familiar to you?' Ray persisted, spelling out separately the letters of the word in the hope that Pearl might recognise the spelling rather than his pronunciation of the word.

Alice and Emma exchanged furtive glances, both alarmed at the way the conversation was going.

Pearl thought for moment and then answered. 'No that isn't a word I recognise Ray. Sorry. And if there was other coloured paper in the dustbin, then I didn't see it. What's more, unfortunately, I think the dustbin men came first thing this morning, so there now won't be anything left in the bin were you thinking of checking.'

Ray did not say anything for a moment. He looked at each of the women in turn as if sizing them up and reaching a conclusion.

'What I tell you mustn't be shared with anyone else, just between the four of us – do I make myself clear?'

The three women all nodded, each individually wondering why he was being so assertive and discreet.

Ray glanced quickly over his shoulder to check that nobody was immediately behind him and leaned into the table. He then twisted his head slightly towards Alice. 'Look after my back.' This was clearly expressed as instruction, not a request. He then addressed all three women earnestly, looking at each of them in continuous rotation.

'As you know I am a linguist. I specialise in several languages including German. Let us just say it is my job to understand Germany and Germans. OK?'

The women all nodded silently.

'Pertrix is made by The Pertrix Company, a Berlin enterprise that makes dry batteries and torches for the Wehrmacht and Luftwaffe. Its batteries are labelled Diamon, spelt D-I-A-M-O-N. They have a logo on them of a little cartoon sailor boy struggling to shine a lamp in front of him. They are predominantly orange and are flat 4.5-volt dry batteries. On the back of the batteries they have printed on them a full Morse Code. This is printed on an orange background.'

On hearing this Pearl's hand flew up to her mouth of stifle an exclamation of surprise.

Ray continued.

'Pearl, the Pertrix No 679L torch that you have seen has what is known as a stealth slider. It is not a mere low light setting lever used in theatres to read stage directions. The stealth slider is used for dark hours signalling.'

Ray held Emma, Alice, and Pearl in rapt attention. He hesitated for a moment and then decided it was safe to carry on.

'Ladies, Pearl has used an original German and, importantly, German-powered, torch when she smoked her cigarettes. Worryingly, this *may* now suggest a current and ongoing German connection with the torch, otherwise I would have expected the torch to have had an English 4.5-volt battery replacing a dead German 4.5-volt battery, not a Diamon battery ... and which the user seems very much to have wanted to conceal.'

It was Alice who spoke next.

'Ray, given what you have just said, I think there may actually be a bit more to all of this, if we join up the dots.'

Ray looked quizzically at her. 'What do you mean join up the dots? Have there been other things happening that you now think might be connected to this torch and the battery?'

Alice looked at Pearl, who looked back and nodded her assent. Ray followed their eye contact like a hawk.

'Pearl and I know that some naval uniform that she was mending for a costume went missing on Tuesday and ended up the following day on the body of someone getting on a train in Shrewsbury heading for London, yesterday. Is that a coincidence, or is it connected?'

Ray moved his head forward and opened his eyes wide in disbelief, not speaking. Alice went on.

'And, when Pearl and I were chatting in her workroom at the theatre the other day – um, again, on Tuesday – I recognised one of the engineers from the air station there.'

'What, at the theatre? Really? Who? What was he doing there?' Ray asked.

Pearl cut in. 'Well, that was the strange thing. We overheard them–'

'– And fleetingly saw him as he passed our door too Pearl, don't forget that.' Alice interjected.

'Who do you mean 'them?' Ray persisted with yet another question.

Pearl corrected herself. 'Oh, sorry, yes, well it was this chap from the base that Alice recognised and Lawrie Sumner, who is our theatre's Technical Manager. They were chatting about our broken theatre microphones that the RAF engineer said he could help to mend once he had

136

access to some equipment or other that was currently on an aircraft. But that's the strange thing. I don't understand why Lawrie told him that the microphones were not working because Lawrie had tested them himself only that afternoon. And they were all working fine then. I know this, because I was there when he did it.'

Ray turned to face Alice. 'Do you know the name of this engineer from the air station?'

'No sorry I don't Ray, but I have seen him many times in the Canteen. He usually carries bits of equipment around with him in a canvass grip. He has a good rapport with the Czech aircrew if the banter between them in the Canteen is anything to go by. He is a nice man. Private. Comes across as very competent – and always willing to be of help. I am sorry, but he doesn't wear military uniform or rank or any name badge and so I don't know who he is exactly. But I know what he looks like.'

'OK.' Ray said cautiously. He slowly looked around the table before speaking again.

'Is there anything else anyone else wants to share?'

'And they're probably meeting in The Sutherland Arms in Tibberton on Saturday lunchtime' Alice suddenly blurted out.

'Who, Sumner and this engineer? How do you know that?' demanded Ray.

Alice amplified. 'I have just remembered. The engineer proposed it, didn't he Pearl? While they were talking?'

Pearl was not so sure and just shrugged her shoulders.

Alice insisted, 'Ray, I am sure. Absolutely sure. The Sutherland Arms was mentioned. Absolutely sure. And I am sure that Saturday lunchtime was mentioned too. And noon'

He looked across the faces of all three women to see if anyone else had something to add to the discussion.

Emma spoke next, clearing her throat before she started to talk. 'Um, it may be nothing ...' she said nervously, allowing her voice to tail off.

'Go on.' Ray quietly encouraged.

'It's probably nothing–,' she tried to insist, '– but when Dad and I were in the pub here last night, after I had arrived back from Pompey, we overheard Dougie Newton from Home Farm asking around the other farmer workers whetting their whistles if any of them had been having problems from poachers or gypsies. What you need to know Ray is that I have known Dougie ever since we were at primary school together. His family has always worked for the Garth-Williams family. The thing is that, as best I understood, something went down this week between some people up by Upper Field in the woods up there – you know Pearl, that bunch of fields a little way off Mill Road ... up by the Heath?'

Pearl nodded. 'I know where you are talking about.'

Emma continued. 'Dougie thought he saw a handgun there too. He guessed it was some black-market deal taking place, which of course, being Dougie, he doesn't have a problem with. However, what rattled him was the handgun and the fact that someone was shifting a package that required a weapon.'

Alice timidly half-raised her hand asking permission to speak. Everyone turned their faces to look in her direction.

'Well, like Ems, I don't know how relevant any of this is ... but I have been asked if I know the names of any of the Czechs on the air station. Could that be relevant?'

Once again Ray jerked his head forward in surprise and opened his eyes wide 'I should say! Who was doing the asking? And what were they asking?'

'Well, it was Pearl's Theatre Manager, Bernard Miller. It was only in passing, the other day when he was on the air station, but it was a bit intense questioning all the same, wasn't it Pearl?'

Pearl again nodded.

'He wanted to know if I fraternised with the Czechs and wanted to know their names so that he could approach them for acting in the Gang Show that the theatre is putting on there.' Alice explained.

Pearl, whose mind was clearly racing and now starting to connect things together then piped up breathlessly. 'And Lawrie Sumner has had to make a second visit to the air station to sort out production technicalities. He has also visited other military bases.'

Ray blinked. 'You need to explain that comment a little more Pearl,' he urged.

Pearl took a deep breath to compose herself before saying anything more. 'Since the theatre arrived here around a year ago, we have put on films, concerts, ballets, operas, and plays. The other day, however, Bernard announced that we would also do some outreach variety productions, like Gang Shows, on local RAF and army camps in the area – rather than run the shows centrally in the theatre itself. And we would start by running three outreach shows. It's those places that Lawrie and Bernard have been visiting recently to check them out and make plans.'

Ray was listening intently and nodding, deep in thought. 'So, just to pick up on your phrasing Pearl. You just said, "since the theatre arrived here a year ago". Did the theatre not exist before then? And does anyone know where Mr Miller and Mr Sumner hailed from before they arrived here?'

Pearl replied. 'No, neither the theatre nor even the theatre company existed a year ago. And I think two of them are Cornish. They certainly regularly talk of having strong roots in the county.'

'Cornishmen, eh? And what about these outreach visits? Do you know where they have visited?'

'I only know of RAF Rednal as one of the planned outreach sites, though I am not sure. There might also be one planned for the rail workers working on the railway line construction site between Maesbrook and Ford. That activity all has something to do with the War Office or Ministry of Defence or something. Bernie asked me the other day why there was construction taking place there – but I couldn't tell him as I did not know. All I know is that there is some good money for labourers coming out if it.'

Ray didn't say anything for a moment. He ran his hand through his hair and sighed and slouched back in his seat. He then quickly glanced left and right looking over his shoulders to check again to see if it was still safe to talk.

Alice spotted this and leaned slightly in his direction and gently squeezed his interlaced hands on the table. 'You're still OK Ray. It's still all clear,' she assured him.

He smiled at her in thanks, straightened his back, sucked his teeth, and once again leaned forward into the table before speaking in hushed tones.

'So, to summarise, there appears to be some form of German connection with the theatre – possibly, or probably, with the Manager and possibly, or probably, with his sidekick too. They both claim to be Cornish – and turned up out of the blue a year ago. What certainly seems the case is that they currently have almost unfettered access to military bases in this area and are mooted to have a very developed curiosity in what is going on locally? Additionally, of concern is a suggestion that they may be lying to an air engineer who is maintaining aircraft on the base. Meanwhile, separately, or perhaps they are connected, there are some strange goings on with theatre props and equally unusual armed black-market activities are taking place on one of the farms nearby. Oh, and Alice likely fell across someone signalling using a torch ... while the local Theatre Manager owns a most interesting

German torch, whose primary use is signalling. Would that just about sum things up do you think?'

Alice looked around the table to garner agreement, which Pearl and Emma both readily gave back with vigorous nods. 'You have a decent precis there, Ray,' she confirmed.

He took time to scrutinise and acknowledge each of the women in turn.

'OK. I suppose the question now is how to proceed from here. Thinking aloud. I've obviously got to talk to our seniors about all this and ask that you all keep this meeting secret and not mention it to anyone. I am quite certain that there will now be intense interest in the theatre and the two managers and their possible links with Germany. I am also sure that the Group Captain will want to prioritise flushing out the identity of the air engineer offering to help mend theatre microphones that aren't broken. Meanwhile I warn you that everything else is likely to be of secondary importance, at least for the time being. I am sorry I can't explain why I think this: you'll just have to take my word for it.'

All three women nodded again.

'Alice, darling,' at which point Alice immediately flushed, not with the warmth and realisation that he completely trusted her even after such a short time, but because he was confidently so willing to show this affection to her friends, 'would you be willing tomorrow, Friday – and the day after if necessary, or for however long it takes – to keep a watch for this man and identify him to me when he comes into the

Canteen? I am thinking of proposing a plan to co-opt the assistance one of the senior Czech aircrew to help me out, as he knows all the engineers working on their airplanes. We could park ourselves on one of the Canteen tables and you could then tip me the wink when this guy sits down?'

'Yes, I'd be happy to do that. I am on shift tomorrow, but not due to work on Saturday but could find an excuse to do so if necessary if you needed me to.'

'Good, let us go for that plan.' Ray then downed the remainder of his pint which he had only been sipping until then. 'Anyone for another or call it a day as this evening of relaxed bonhomie and laughter doesn't appear to have gone entirely to plan!'

All three women shook their heads, laughing politely at his dry humour.

Emma departed first closely followed by Pearl, leaving just Ray and Alice at the table.

For a while, neither of them spoke. Alice then softly brushed the left side of Ray's face with the back of her right hand and could feel his stubble starting to appear. He turned his mouth onto the back of her hand and kissed it gently.

'Let's do this again, but, please, not quite like this evening next time.' he joked.

Alice giggled. 'You look tired Ray,' she said, her eyes mapping the contours of his face.

'So do you Alice-Peters-from-the-Canteen.' He held her gaze. 'We have a busy day tomorrow and a need for clear heads.'

She agreed. 'We do.' And then she leaned forward and slowly kissed his lips once, each breathing in the other's scent.

Four eyes shut, both transported.

Chapter 22

Day Five (Friday)   16th May 1941

The following morning, well before dawn, Dougie Newton heaved himself out of his warm bed. It was freezing cold and there was water streaming down the inside of the bedroom windows, the condensation of body heat and breath flowing over now rotting wooden windowsills.

Sleeping on the window side of a double bed, he swung his legs onto the wooden floorboards, lifting his bulk quickly to pull the opened sheet and blanket back under his bottom, which he then sat on to keep the heat in the bed.

He rubbed his eyes with both palms, smoothed his hair down and sighed once, girding himself for the new day.

He then stood up and nudged open the curtain an inch to check what the weather was doing. It had ended up being a clear evening and starlit sky and so the temperature had plummeted overnight. He could just see ice crystals formed on the edges of the puddles from yesterday's rain. On the field rising opposite he could see sparkling hints of frost and ice reflecting the now gradually diminishing glow of the night-time moon.

Dougie closed the curtain again and stole a quick look back at the hair-tousled slumbering shape of Marion, the current girlfriend, and gingerly stepped out of the room, grabbing his clothes from a chair as he moved, avoiding all the floorboards that creaked that might wake her up.

He crept down the narrow stairs, wishing he had put his sweater on sooner, and emerged into the woodfire-infused atmosphere of the small ground-level parlour that doubled as kitchen and lounge.

The embers of the fire were still just visible, and its warmth was slight, though welcome. He bent down, prodded the fire, and put on another log hoping that it would catch and keep going long enough for Marion to build it up again once she was awake. He gave up on being able to heat water for a cup of tea, turned on the tap over the kitchen sink and cupped some ice-cold water in his hands, dousing his head and face to wake and freshen himself up.

Next, he got into his clothes in front of the fireplace and went to the back door to put on his coat and boots.

Lifting the latch on the split-level barn door and stepping outside to take a leak in the outside toilet, he felt the icy strike of early spring and a cloudless night hit him. But it was a wonderful sensation of fresh air and temperature which was invigorating and so he stood for a moment drawing in the air deep into his lungs, welcoming in his lot, before turning towards the privy.

Dougie went back through the back door and closed it so that he could then open a wall cupboard hidden behind it. From the cupboard he extracted one of the two shotguns he had in it, one a gift from his late father and the other a gun supplied to him by the farm's owners. This morning he took the farm gun and opened a box of cartridges to check how many were in it. He then put the cartridge box in one of his waxed coat's deep pockets, closed the cupboard and turned to leave the cottage. Having seen a weapon being handled by the men in the northern coppice, Dougie had decided that he wasn't prepared to take any chances.

Walking the path around the open right side of the cottage to the front gate and immediately onto the road in front, he could feel the ground was icy and so knew he had to tread carefully. He moved to the steps up the bank opposite his row of cottages and clambered up onto a rise and started to head off north away from the farm complex. After about five minutes of walking over still rising ground, he realised he was beginning to look like puffing train as he breathed harder and as his breath condensed in clouds around him in the still air. He realised that what with the crisp ice-cold ground and the condensation of air from his lungs, things were not going to be quite as easy to be concealed as he had originally thought they would be when he had first agreed to get up earlier than usual.

147

It had been around 10 pm, late the previous evening, when there had been a tap on the cottage door. When he had opened it, he had found Colonel Parry and his now extremely good-looking daughter Emma standing there. The two of them had seemed agitated and so he had invited them in.

The Colonel had let Emma do most of the talking.

To cut a long story short, Emma said the Parrys had overheard Dougie asking around the pub if anyone had come across increased poacher or gypsy activity. He was given to understand that Colonel Parry had been asked by the authorities to monitor and coordinate the local response against black marketers. The Colonel wanted to know if the incident that Dougie had witnessed was a one-off. Emma, meanwhile, had asked if Dougie could establish a hide in the same area, to see if there was any repeat behaviour that the police could then act upon.

Dougie had, of course, readily consented, and suggested that before light he would need to set up the hide so that he could move in and out of it without being seen. He knew exactly where he would set it up.

Putting all thoughts of lascivious Marion and their burgeoning relationship to the back of his mind – which was hard to do at times, he frequently randomly mused while seated on one of the tractors or while mucking out the cattle – Dougie headed for the southern of the two coppices, close to Upper Field.

As his head began to reach the summit of the hill, between the two coppices and the gentle downhill sweep right to Upper Field's gate where he had brought the Herefords the other day, he crouched down and moved slowly and carefully to his right. He positioned himself alongside the wood with the woodland becoming his backdrop should someone in the northern coppice be looking in his direction across the summit towards the southern coppice opposite.

It concerned him that the ground was so crisp and icy, risking the noise of his footsteps giving his position away. During his passage up to Upper Field he had worked out a temporary method of suppressing as much as he could the vapour that he was exhaling. His mouth and nose were now buried inside a tightly wrapped scarf around his neck and his face and his beanie were now pulled down around his neck and ears so that only his eyes were exposed to the air.

As soon as he reached the point of entry to the southern coppice that he had been looking for he ducked into the wood and then stood motionless for a full ten minutes facing north looking across the northern coppice. He lifted the beanie off his ears and strained to listen for any noises that might indicate movement or danger. He heard only wind, barn owls, fox screeches and the occasional distant dog bark.

Content, he leaned his still un-cocked and broken 12-bore gun against the base of a young tree and then started to pick up logs and cut branches that only a few days earlier he had cut as part of his coppicing work in the southern wood. He did not need to move more than a pace from his observation point and soon had built a rudimentary wooden igloo structure, the rear entrance of which faced into the wood. He stopped again for another full five minutes and repeated his acoustic vigil. Still silence.

Dougie used as many of the discarded leaves and branches around him to fill in the gaps and make the hide as camouflaged as possible. Extremely happy with his work – his father had taught him well when they had gone poaching – he stepped carefully away a couple of paces from the hide to empty his bladder, and then retrieved his gun and slowly and silently crawled inside the structure. He cleared a few leaves from his line of sight of the northern coppice and then settled down for sunrise and beyond.

He only had to wait about twenty minutes before he heard the distant noise of a car driving up Mill Road. The engine noise did not gradually disappear back into the background as you would expect it to do as it closed and then re-opened range. It just stopped, and it was the sudden stoppage of the noise that nudged him awake from a comfortable dose that he had been enjoying.

The sky was still full of stars. The first hints of a new day were just beginning to show to Dougie's right in the east, the horizon starting to become defined and a horizon-level orange hue just hinting of a dawn soon to follow.

Dougie could hear foot movement over the ground to the front and right of him coming from the north-east of his hide's position and where he estimated was probably the closest point of approach from a vehicle parked up and just off Mill Road. He strained his eyes and hearing to see if he could identify the source. Suddenly he saw four flashes of a torch in the distance pointing north-west to the left-hand side of the northern coppice and then another four after a few seconds. Almost immediately and clearly in reply and from the middle of the northern coppice he saw a double flash of a second torch pointed towards the first torch source.

He could just make out three figures closing on each other, two from the right and one from inside the northern coppice. The two people who came from the right passed over a large parcel to the person who had emerged from the northern coppice. Dougie could just about hear low male voices on the wind but could not make the details of any speech out.

He watched one of the figures track back right towards the far right-hand side of the northern coppice and disappear back down the incline, presumably back to the car parked in Mill Road. The other two bodies moved a little towards his position along the southern edge of the northerly coppice and then changed direction and tracked sharply left all along its southern edge to its far left-hand side. Once they reached the left had side, one of the pair of figures slipped back into the trees and vanished.

The remaining figure then set off in a brisk walk, straight towards Dougie's position.

Dougie swore under his breath. Surely he hadn't been spotted? He suddenly felt very clammy.

Keeping his eyes fixed on the person who was now closing the distance efficiently at a fast-walking speed, Dougie used his fingers and his sense of touch to search for his gun. Finding it still in a standby state, Dougie realised with dismay that he had omitted even to load let alone cock the gun and knew he was now at a rather key decision point: should he do so and almost certainly give away his position in the southern coppice, or should he keep it unloaded and un-cocked and just hold his breath and hope that the man bearing down on this position still had not seen him.

His heart was pounding fast. His lips suddenly felt bone dry. He started to feel a bit giddy from a surge of adrenalin coursing through him.

Dougie kept his eyes fixed on the approaching individual. Then, maintaining a static upper body shape, he imperceptibly used friction between his right-hand glove and his jacket to grind the glove off his hand. He then moved his exposed hand slowly into his pocket and rummaged around for the cartridge box until he had grasped two shotgun cartridges.

A nano-second later Dougie made his decision and acted. He slipped the two shotgun cartridges into the gun's twin barrels and cocked it in an almost single motion, while calling out to the unwanted visitor in synthetic anger.

'Hey man, what are you doing spoiling my shot at the rabbits?'

Dougie then emerged from the wood with his gun aimed at the ground in front of advancing person.

'Who are you?' the man from the northern coppice asked. Dougie could see that he was not dressed for country pursuits and was wearing muddy brown brogues.

'I am the gamekeeper on this estate, sir. Far more the point, sir, who are you?' Dougie knew that he had seen the man's face before, but just could not place it.

The man ignored Dougie's question. 'What are you doing?' he shouted out, with considerable venom.

Dougie stopped and started to raise his gun to threaten the man who stopped his forward trajectory but who then moved sharply right to, once again, track left around Dougie.

'I think you have come quite close enough, mister. I would stop right there if I were you.' Dougie cautioned.

The man took a couple more steps to his right, moving further to Dougie's left, forcing Dougie to swivel even more left as he held his ground feet rooted and apart ready to shoot, his body language indicating his readiness to raise and fire the gun. The man stopped. He then turned to face Dougie.

To Dougie's surprise, given that Dougie was self-evidently armed and primed, the man continued to act with hostility, rather than just stop and shut up. 'I asked you lad, what you think you are doing up here?'

Dougie had come across people like this before and did not hold them in high esteem. However, he was nervous. He knew that although he was posturing with the gun, he would not use it against anyone, though he would be prepared to fire one barrel into the ground to show intent.

Then Dougie made his mistake.

'I know you,' he blurted out, 'you're from that picture house, aren't you? What are you doing up here at this time of day?'

The man looked at Dougie, held both of his hands out and just shrugged his shoulders, one second before Dougie's head was yanked back, his throat was cut with a single sweep of a knife-blade and his gun was knocked out of his hands.

Dougie realised far too late – but sadly for him, he did momentarily – that the Theatre Manager had tracked left to allow the other man, who had tracked right and then disappeared, an opportunity stealthily to return to close to an attack position immediately behind him.

Hair released, Dougie slumped forward as he lost consciousness and bled out.

Chapter 23

Miller looked at him with undisguised disdain, 'What a pity, such a shame. Bury the body in these woods.' he ordered.

Sumner wiped the blade of his knife on Dougie's jacket to clean it. 'How did the PoW know he was here?'

'He got to the rendezvous earlier than he expected and was hiding in those trees over there.' Bernard Miller pointed to the northern coppice. 'He saw him arrive and build himself a hide.'

'Just as well the sun came up and started to melt the ground ice, otherwise I think he might have heard me moving towards him along the tree line.' Sumner observed forensically. He looked up at Miller. 'He said he was shooting rabbits and was the gamekeeper – a coincidence, or for our benefit do you think?'

'I don't know. What do you think – stop running the repatriation route, at least for a while? They will be looking for this man or will already know that he was coming here. Either way it is a problem for us we do not need. There is nothing to link us with this, so we now keep clear blue water between us and the PoW network. Agree?'

'OK. I agree to stop the repatriations – for the time being, but only temporarily, otherwise why are we here in this bloody country? We need to radio Berlin to notify of the suspension. I will signal the suspension this morning. By the way,' he added nonchalantly, wafting his hand in front of Miller's right cheek, 'you have some blood splatter on your face.'

Bernard Miller used his hand to wipe the area Lawrie Sumner had pointed to and swore when he saw blood on his fingers. He then looked down his front and could see he had stood far too close to the dying gamekeeper. He sighed. 'Right, let's process this guy underground and get off the heath.'

Lawrie Sumner, or rather Lorenz Sommer, which is what his mother called him, could not disguise his contempt for his Field Office-in-Charge, Bernd Müller. They came from different stock and had completely different backgrounds and outlooks on life.

In Sommer's eyes it was unusual to encounter a military man like Müller who preferred procrastination and oversimplification to active management or clear decision-making. While Sommer himself was a civilian radio and engineering specialist with practical and motivated skills, Müller seemed far too used to being part of the gilded officer class of an ill-defined skill set and being expectant of people around him, rather than he himself, to focus on the detail and do the grafting.

He personally thought Müller was out of his depth leading the *Abwehrstelle*, given how much hands-on work needed to be done to establish the intelligence cell and launch and operate its various covert activities – though Sommer did appreciate that Müller possessed far better social skills than he did.

While Müller had been brought up in Mannheim and an urban, university, existence, Sommer had spent his whole life in Bautzen in the far south of Germany, until being spotted for his maths and engineering ability in his last year at school and being sent away to be taught the dark arts and science of espionage.

The historical capital of Upper Lusatia reaching back generations, the town of Bautzen sits astride a poor agricultural region, far enough away from the Polish coal mines to the north and close enough to the source of the Spree and Lusatian Neisse rivers in the granite Lusatian Ridge to the south. Living quite a simple basic life, as a child and teenager Lorenz and his father would regularly spend days at a time close to the Hochwald and Lausche peaks in the Zittau Mountains on the Lusatian Ridge where they camped, hunted, and survived. He quickly learned to become self-sufficient and to deal with problems swiftly, quietly, and efficiently. Lorenz also found the process of killing animals an intriguing exercise in maths, engineering, and risk assessment – and by his fifteenth birthday was already a very proficient hunter, never displaying emotion, only ruthless efficiency in the task and execution of the task.

Lorenz mused that he and Müller were strange travel companions who would never associate back in Germany. He knew Müller over-depended upon him – but that suited him because, even though there was demanding work and long hours at times, at least he could be satisfied that their route ahead was safe and that the tracks they left behind them were properly covered.

Fifteen minutes later they were both back in the car and driving back towards the theatre – having quickly covered their tracks in the fields.

It still was not even 6.30 am.

Chapter 24

Around the same time Alice was heading into work from home and Ray was almost at the Criggion radio intercept station having left his lodgings near Shawbury in the dead of night.

They were each glad the sun had risen and, with every minute of warmth, making the roads less hazardous.

Ray had been concerned that driving up the Breidden Hills that morning might prove to be a dangerous occupation in his ancient Wolseley, as its brakes were not great nor his tyres new.

For Alice cycling in perfect weather could sometimes be a challenge while cycling in icy conditions was something that scared her should her bike fall the wrong way and her weaker leg be forced to absorb the force of any crash.

* * *

As soon as he was inside his office Ray grabbed the overnight airborne intercept transcripts from his in-tray that he would evaluate and precis once he got back to the air station. Thankfully, it had been a quiet night over Britain and so the intercept numbers were ridiculously small, most probably due to the clear skies that there had been over the country overnight and the Luftwaffe's unwillingness to fly in such clear conditions.

By the time he later arrived at the gates of RAF High Ercall, it was just before 8 am and a busy time of day for the changeover of watches and shifts. It was very much the start of the military day.

There was a longer queue of cars waiting to get on the base than normal when he got there, not helped by a lorry leaving the establishment had turned too sharply into the exit channel and had impaled itself on some of the low-level signage. The gate staff had stopped the inbound vehicle channel in order the help free the lorry and to get it to reverse off the now splintered signs and straighten up for a cleaner exit.

While waiting for his turn to move onto the base he mulled over the conversation the previous evening in The Plough and started to imagine what format his report to Bletchley Park would take. He reviewed his choice and decision to prioritise the identification of the air engineer and concluded that clarifying the threat to the RDF-2A programme had to be a priority as many lives, civilian and military alike, depended upon the successful introduction of the equipment into the air defence organisation.

When it was his turn, he got out of the car, signed the Visitors' Log and then got back in and drove onto the base, straight to the Command Building again. Parking in the same bay that he had used previously, he quickly scanned his eyes over the thin sheaf of overnight intercepts and scribbled a quarter-page summary on a note pad for his briefing to the Group Captain before heading into the building. He showed his pass at the entrance and then again inside before heading over to the Commanding Officer's office.

The CO was away from his office attending a technical briefing when Ray arrived at his office door, so he said to the Group Captain's secretary that he would come back later and then strolled across to the Officer's Mess to pop his head into the dining room to see if anyone was still having breakfast. To his relief Jakub Novák was just finishing reading a newspaper, and so he went over to his table and slipped into one of the empty seats opposite him.

'Sorry to disturb you Jakub, but could I borrow you this morning? It's rather important and urgent I do.' he whispered without fanfare.

Jakub was surprised and pleased to see him. 'Hi Mister Ray. I give tactics training for Czechs this morning.'

'Is there any chance, please, that you can delegate that to your Number Two? It really is especially important.'

'If you and me smoke a cigarette outside and I teach, no, I school , no, I learn what important, then maybe?'

'I am ready when you are. Now?' Ray asked, continuing to impress urgency of their conversation.

'Ja, now good.' Jakub replied, putting down his newspaper. They opened the dining room's French windows and walked onto the ceremonial patio at the rear of the building.

'Cold.' was all Jakub could say without outer protection from the still cool morning air. He fumbled in his trousers and extracted a cigarette packet and matches, lit his cigarette and then, as an afterthought, offered Ray one. 'You want?'

'No thanks Jakub, I don't.'

'OK, you speak now quick. I bloody cold.'

'I can be very quick now and explain more if you help me. I need you to help identify one of the engineers working on your aircraft. Something has happened which requires us urgently to identify this engineer, or there is a danger that aircraft safety or operational advantage might be compromised.'

'Aircraft?'

'I don't know which ones, Jakub, maybe all of them.'

'Many aircraft, many engineers. How you say, needle something.'

'A needle in a haystack.' Ray explained.

'Ja, that is it, needle in haystack!' Jakub was pleased to be reminded of the idiom.

'No, it is *not* a needle in a haystack.' Ray insisted.

Jakub frowned. 'But you say now, needle in haystack!' he protested.

Ray became exasperated and held up his hand to indicate that the conversation should stop.

'Just listen to me for a moment Jakub. Let me explain it using different words. Yes, there are

162

many engineers working on the airframes on the air station, but I know someone who also works on the air station who knows who this person is, by sight, by eye, but who does not know his name. So, what I need is for this person to identify this engineer and for you to tell me who the engineer is. If we can do that then we will have an idea of what the threat to the aircraft or aircrew is.'

Jakub sucked on his half-smoked cigarette and then threw it on the ground extinguishing it with his shoe.

'Ja, OK. When?'

'Now?'

'You give me 10. I help you. I meet you at Hall Porter, ja?'

Twenty minutes later both men arrived at the Canteen and chose seats at a table on the opposite side of the hall to where Alice had suggested was the engineer's habitual preference.

On the way over, on an assurance of secrecy, Ray shared with Jakub knowledge that had surfaced the previous evening that both theatre managers, in different settings, appeared to be trying their hardest to identify the family names of the Czech aircrew working out of the air station. However, Ray elected not to share with Jakub that there was a potentially live German military connection to them, nor that it was suspected by Bletchley Park and his own intercept team that there was an Abwehr sleeper cell now active in the locality.

Chapter 25

Alice busied herself from the moment she had slipped, almost unnoticed, into the Canteen.

The day shift had completely changed by 8 am and so nobody knew that Alice had already been there an hour keeping her eyes open for the engineer.

Shortly after the shift started, as casually as she could manage and trying not to be too self-conscious, she sauntered towards the Canteen Manager's cramped office situated immediately behind the main dining hall at the head of tight corridor connecting the backroom stores and kitchen area with the front of house servery. Tapping on Margaret's door and entering without waiting for a reply, Alice grabbed a quick look to her right into the main hall before ducking into the office to check again whether the engineer had yet appeared. She knew couldn't afford to spend more than a minute or two in Margaret's office if she was to keep a reliable watch in the Canteen's many visitors.

'Good morning, Margaret. I wonder if I might have a very quick word?' she asked.

'Promptly on shift Alice I see today – thank you,' she pointedly, but graciously, said. 'I fear we may be a little under-staffed this morning, as Hilda's son is back from sea on a 24-hour pass and so I told her yesterday that I was happy for her to take a half day from late morning to spend time with him. What can I do for you?' the Canteen Manager enquired affably.

Alice's heart sank a little hearing that one of the kitchen staff was taking some of the day off, even though in theory that wouldn't normally affect her own work routines, running the canteen till, clearing, and cleaning tables and selling goods from the NAAFI shop.

'I think I met him once –,' Alice commented, '– he's a really nice polite boy.' Alice then hesitated, causing Margaret to glance up at her from her previous position concentrating the following week's menu design. Alice wasn't sure how now to position her request, 'Um ... well err ... I was wondering, Margaret, if you could allow me to spend more time that usual seated this morning, operating the till rather than have to do my usual running about. Unfortunately, earlier I came off my bike on a frozen puddle I hadn't spotted and ended up banging my bad leg in the ground in the process.'

The Canteen Manager immediately leapt up with sympathy and insisted that Alice sat down in her chair, 'Oh goodness me Alice, that's awful. Are you alright?' Here, sit down and take the load off the leg. Do you need to go to the Medical Centre?'

Alice felt very guilty about lying to Margaret and consequently found it difficult not to look flushed, as she guessed she must be blushing. Desperately not wanting to catch Margaret's eye and give herself away, she theatrically focussed her attention on her damaged leg rubbing it.

'No, I'm fine really. It was only a slip, and I was going very slowly at the time because of the ice on the road. It all sounds far worse than it was, but my leg did take a knock and I think I ought to try to rest it as much as I can this morning. It's not as if I can't use it or anything, or that I won't be able to do my job, but just that resting it for an hour or so by sitting at the till would help me immeasurably.'

The Canteen Manager was predictably compassionate. 'Of course you can Alice. I'm sure we can manage for an hour or two with you on the till.'

Alice thanked her and quickly made to leave the office, ensuring that she rubbed her leg again for the purpose of theatre. She then headed straight to the seat by the till, which gave her a commanding view of the whole eating hall.

She had only been in her manager's office a minute or so and in that time nobody had come along the servery to pay for their food. Once she perched on the till seat, she craned her neck to look around the main hall and was relieved to see that there was also no sign of the air engineer she was on the look-out for.

A little before 8.30 am she saw Ray come into the Canteen with one of the Czech aircrew officers. They sat down at a table a slight distance

166

away to one side. As Alice had not yet had a chance to speak to Ray, she didn't know the connection between the two men. However, she deduced from the way Ray had been at pains not acknowledged her presence when they entered the dining hall that he didn't want to share her identity with his associate.

Alice leaned to her right and called behind her for one of her colleagues, 'Georgia, could you give me a hand for a moment please?'

Georgia Mason, one of the Canteen's Earth Mothers with a cluster of children and a wicked sense of humour to her name, was one of those women who never said no – probably the reason she was the mother of a large brood many had been heard to mutter about her in the past, though always out of earshot. 'No problem Al, is your leg causing you gype again today?'

'Oh Georgie, you are a life saver, yes rather. I came off second to an ice puddle this morning on the bicycle, but thankfully without anything more than thumping it.' Alice hated lying to her too.

She continued. 'You see those two men over there at that table?' She nodded in the direction of Ray's table.

Georgia glanced over her shoulder looking into the dining hall, 'Yes, sure.'

'Could you please take a clipboard with you and ask them for their names to check whether they are the ones who have reserved that table. Then, when they do, tell them that the table they are seated at is, unfortunately, reserved under a different name... and ask them to move to the adjacent vacant table.'

167

Georgia blinked, 'But none of the tables are –' then grinned broadly, ' –you're a wily dark horse you Alice,' and then set off in Ray's direction, grabbing the clipboard as she went chuckling to herself and adjusting her clothing in the process so as to present an image of being as officious as she could.

Alice could barely stifle a smirk and hoped that she was not showing any external signs of belly laughing within.

She watched Georgia walk up to Ray's table and lean down to talk to the two men, initially writing down some words and then gesturing that they should switch tables, which they duly did.

Just before they got up from their seats, Ray looked across to Alice and caught her eye, but without showing any emotion or indication to his guest that he knew her.

Alice herself had to look away and pretend to busy herself with chores at the till, otherwise she would have burst out laughing. It hugely amused and excited her that still nobody in the room had any idea that Ray and she knew each other – and that even though they were not talking they were still very much connected and communicating.

Georgia scuttled back to Alice's post, pleased as punch with herself. She made a play of consulting the paper on the clip board.

'One of the gentlemen is called Jakub Novák and is one of the Czech pilots – and is dishy if you ask me. The other one is called Gerald Higginbottom – what a stupid name that is! But I take my hat off to you girl, that was an inspirational move ... I wonder which one you have a beady eye on ...'

For a brief second a flash of confusion crossed Alice's face. Then she glanced across to the men's table and saw Ray desperately trying to hide a broad grin with his hand by pretending to yawn.

Alice looked back at Georgia. 'Georgie, you are an incorrigible stirrer. But thank you, that was fun, wasn't it? It's so dull just sitting on a seat taking money.'

Georgia winked and grinned at Alice as she went back to what she had been doing, cackling with laughter. 'Hmmmm, sure, I believe you!'

* * *

For the next three hours, regularly interspersed with suppressed grins both in the hall and at the till, the vigil continued, but with no sign of the engineer. Periodically Ray and the Czech exchanged words about individuals entering the hall after which Ray then stole a glance towards Alice, in case she might signal the unknown engineer's arrival.

Alice remained imperiously impassive, appearing to everyone else in the Canteen only to be working the till rather than the room.

Towards 11.30 am the first of the lunchtime customers started to trickle in. Alice knew that the trickle would soon become a flood and hoped that the engineer came soon – none least because she was also busting for the toilet and had enviously watched both Ray and the Czech take turns to relieve themselves.

169

Ten minutes later Alice was totting up a tray of food and was about to take the money from the customer when she noticed someone sit on a table on the opposite side to Ray and the Czech officer. Unfortunately, she could not see his face as he had positioned himself with his back to the servery and her cash till seat.

'Well dear, are you going to take my money, or not? I know there are lookers here, but how about doing your looking in your own time?' protested one of the civilian secretarial staff who she was serving.

Alice flushed. 'I am so sorry,' she said, 'my mind wandered for some reason.' In response the secretary muttered something about 'less wandering' and 'more focus' as she grumbled her way to her own table at the far end of the hall and sat down to eat her meal.

Alice grabbed another quick flick of her eyes towards Ray and saw that he had cocked his head slightly at her, asking her to amplify.

She snatched another look at the new arrival but still could not tell if it was the engineer, as he was hunched over the table reading something. If he had come along the servery, she would have immediately recognised him. But because he had not yet come up for food and was also seated facing away from her, she knew she had to try to check him out.

So, Alice got up from her seat and politely but brazenly apologised to the next in the lunch queue to please wait a moment while she took a receipt to the lady she had just served. Then, before the next customer could complain, she picked up the receipt book by the side of the till and filled out the amount the secretary had just paid and tore out the page. She then boldly walked to the very end of the hall and gave the secretary the receipt just as the woman was taking the first bite of her sandwich. Alice threw her a synthetic smile and without saying anything or explaining her action, she turned to head back towards the servery.

Alice kept to the side of hall the engineer was sitting on, and as she walked forward, she checked the face of the man who was engrossed in what looked like a novel. Sitting on the seat on the opposite side of his table was a large RAF holdall with metal boxes inside it – the same items that she had seen before.

She did not break pace. Just after passing the man, she glanced left to give an almost imperceptible nod to Ray, who acknowledged her in the same non-verbal manner. She then resumed her position on the till and, after further polite apologies to the next customer, she got the lunchtime queue flowing again.

Shortly after Ray and the Czech officer rose and left the Canteen.

Chapter 26

Pearl Simpson also had a disturbed sleep and early start to her Friday. The revelations the previous evening and realisation of the reality of things had been hard for her take.

She realised that she would have to walk away from a precious job which she not only liked but was also good at.

On her way home from The Plough she had wondered how she was going to explain the sudden need to leave a decent job to her parents and feared the third degree questioning that she would inevitably get.

But equally, given the facts, she also knew that she had to separate herself from the theatre immediately as she could not guarantee inadvertently giving away a change of attitude towards Bernard, which she was sure he would easily spot, and which might place her at physical risk.

However, for the moment she decided that she would not tell her family anything.

She got up around 6.00 am and made herself a cup of tea.

While still in her night clothes she went back to her room with the steaming brew, grabbed her writing paper and drafted a short letter to Bernie apologising for having to let him down at short notice, using the excuse of her mother having unexpectedly been taken gravely ill. To conceal her genuinely urgent need to completely terminate contact, Pearl offered to return to the theatre to take up her position once her domestic situation was back under control, should a vacancy still exist.

She then made a fair copy of the final draft and signed the letter and put it in a matching envelope addressed to Bernard Miller and put it in her bag.

Pearl washed and dressed in increasing apprehension at the prospect of having to go to the theatre again. However, she knew she had no choice and so steeled herself to walk there to collect a few of her personal belongings from her workbench and deposit her note on Bernard's desk as she departed.

Setting off just after 7.00 am and well wrapped-up against the cool air, she briskly walked the lane towards the centre of Crudgington. As she arrived back at the converted school, she heard the village church clock strike the half hour time mark.

She also heard a car door slam behind the building. She checked her speed and slowed just before the last right-hand corner before the road swept around right past the front entrance of the theatre. She slipped into the shadows afforded by

173

the trees and hedgerow which abutted the rear of the building and its parking area – and stood still.

Pearl could see Bernard's car there – which she thought was unusual for the time of day. He never normally appeared until 10.00 am, unless he had an external appointment.

Hiding in the trees she agonised what her next move should be. Should she stay where she was and risk being seen, or should she now turn around and head back home and risk being seen doing that just as she was breaking cover?

Almost immediately this binary decision was superseded by events. While she was deliberating, the back door of the theatre opened, and Bernard Miller suddenly emerged carrying files in his arms.

Fascinated, she watched him making three swift trips between the theatre's back door and the metal dustbin, taking a moment to tear up the paper he carried each time he reached the dustbin. She watched with curiosity as he fastidiously made sure that everything was torn up and went into the bin, occasionally picking up wayward pieces of paper that had fallen to the ground.

Every time he emerged from the building, he looked around outside, as if to check if anyone was watching him. Pearl remarked to herself that he looked like a man under stress, because he was trying to do things quickly and was not displaying his usual cautious and controlled demeanour. And he was also, self-evidently, not being as careful as he might normally have been to take the time to check his surroundings, to spot her. She was grateful for small mercies.

On the fourth and final trip from the back door he carried what looked like to Pearl to be a parcel of cloth, placing it down on the ground close to the dustbin.

'What on earth are you up to Bernard Miller?' Pearl whispered very quietly to herself. 'Why could you not have been genuine? Why in God's name am I hiding in the bushes?'

Pearl watched Bernard Miller then bend down and pick up a container of liquid which he shook over the contents in the dustbin. It did not take long on the breeze for the aroma of paraffin to reach Pearl's nostrils.

'Oh God Bernard, what happens if the smoke comes this way?' Pearl asked herself in another quiet whisper, increasingly alarmed that she might be smoked out.

Miller stepped back from the dustbin, ignited the contents with a match and stood for a moment observing his handiwork as the fire caught.

Pearl could see that he took off his jacket and folded it with one hand into the dustbin. He then bent down to the parcel on the ground and lifted up a sweater, which he proceeded to put on. Next, he undid his trousers and slipped them off and put them in the dustbin too, allowing them slowly to concertina into the dustbin so that they could catch fire also. He bent down a second time to the parcel on the ground, this time lifting up a pair of replacement trousers, which he then put on.

Next, he poured more paraffin over the clothing in the dustbin, which started to burn very fiercely.

From her concealed position Pearl could see from the bright light of the intense fire that reflected on his face that Bernard appeared almost to be in a trance, impassively gazing at the fire and watching – and waiting for – the contents of the dustbin burn.

Fortunately, the majority of the smoke from the brazier was floating away towards Pearl's left and well ahead of her concealed vantage point, but she could already start to taste the smoke in the air and knew that only a slight eddy in the air or change in wind direction could easily swamp her position and cause her to cough and reveal her presence. Meanwhile, not wanting to be seen, she dared not move a muscle or make any attempt to put a handkerchief in front of her nose or mouth.

In her mind Pearl hurled abuse at Bernard while she watched him from the trees with an almost icy disconnection. She kicked herself for not spotting that what the theatre offered had obviously been too good to be true. She castigated herself as to why she hadn't asked more questions. But she also protested, in her defence, that she had been duped, along with everyone else – and rationalised that she shouldn't blame herself or be blamed for not realising that something wasn't right, particularly where the missing props and clothing was concerned. After all, Bernard's explanation had been entirely plausible ... and who was she to know it was anything different to the way he explained away the wardrobe losses or his torch: indeed, how on earth was she to know that Pertrix was a German name? She was a seamstress, not a bloody spy!

Bernard Miller added paraffin to the fire a third time and used a stick close by to him to prod and move around the burning entrails of the dustbin, Pearl presumed he did this to ensure that it all burned.

He then replaced the dustbin lid and returned inside the building.

Pearl stayed motionless for what seemed an age, but which was in fact no more than five minutes. She had just about decided that the coast was now clear for her to turn tail and head back home when Bernard suddenly reappeared from the back door, this time in a coat. He closed and locked the door, checking it was locked by shaking and pulling on the door handle a couple of times. Satisfied that it was, he turned to his car, got in and started the engine.

Immediately he stopped the car engine and got back out of the vehicle. He walked over to where the clothes parcel had sat on the ground close to the dustbin. With light conditions very much improved by Pearl now watched Bernard bend down and with his right hand pick up a pair of shoes from the ground which he next thoroughly inspected as if he was sniffing them. He then walked to the rear of his car, released, and lifted the boot lid with his left hand and placed the shoes in the boot before shutting it, getting back into the vehicle, re-starting it, and then finally driving off.

The moment Bernard's car was out of earshot, Pearl decided to move. With nobody in the school she decided now was her chance to nip in and out.

She quickly worked her way down a low bank into the car park and used her keys to unlock the door and enter the building. Immediately she was struck by how much dirt and mud there was in the corridor. She could see the imprint of footprints entering Bernard's office from the back door – a single set going in one direction into the office.

She nipped past his office and went into her workroom which had clothes laying over every surface and all over the floor. Clearly someone had wanted something fast and so she guessed Bernard's replacement clothing had originated from one of the costume sets that she had made.

Pearl grabbed a photo of her parents from her desk and opened a side draw to take out her personal design notebooks and a secret packet of cigarettes that she stored at work.

She opened her bag, took out her letter to Bernard, and stuffed her personal belongings into it. She picked up the letter and on her way past Bernard's office, put the note on his desk. His office was, as usual, immaculately tidy. Pearl then headed for the back door.

Just as she was reaching for the handle, she heard over her shoulder what sounded to be big band music. It was noticeably quiet and very tinny, but it was also very real and sounded to be coming from the auditorium. She was confused because the building was empty, and she had seen Bernard lock up.

Pearl turned and crept back towards the sound, reaching the doorway into the auditorium which she cracked open to listen better. She knew that it was a well-oiled handle and door used by people to move unheard in and out of the side of the auditorium during performances.

The noise was stronger and now included tinny voices giving way to bleeps which then gave way to more tinny music and then the unmistakable sound of morse code. It was very obviously a radio that she was hearing. The sound appeared to be coming from the eaves of the auditorium immediately above the stage and lighting gantry. As quiet as possible, Pearl screwed her head to look up. A ladder rested against the rear wall of the stage. And standing high up on the ladder looking into a small trap door was the unmistakable form of Lawrie Sumner with a set of headphones on. She assumed he must have had the volume high otherwise he might have heard her.

Pearl immediately ducked away and moved quickly to the door she had just passed through into the auditorium. Praying Sumner did not decide that moment to come down the ladder she opened the door and slipped through, shutting it carefully and quietly. She then ran as quietly and as quickly as she could back down the corridor towards the back door. However, as she passed Bernard's office she hesitated, nodded to herself and the ducked into the office to retrieve her letter which she stuffed back into her bag. She then headed for the rear entrance and freedom, locking the door behind her.

Crossing the car park, she went up the bank and emerged on the road – and then ran and stumbled her way home. When she got there, she was grateful that her parents were both at work and so didn't have to explain herself. She then ran into the garden and pulled her bicycle from a shed and set off for the air station, hoping beyond hope that either Alice or Ray were on site.

Pearl's world was crashing around her, and she didn't know what to do, or in what order to do it.

The first hour back home she lay faced-down on her bed sobbing ... and listening. She knew that if either Miller or Sumner tapped on the front door she would have an immediate heart-attack. So, between sobs, she briefly lifted her head an inch to listen for the slightest sound of anything that might signify danger.

Once she had calmed down, she debated calling the police, but couldn't imagine for a moment what she would say to them, or where to start the story. She then reminded herself that only the previous evening she had told Ray that she wouldn't talk to anyone about what she had discovered until he had had an opportunity to brief his superiors.

But, having seen what she had seen that morning, she knew deep down that she needed to get a message to Ray Thomas to alter him. She assumed that he worked at RAF High Ercall from the little that he had shared with her and the girls the previous evening. And then fretted: what if he didn't work there? How might she then contact him?

Eventually calmer rational thought dominated proceedings: she was sure Alice would know how to reach Ray and so fixed her attention on the need to cycle as fast as she could to the air station to speak to Alice, whom she knew would still be on shift.

Chapter 27

It took Pearl thirty minutes to reach the air station.

She had been peddling so furiously and was so mentally absorbed, constantly replaying in her mind what had happened earlier, that she misjudged the sharp left-hand turn towards the entry barrier. Flustered, she then applied the front rather than the rear brake block hard, immediately causing her to almost catapult over her handlebars.

For a moment she sat astride the bike frame legs apart, panting. Just sucking in the air. Her lungs were burning. Her legs felt numb. She was sweating profusely.

One of the guards stepped towards her from the Guard House, approaching her with trepidation, his fingers positioned close to the trigger of his .303 Lee Enfield gun, its barrel pointing towards her.

'We're in a bit of a hurry today aren't we Miss?' he suggested, albeit slightly cautiously.

'I'm sorry,' she sucked in more air. 'Yes, in a hurry. In a big hurry,' Pearl managed to say before needing to pant and gulp in yet more air.

The guard stayed motionless and silent, still with his gun pointing at her, waiting for her to speak. Gradually Pearl's heart rate started to subside and she began to feel better able to talk.

'It's really urgent, Sir, I need to see Alice Peters who works in the Canteen. It's really important.'

'Alright –' he cautiously responded, '–but you'll need to show me your identity card and security pass.

'But I don't have a security pass, I am not in the military, nor do I work at the air station,' she replied in frustration.

'Well in that case, Miss, I'm afraid you can't come onto the base. Only people with authorised access can come onto the base.'

'I know that. I implore you. You must telephone for her to come to the gate. Please. It really is especially important. It's very urgent,' she urged.

The guard told Pearl to wait on the side of the access road and went inside the Guard Room and spoke to the Duty Corporal.

Owing to the incident with Alice and Private Harris earlier in the week the Guard Room staff all now knew who she was, so it only took five minutes to track her down and for Alice then to cycle over to the gate.

Alice was incredibly surprised to see her friend there. Additionally, it had only been a few minutes since Alice had been able to leave the Canteen's main hall having identified the mysterious air engineer to Ray.

Seeing Alice, Pearl threw her arms around her and sobbed into her shoulder before calming and explaining herself. The duty guards left the two women alone standing outside the air station's boundary.

Though burbled and incoherent Alice gathered enough from Pearl to know that she needed help. She then went into the Guard Room and telephoned the Officers' Mess and spoke to the Hall Porter to see if Ray was still there with Jakub Novák. After holding the line briefly, she was told that he was now in a meeting with the Commanding Officer.

She came out of the Guard House and instructed Pearl to stay exactly where she was – and not move or talk to anyone. She then ducked back under the barrier, grabbed her bike and, as quickly as her legs allowed her, cycled over to the Command Building.

As she approached its security cordon around the Command Building's main entrance, she braked and stood astride her bicycle. The armed staff manning the cordon had already been alerted that some form of incident had just taken place at the Main Gate and that one of the air station's civilian staff was on their way over to them on her bicycle. Not sure what was going on they elected to stay protected behind their sandbags, one of the two soldiers on duty holding a machine gun while the other manned the field telephone.

Alice called out towards them.

'Gents, I am Alice Peters from Building Charlie. I urgently need to speak to the Commanding

Officer's secretary. Could you please see if she is available and, if so, kindly ask her to pop out of her office to meet me here?'

A couple of minutes later the Group Captain's secretary emerged from the building, initially uncertain as to why a civilian from the Canteen was acting in the way she was.

Alice chose her words carefully. She briefly explained the vital need to talk to Ray Thomas and explained that she had urgent information for him. She asked if he could briefly come out of his meeting to speak with her.

Ray then emerged from the Command Building one minute later.

'What's wrong Alice. Are you OK? Has something happened?'

'It's not me Ray, it's Pearl. She is at the Main Gate and can't get on the base. You really need to hear what she says.'

Ray shouted at the duty security sentries to put Alice's bike to one side of the Command Building entrance and instructed her to get in his car parked a few yards away. He reversed it hard, spun the car around and then drove fast to the Main Gate.

Screeching to a halt he called the Corporal over to his window. The Corporal wandered over to the car and bent down to check the driver's window.

'Yes sir?'

'This is my War Office pass. Please allow that woman, over there, access onto the base,' pointing to Pearl who was sitting quietly, looking ahead of her, 'I will vouch for her and sign her in,' which he then did.

Alice and Ray then swept Pearl up and drove her back to the Command Building at speed. In the short journey from the Main Gate Ray extracted the succinct precis of the events she had witnessed that morning.

They arrived back and parked. Ray walked them to the access control post. 'Wait here both of you – I will be two minutes.'

Less than two minutes later the Group Captain himself appeared at the entrance to the building. The senior RAF officer instructed the security team to let the two women pass and curtly invited both females to follow him.

Once into the lobby they turned and were ushered into a conference room in which several people were evenly seated around a long table.

The Group Captain took a position at the head of the table and addressed the assembled company.

'Gentlemen, I have no idea what this is about, but I am assured that we need to hear what these ladies have to say. So over to you Mr Thomas.'

Ray was standing near the Group Captain's chair.

'Thank you, Group Captain Percival, Sir.'

He cleared his throat.

'Gentlemen, as you know from my briefing to you a few minutes ago, a series of seemingly completely unconnected events have taken place in our area over this past week. These two ladies have provided some of the intelligence that now results in us all seated around the table this morning – and we are in their debt.'

There was a murmur of agreement from around the table. Alice and Pearl blushed.

'As you also know, after piecing some of this intelligence together, it is now believed that an Abwehr cell is currently active in our locality. Backing up this belief up we also have signals intelligence and triangulation data that my group and Major Burton's army signals intelligence group have been jointly working on over the past few months. Our collaborations now house Abwehr transmissions close by and to the east of this air station. Hitherto we have not been able to be more accurate. At least not until today – more of which in a moment.'

'There are strong indicators that two of the Abwehr antagonists are Bernard Miller and Lawrence Sumner, currently of the Crudgington Theatre Company. There may, of course, be other antagonists whom we do not yet suspect.'

'The evidence we have against these two characters is all still rather circumstantial, albeit more than highly probable and mostly detected through either carelessness or lack of awareness. As I briefed earlier, I believe these tell-tale transients on display, once mapped and analysed, signpost us towards surfacing a real and present threat to our military infrastructure, our national air defence system and even to British society through a potential propaganda threat. I know that sounds a grandiose statement, but the facts do not discount the possibility.'

'Where these people have materialised from and how they have managed to achieve such a deep reach into our civilian and military societies needs to be carefully explored and understood, but that is for another time, not right now.'

'Gentlemen, we appear to have a partial breakthrough this morning nailing some of this circumstantial evidence down. At 0730 this morning this lady here, Miss Pearl Simpson, who works as a seamstress for the Crudgington Theatre Company, encountered Lawrence Sumner high up in the loft of the theatre house operating a radio and listening for Morse Code. Pearl, could you please narrate everything you witnessed, first-hand, this morning,'

Pearl did as she was asked, without embellishments. She held the attention of the whole room.

Ray allowed a moment of complete silence to fall on the room before once again taking control.

'It is clear that we need immediately to secure the theatre and take possession of the radio. It is also clear that we need to lift both Miller and Sumner at the first viable opportunity.'

'However, it is equally clear that we cannot pick Sumner up yet because we still need to try to determine whether this intelligence cell has already secured the services of John Crawley, the senior engineer from the Telecommunications Research Establishment who has been installing RDF-2A onto the night defence aircraft and who has now been established and positively identified as having had off-base contact with Lawrence Sumner. If we were to pick them both up at this precise moment ... and if they were operating in collusion ... then they would assuredly conceal the nature and extent of their relationship. This said, I would add here, having worked with him from the inception of the RDF programme, Wing Commander Jakub Novák here –' Ray indicated Jakub with a hand gesture, '– doesn't believe that John Crawley is a bad apple, though he agrees that he may perhaps be a tad naïve, or is not mindful enough of his importance to Britain's defence at this time.'

'For the record we need to know if there are any others involved with this undercover unit. To take Sumner and Miller off the street too quickly or too overtly risks the cell immediately going to ground. Additionally, we need to know who the cell is in contact with – not only to evaluate the type and extent of operational threat they have so far posed, but also to understand the location and reach of their intelligence sources and network supporters – and their interests. I don't need to state the obvious, but to run a POW aircrew repatriation route, which is a strong suspicion of Military Intelligence, notwithstanding running a parallel area intelligence gathering operation, requires an extended resource infrastructure and takes more than just two people to feed, clothe, accommodate, and move airmen along a line. Neither Miller nor Sumner are ever likely to tell us that if we confront them, so we have no choice but to monitor the theatre's post, phones and its people and visitors to see what creeps out of the woodwork.'

'We would also like to know if Miller and Sumner are connected to the field rendezvous that was seen at Home Farm on the outskirts of Tibberton the other day, which we currently assume they are. We also need to know what the field rendezvous actually signified and involved. It remains a possibility, if not a probability, that the field sighting *and* the use of clothing from the theatre wardrobe *and* the movement of POWs are all connected.'

'Finally, we need to try to get a handle, if we can, on what the intelligence cell has been targeting and passing back to Germany about this part of Britain. We must prioritise our actions and move swiftly while accepting certain levels of risk.'

Ray concluded his monologue with this statement of fact and then looked for feedback from around the table.

Everyone's else's eyes were on the Group Captain waiting for his leadership.

'Thank you for that synopsis, Mr Thomas. We must move quickly and accurately – that much is truly clear. So, gentlemen—' he nodded graciously to Alice and Pearl '—and ladies too, can I please go around the table, at pace, for observations or recommendations.'

Over the next ten minutes different various people contributed a range of opinions and comments, none of which altered what emerged as an emergency action plan. The Group Captain eventually brought the meeting to a close.

'Ladies and Gentlemen, 'he announced,' 'we have an agreed plan.'

He first turned to face the army major.

'Major Burton, your intelligence team will place the theatre site under immediate covert surveillance and will very shortly secure its dustbin, as it may still hold vital evidence.'

'On Saturday morning , tomorrow morning, once it has been determined from your surveillance teams on Miller and Sumner that neither are in the theatre nor heading for it, your covert entry team will effect an entry of the establishment, using keys provided here by Miss Simpson, initially to sweep it for the presence of anyone on the premises, for example for a nightwatchman whom we do not know about. Your primary task is to locate and secure the radio equipment, believed to be somewhere in the roof space – and to search for associated code books or paperwork. I am sure I do not have to remind your staff to proceed with caution and to check for booby-traps that the Germans may have left in place overnight to protect their equipment in the absence of an actual nightwatchman.'

He looked around the table to lend gravitas to his words, 'I agree with Mr Thomas that covert entry and search is required to deny Miller, Sumner, and any other unknown associates the chance of being alerted of unusual activity taking place on the old school property. Were this to happen it would almost certainly also affect the lunchtime Sutherland Arms rendezvous between Crawley and Sumner, which we must not jeopardise if we are to establish the nature of the risk to the RDF-2A installation programme and the security integrity of the Telecommunications Research Establishment staff.

The Group Captain continued.

'The moment your surveillance teams on Miller and Sumner clear the way for the covert entry of the building, the police will establish a defence perimeter with roadblocks on all access roads to the village. These will then prevent Miller and Sumner – and hopefully any other undesirables – from entering the secure zone and making mischief.'

Major Burton confirmed his understanding of his responsibilities and then immediately excused himself from the meeting. He left the room to task his team who were parked up alongside the closest hangar.

The Group Captain then turned to face Ray. 'Mr Thomas, you have undertaken that it will be your responsibility to arrange to place Crawley and Sumner under audio surveillance when they meet tomorrow lunchtime at The Sutherland Arms – and not to lose them afterwards. I agree that it is imperative to know if this engineer Crawley is conspiring with the Germans and whether our RDF-2A programme has been compromised.'

'While I hear your request not to lift either man until after that meeting, just in case doing so jeopardises the intelligence gathering opportunity, I judge that I simply cannot permit either man to depart the meeting out of custody.'

'If you cannot establish Crawley's relationship with Sumner in the meeting, then I can assure you that this *will* be determined from position of custody. And, if as you believe, Crawley is innocent, then a period in custody will probably not do him any harm – indeed it might provide a valuable kick up the arse that there is a war on and that bad actors can emerge from anywhere. It's about time these rarefied engineers and scientists threw a six and joined the real world in which the rest of us live!'

The Group Captain rose to leave. 'Please continue to use this conference room as your operational office – and feel free to use my assistant, Helen Lockyear, to help you to fix or arrange anything – she knows her way around most places. My door is open 24 hours a day. Good morning.'

He swept out of the room leaving everyone left in no doubt of what needed to be done.

Chapter 28

It did not take long for Major Burton to task and deploy his team to give himself 360-degree coverage of the old school buildings in Crudgington.

The moment they were given clearance to move, the Major and his team all climbed aboard their military truck and drove the three miles between the air station and the Old School as swiftly as the roads would allow, arriving close by only a matter of minutes later. They parked up a few hundred yards short of the Crudgington Theatre in the yard of a local farm, taking care to ensure that the truck was not visible from the road.

Looking around for signs of life, a surprised farmer clearly needed to be placated by the Major. Telling everyone to stay in the vehicle until he gave the green light, Major Burton clambered down from the driver's cabin of the lorry and quickly crossed over to a barn entrance to talk to the farmer. He had been washing out milk urns when the army vehicle had unexpectedly appeared in front of him.

'Sorry for the intrusion Sir, but we are parking here on War Office business. We should not be here too long, but I am afraid until we leave, neither can you.'

Politely batting off a multitude of questions from the farmer and establishing that there was nobody else on site on the farm at that moment, Major Burton then thumped the side of his truck three times to signal that everyone could disembark. The team of eight all gathered around the rear of the lorry to await his briefing.

'OK guys, not the most ideal location but it's the dice we have been rolled. Just to remind you. Jez and Frank off you go – stick to the tree line and approach from the rear after you have dealt with the neighbour's bin. Nancy, front door. Nutter, Geordie, Tank and Spider, use the hedgerows to deploy to your obs positions on each corner of the building – you all know which corner's yours. Don't fuck up. Don't be seen. Quick job. Remember the aim is to simply to secure the theatre dustbin and not be seen doing so. You've done this type of operation successfully before, so let's do it successfully again. Sergeant Collins, please check everyone is clear, prepped, and swift.'

With that he saluted and turned to head back to talk to the farmer. Although all operations carried risk, he was confident of executing a successful operation because he had hand-picked every member of this signals intelligence unit and they had worked closely together for a year now, frequently deployed at no notice to set up direction-finding or intelligence observation positions of target locations.

Knowing that there remained a high possibility that Lawrie Sumner was inside the theatre building and that he was, therefore, potentially able to see out, Major Burton had had to accept that it would be impossible to drive onto the site unnoticed. So his only option to secure the dustbin had been to plan for sending two men down to retrieve and replace it with a similar one, stealing an identical council-issue bin from one of the immediate neighbours on the way, emptying it out of sight, and then switching it for the target dustbin that they wanted to recover. A drive-by earlier that morning had confirmed that the bins were identical.

As for the front door, he was using one of his female corporals to act as a decoy. He had agreed with Nancy that she would knock on the front door of the theatre and pretend to be a local mother asking if it could host a local school singing competition. The aim was to distract Sumner and oblige him to be in the front of the building – and be physically unable to observe any of the bin switching manoeuvres that needed to take place in the rear car park.

* * *

It took a while for the front door to open – presumably because Sumner was being cautious, or had been busy with the radio in the roof space – but eventually he opened it and politely deferred the request to his manager Bernard Miller, recommending that the lady visitor write to him with details of her requirements while assuring her of a prompt response.

But this was all the time Major Burton's team needed to run into the rear car park and switch dustbins. In a matter of seconds, the switch had taken place and the seized dustbin was carried away into the undergrowth.

Shortly after Jez and Frank jogged back to where the Major was in the farmyard, carrying the theatre's dustbin between them. Both were sweating profusely. As they placed it on the ground by the tail gate of the unit's lorry Private Frank Potts puffed out his cheeks. 'Jesus Boss, you didn't tell us the bin would be almost full. It weights a ton!'

Major Burton smiled. 'That'll teach you to question why we all must go for those early morning runs Frank! Can you just lift it into the lorry lads please.'

Between them Frank and Jez soon had the dustbin standing on floor of the army truck.

Immediately Sergeant Collins, the intelligence unit's senior NCO and Major Burton's assistant, started to unpack the dustbin onto the floor of the vehicle.

Lifting the dustbin lid caused the NCO to cough – as he lifted it, he was hit by strong fumes mixing burnt contents with a residual aroma of a paraffin accelerant. It quickly became apparent that some clothing had been the last thing to enter the dustbin, but that the fabrics had not fully ignited even though they had had paraffin poured over them.

Lifting the burnt material remnants out it also became clear that whatever the clothing had possibly been, a jacket and some trousers, the clothing had prevented what had been burning below it from being entirely consumed. It was also evident that replacing the dustbin lid had also helped to extinguish the fire quite quickly, starving the container of oxygen. Basic schoolboy errors the Major decided.

The team discovered that what had been burning below it had been a large, folded, map of the area on which various hieroglyphs were marked. The large map was seriously damaged from the heat but enough of it remained to show that it had been made up from pasting together smaller map pages, carefully cut so that landmarks and roads did not overlap. The map covered a land area from Eccleshall in the east, Market Drayton in the north, Halfway House in the west and Bridgenorth in the south. At first sight it appeared to identify several PoW camps in the region that Major Burton knew about, such as Wern, Donnington and Condover. But it also appeared to be a working map with the owner using alphanumeric codes to identify different map locations. One set of notations caught the Major's attention, as the map position was close by. Four sets of alphanumerics coalesced around a map mark to the north of their position, north of Home Farm which he recalled had been a focal point of signalling and unusual field activity.

He called Nancy over to the truck having just seen her arrive back at the farmyard.

'Corporal Lightness, Nancy, come and look at this.' The junior NCO walked over to the rear of the lorry and got in.

'All OK Nancy, with Sumner?' the Major quickly enquired.

'All fine boss,' she confirmed. 'A creepy guy though. Let me know when you want me to chat about him.' Then she pinched her nose. 'Bloody 'ell sir, that's a strong stink.'

'Yes, a bit over-powering, but not what's important. Have a look at this, here.'

He pointed to the map.

'You see these notations here? They all are referring to a place about two miles from here up Mill Road heading onto the Heath. Call in one of our unmarked sentry vans – there should still be one parked up about quarter of a mile from here. Take the van with a couple of big bodies – I suggest you take Tank and Spider when they are back, which should be in a minute – and go and see what's at this map location. Have a good sniff around as there may be things being left there for collection. Just in case it is still a live location I suggest you park well short and tab over – and be prepared for a firefight. Take one of the radio sets with you and let me know what you find the moment you have secured the location.'

The corporal was gone after five minutes with her two colleagues.

Twenty minutes later the radio came into life to say that a body of a murdered man had been in one of the woodlands adjacent to the datum point that they had been sent to investigate.

Chapter 29

After the Group Captain had left the conference room in the Command Building Ray, Alice, Pearl, and Jakub sat for a brief time not speaking, each deep in their own thoughts.

Alice's own mind was racing. By rights she ought to have felt completely out of her comfort zone – but she didn't, and she couldn't work out why, try as she might.

The discussions and conversations over the previous few days were a million miles from her usual existence and daily routines. But perhaps, she contemplated, it was because there was connectivity with normal life that made the insights she had and confidential knowledge that she now possessed all the more acute, fascinating ... and exciting. And curiosity about how life is structured behind a façade of how people choose to portray their existence, was starting to grow in her, at pace.

But she also felt conflicted.

While the urge to peel back façades and reveal reality was more than appealing, the reverse side of the coin worried her immensely, that there was a danger that she might now never believe anything or anyone unless empirically or evidentially proven. Nor ever again take anyone at face value. She knew from her own personal experience that there were always things that people wanted to conceal about themselves: and doing so didn't make someone a bad person or immediately justify an accusation of seeking to mislead or misdirect.

But there again, she reflected, as she stifled a slight smile, she could not deny to herself that lifting stones and looking underneath them beat stacking shelves with sandwiches and cigarettes any and every day of the week.

Alice was awoken from her musings by Jakub who had decided to break the room's silence.

'So, Mister Ray. Your plan please.'

'Ah yes, my plan. I am glad you asked me that. Let us just say it is work in progress.'

'Work progress? Not understand Ray.'

'It means that I have not got a clear plan yet.'

'But Group Captain think yes.'

'Yes, Jakub, he does. But I am still trying to work out how to do it. The problem is that we have no technology, no bodies, and no time ...'

'Oh, bloody bugger' Jakub retorted rolling his eyes in exasperation.

'Yes, Jakub, oh bloody bugger' Ray confirmed.

The four of them sat a further two minutes in total silence absorbing the exchange, until Alice spoke.

'Well, it's not true.' she pronounced.

'What isn't?' asked Ray.

'None of it.'

'None of what, Alice?' Ray asked, discernibly tetchily. Alice could see Ray was getting frustrated, but she was enjoying herself.

'It is not true that you have no technology to listen or record the rendezvous. It is also untrue that you have no spare bodies to help at the rendezvous. And it's not true either that you have no time – you have all today to sort things out.'

She enjoyed lecturing Ray and loved the slightly school-mistress tone of voice that she had found inside her.

'Go on then.' Ray invited cautiously.

'In the absence of Pearl being able to get hold of one of the spare theatre microphones, I don't know Ray, use a main broadcast microphone from the air station, or even use a cockpit microphone, transmitting to a speaker with a shorthand secretary or a stenographer taking verbatim notes of what is said. Take a feed to a recorder too. Ray, that is your world not mine. It just seems to me that you have an ability to capture sound and transmit it with the solution already here on the base, or already in dozens of cockpits.'

Ray did not interrupt her flow.

'As for getting the microphone close to a conversation between Crawley and Sumner, you need someone to help you that no one will suspect. Pearl cannot do it, obviously, and no man would do. Sumner doesn't know me. So, use me. And even if Crawley does recognise me, which I doubt he will because I wouldn't be in my Canteen smock, I am just Alice-from-the-Canteen, as you so often tell me.'

She stuck her tongue out at Ray playfully. He smirked back at her. 'And as for no time, as I say, you have all afternoon to design and test a solution.'

Jakub interceded, making a long whistle 'She shit heat Mister Ray. You have a match.'

Ray's eyes stayed focused on Alice's face as he replied to the Czech officer. 'Jakub, the English idioms are "I have met my match" and "shit hot" ... and yes, you are quite right.'

Alice waited for his reply and then winked at Ray. He pursed his lips to try to conceal a smile.

And then it all got profoundly serious suddenly. The Group Captain's secretary knocked on the conference room door and walked over to Ray, handing him a note, which he opened. He waited until she had left the room and closed the door behind her.

Three sets of eyes were on him.

'A body has been found up by North Field. It is Dougie Newton. His throat was cut.'

Jakub sat bolt upright from his habitual slouched position. Pearl started crying. Alice looked stunned.

'So, let's get on with this, Ray,' Alice said quietly. 'These people need taking out.'

Chapter 30

Ray and a team of RAF radio engineers had worked until mid-evening perfecting and testing an audio pick-up and monitoring system that used both the air station's primary broadcast microphone and a modified cockpit microphone.

This had amused Alice who did not know the first thing about anything technical. It had only been a passing idea ...

At one point, in the earlier evening, she had sat on the edge of a table and swung her legs beneath her as she had done years ago as a schoolgirl and looked around her.

To her right was a group of technicians with wires, batteries and microphones ranged around them on the floor and the tabletop. Earnest huddled discussions were taking place between them. The testing of circuits and measuring of voltages and currents was in full swing. Occasionally someone would hold a microphone pick up close to their mouth and say something, while another engineer with headphones on, sitting in front of a green-painted receiver unit at the side of the room, would periodically give either a thumbs up or a thumbs down signal back to the engineers.

Ray was part of this group and at one point took a moment to look across the room to see what seamstress progress was being made by Pearl. He caught Alice's eye momentarily in the process. He rolled his eyes and briefly nodded his head towards his RAF group, suggesting that it was all getting quite technically complicated.

Alice giggled and made a face at him miming her innocence at the problems she had caused. He smiled and winked back at her and then turned back to the engineering task in hand.

To her left, close by her side, was Pearl, surrounded by seamstress paraphernalia, busily adjusting a dress that she had earlier attempted to fit to Alice's frame.

Pearl sensed that Alice was once again looking down from her tabletop at her progress, conscious too of the time of day and the need to get the clothing perfect.

'Al, I will be ready for the next fitting in around ten minutes. Sorry it's taken me a bit longer to do this than I had expected it to,' she garbled from one side of her mouth because she also held a pin in it that she was about use on a seam.

'It's OK Pearl, I am not going anywhere.'

Pearl grunted her thanks. 'The biggest problem are the wires feeding the cockpit radio set pickup that I have sewn into your dress. I have concealed all the wires in the seams of the dress so you can't see them, but only down to the waist. The wires will then have to snake free inside the dress around your waist to the dry cell battery and transmitter pack that you are going to have to insert in your knickers at the base of your spine. It's going to be a very uncomfortable but at least nothing should show from the front ... and only a slight bulge should show at the back above your bottom, as you have a decent spinal curve ... which, of course, gentlemen should not be looking at anyhow. But I was thinking that if you wear a cardigan or a coat nobody is likely to notice the rear bulge anyway.'

'That sounds to be quite a work of art Pearl, thank you. Yes, I was just deliberating how I might hide the bulge behind me should these chaps catch sight of me in profile. I agree a coat, or a long woollen cardigan, might just do the trick. What about the microphone in the bag? Are there are similar problems?'

Pearl stopped what she was doing, took the pin in her mouth and put in in seam of the dress that she was about to sew and then laid the dress down on the table in front of her. She then leaned to her right and grabbed the shoulder bag that Alice would take with her into the pub.

'Slightly different on the bag Al. Look–,' she proffered the bag to Alice, who lifted and examined it carefully, lifting and dropping the bag flap repeatedly looking at it from different angles, '–the pickup itself isn't muffled when the flap is down and is invisible to any casual observer when the flap is open. I'm actually quite proud of that bit of work there, Al.'

Alice nodded and handed the bag back to Pearl. 'It looks very neat and clever Pearl, thank you so much.'

The decision to use two sets of microphones and two transmitters had been decided earlier in the afternoon to ensure that the antagonists could still be heard should background noise conditions in the pub not suit the frequency range of one of the pickups – and additionally to ensure there was a safety fallback, should one of the pickups completely fail.

Alice next glanced over her left shoulder to see what the third and final cluster of people in the long room were up to. She could see that Helen Lockyear, the Group Captain's assistant, and a couple of RAF communicators were hard are work and concentrating on practising their stenography skills, oblivious of the murmurs and chatter going on in the middle and far end to the room to them. Helen had willingly been co-opted into acting as the primary stenographer along with two of the more capable girls from the air station's Communications Centre acting as back up recorders. During the late afternoon, the three women had been given practice conversations recorded onto a magnetic tape to listen to and record using shorthand notation. All three already knew how to write in shorthand, but none of them had ever attempted to generate shorthand transcripts from a taped source that was talking at normal speed. However, by 6 pm they were each achieving a 90% pass rate in every test that they attempted.

While Alice didn't know how well they were faring, she elected not to wander over to interrupt them as it was vital that they practised as much as they felt they needed to get up to speed and be ready for the following day's pressure.

By the end of the evening Ray and his group had jury-rigged and tested and proven a recording system for the primary pickup in the bag. Meanwhile the stenographers had all packed up and gone home – primed and ready for the following day.

Around the same time that Helen and her staff left, so Alice and Pearl too made their excuses, but only after a final dress fitting had taken place.

Later an RAF driver deposited Pearl back at her house first before stopping and repeating the process at Alice's home. Neither woman spoke in the car. Each was in their own thoughts; both were tired out; and neither of them dared inadvertently to reveal anything of what was about to happen.

Arrangements were in place for a driver and car to collect Alice again at 8 am the following morning from her Kynnersley lodgings.

Chapter 31

Day Six (Saturday)   17th May 1941

Long before dawn on Saturday morning Major Burton's unit had Bernard Miller and both actors of the forthcoming rendezvous under close tactical surveillance.

By the time dawn had broken and the weekend had begun in earnest, his team had switched itself around. The tired night-time watchers had been relieved of their duties and allowed to go off to sleep, replaced by fresh faces and new energy for the day.

Major Burton was used to running lengthy surveillance cases but was always short-staffed. No surveillance ever went without a hitch and, he mused from the small office he had temporarily requisitioned on the air station, and there were never enough bodies to run the operations without he himself taking turns on shift.

'Corporal Johnson, Corporal Lightness,' he bellowed from his office into the corridor for everyone to hear, 'My office please!'

Instantly a small man in field clothing and blacked face appeared at his door. 'Sir!' the Corporal announced saluting. Thirty seconds later Nancy Lightness also materialised by his doorway, dressed as an RAF engineer in staff overalls.

The Major smiled at his two NCOs and gestured for them to sit down on the two spare chairs in his office, adopting a far more informal and interpersonal tone in private. 'Come in Dave. Nancy. Excuse the paperwork.' He moved onto his desk a stash of papers lying upon one of the chairs. 'Here, take a seat and update me on Sumner and Crawley. By the way, have you both had breakfast or a cuppa yet?'

'Thanks Sir,' Corporal Johnson replied, 'but I'll survive, thanks. I grabbed a mug of tea the moment I got back. To be honest I don't want to eat at the moment, at least not until I have showered and rested up a bit.'

Nancy didn't speak but just held up her hands in a way to indicate that she was fine too, shaking her head.

'Alright,' the Major accepted. 'So, tell me about the obs then. Dave, you go first – you were on Sumner, weren't you?'

'Well, Sir, there's not a huge amount to report concerning Sumner.' Corporal Johnson suggested. 'He eventually left the theatre yesterday mid-afternoon – we have the detailed timing in the logs of course – and returned to his nearby digs. They are only a ten-minute walk away from the theatre. He didn't carry anything with him from the datum. He stopped on his way back to his

211

accommodation to buy some groceries in the local general store. As you know, we planned for that eventuality, and so already had Private Wilson, who was dressed as a farm labourer, in there before he entered. Sumner didn't meet anyone and didn't appear to leave any messages on any of the shop shelves as a dead letter drop. He briefly chatted to the shopkeeper about the weather and a film that the theatre is shortly due to screen. then, after leaving the shop, he headed straight back to his digs where we housed him for the night and watched for any untoward dark hours movements. Nothing! He was there all night. Jez then relieved me, about twenty minutes ago.'

'And John Crawley?' the Major asked, turning to face Nancy Lightness.

'Well, it all went OK there too, Sir. He's a loner for sure. Well not a sociable person or socialite. He spent most of yesterday afternoon installing another of those RDF-2A airframe kits on one of the Beaufighters. He doesn't appear to suspect that he is under surveillance and is actually a dead easy mark to follow even on the air station. In fact, I would venture to suggest that he is singularly unaware if his surroundings. He tidied up his tools late afternoon, then tested what looked like a theatre stage microphone using an oscillator that is bolted to one of the aircraft service equipment rigs that he uses. Afterwards he locked up what looked like spare airborne equipment not yet installed on the airframes in the secure storage cages. And after he had dragged all his toys into the cages, he then stopped off at the Canteen for a short while to grab a cup of tea and a hot meal before, later, heading off to his room in the barracks, staying there listening to the Home Service on the wireless. He was in his room by 7 pm and only left it twice in the night to go to the loo.'

Major Burton waited a moment to see is either corporal wanted to add anything. When it was apparent that they didn't, he thanked them for their reports and work overnight and bade them happy dreams. Both got up, saluted, and then exited quickly vanishing down the corridor.

He picked up his phone and dialled a number. 'Major Burton for Sergeant Charlie Collins, thank you.' He spoke curtly and purposefully, picking up a pencil from his desk and playing with it with one hand, using his fingers to turn the pencil around and around an imaginary fulcrum while he waited to be connected.

'Ah, good morning, Sergeant, Major Burton speaking. Sorry to take you away from your fried eggs and toast. Can you talk?'

He could hear background noise down the line suggesting that the Sergeants' Mess was well populated for breakfast that morning.

Informed that it was clear to talk and that his Sergeant was taking precautions his end not to be overheard, he, consequently, continued.

'Just to let you know Sumner and Crawley are both under our control. Lightness and Johnson and their respective teams did good jobs overnight to house both actors. How did you get on with Miller?' He then absorbed his Sergeant's report.'

Major Burton frowned and immediately stopped playing with the pencil, instead using it to jot notes down on the back of a spare piece of paper on his desk.

'So just to be clear on this, Charlie, we hadn't a clue of his whereabouts until yesterday evening around six o'clock when he arrived back at his lodging near Sambrook in his car, but since then we have had him housed in the lodgings? And to confirm also, he carried a light brown leather attaché case into the property with him and nothing else when he arrived back yesterday evening ... and that he was careful to lock his car, returning to the car to check that the boot was locked, before then heading inside the house for the night?'

He waited for his Sergeant to confirm his understanding of events.

'OK, thanks for that. Clearly the attaché case would seem to be an item of interest to us, as also is whatever is in the boot of the car. I will let Group know all this. Great. OK, well get back to your food. I will see you here a little later ... OK ... cheerio.'

He hung up the phone, rubbed his eyes with both palms and signed deeply. It had been a busy period and was about to get even busier.

Chapter 32

Alice had a disturbed night.

She kept on waking and fearing that she would let everyone down. She wrestled with the demons she had long burdened herself telling her that she was not as able as everyone else and that she should only have limited expectations or ambitions for her life. However, as the night progressed, she heard other voices arguing with the demons, using facts and arguments to banish doubts and reinforce views. If it had not been for her acute observational skills ... if it had not been for her recognition skills ... if it had not been for her tenacity ... if it had not been for her judgement ...

And then suddenly it was 6 am once again and she was banging her alarm clock to shut it up. She lay still looking at the ceiling, pondering how the day might play out. She rubbed her eyes. She felt invincible with Ray at her side but wondered if she was being too led by his shining light because she was wanting to be led. But she then thought about everything that had happened over the past week. She decided that Ray had not, in fact, led her anywhere – that in fact she had been her own pathfinder. What Ray had done though, without a doubt, was give her the safe space and encouragement for her to find her own voice to unearth the latent skills that she had in spades, but which she herself had always previously dismissed as either unimportant or inconsequential.

In truth – and probably for the first time in her life – she could now clearly see a practical and important value in people like her with latent abilities to identify patterns, connections, and relationships. She had always known she had such skills, but had never been able to capitalise on them. But she also acknowledged an equally valuable role for other people with different skills, like Ray, who are quieter and more contemplative and who examine the world and what goes in it with a far more critical, forensically analytical, eye.

Privately Alice was energised and excited at the thought of blending both together to create far more than the mere sum of two parts, both intellectually and interpersonally. She then immediately castigated herself for daydreaming and told herself to concentrate on things that she could control.

Staring at the ceiling, she lay still for a few more minutes, rewinding all the events of previous few days while checking out the cracks in the ceiling, counting cobwebs and idly contemplating a need to re-paint it.

She then started slowly to nod to herself. One thing she was now determined to ensure: as far as she was concerned, her polio would now become an irrelevance to the way she planned to live her life. She was no longer willing to be defined by her disability. Then, determined and eager to meet a future that she believed she was well-equipped to deal with, she, literally, bounded out of bed.

Her mother was already up and about and was in the lounge clearing out the ash from the previous evening's fire. Alice sat on the sofa on her way to the bathroom by the kitchen and schemed what they would do for their next Shrewsbury visit. Mrs Peters watched her head into the bathroom and smiled, happy and relieved that whatever was going on in her life motivated her and felt good to her, even if she had occasional wobbles, like she had on Wednesday. Alice's mother had agonised about her future from the day her daughter had been diagnosed and could see her usual zest for life draining from her, albeit ever so graciously and stoically, particularly since war had been declared and she had developed an increasing sense of having been left behind.

Alice dressed in the bathroom, nervously, briefly questioning what on earth had possessed her to offer her services to place microphones close to a German spy.

She looked long and hard in the mirror above the basin and asked herself what she saw or what others saw and whether it was the same. She watched her body sway and wondered what tell-tale signs this gave away to others when all she was doing was swaying her torso. She gazed into her own eyes and asked the reflection whether it was hiding secrets and whether it had fears.

'We all hide things, don't we,' she whispered in an admission to the mirror. She then took a step back and looked at herself, head cocked on one side and whispered some more, 'there again, everyone unconsciously gives away something about themselves don't they, every second ... if you know what to look for ... if you are watching and waiting for the signs.'

Alice, the watcher, had had many years of practise, honing her ability to pick up non-verbal signs in people. Too many boyfriends had broken eye contact with her when talking, convincing her of their deceptions even when they chose not to admit to any. She smiled – perhaps it was because Ray never broke eye contact when talking to anyone was one of the reasons that she innately trusted him and had done so from the outset.

She had noticed that she herself and almost everyone else she watched touched their faces in some way when under stress and that women tended to blush, and men tended to display movement of their Adam's Apples when suddenly shocked by something that they preferred to hide. And she knew from her own experience, and from watching families or couples in tea shops or people out at the picture houses, that frequently some of the deceitful turned away from their inquisitors, as if about to flee, while others became theatrical with exaggerated hand movements, or took time to pick imaginary threads from clothing. And then there were those who elected to pick up pens or pencils and inspect them earnestly so that eye contact became impossible.

Alice clasped the basin and leaned further into the mirror until she was almost kissing it. She locked her eyes on her own staring back at her. She could see in her visual peripheries the glass steaming up from her breath hitting the mirror from such close range. She whispered again, purely for her own benefit. 'This is the exam day you have been waiting for Alice Bridgette Peters. Don't mess up the first day of the rest of your life.'

Within half an hour Alice was on her way back onto the air station seated in the rear of an RAF staff car.

Chapter 33

John Crawley stayed in bed until 8.30 am, which was a lie-in for him these days. He got up, washed, and dressed and headed for the Canteen for some breakfast, unaware that someone was tailing him and oblivious to the fact that someone else had slipped unnoticed into his room within seconds of him vacating it.

It had been a long week peppered with equipment installation and equipment commissioning problems. It was not that the air base staff were unhelpful, but more that the aircraft had flown so much over the past week that he was running hard to stand still because aircraft access had been so sporadic. He was sufficiently concerned that during the week he had spoken to his director down at the Telecommunications Research Establishment's headquarters in Worth Maltravers about getting additional qualified installers up to RAF High Ercall to help him speed up equipment commissioning rates.

He enjoyed his weekends off, if operational sorties did not get in the way of them. So, after getting some porridge and toast and a big steaming mug of tea, he sat down and allowed himself the luxury of getting absorbed in a new Penguin murder mystery that his mother had just posted to him.

Around 10 am, after another mug of tea, he sauntered back to his room, put on his duffel coat, and picked up his satchel, checking before he left his room that the theatre microphone was still inside it. His meeting at The Sutherland Arms was not until noon and so he had planned a stroll to the pub to give himself time to grab some much-needed exercise and time outside to enjoy the noises and arrival of an ever more boastful Spring day.

Soon afterwards he started to walk towards the Main Gate and then set off on what he had estimated would be a two-hour walk to the pub.

Chapter 34

Back in Sambrook, Major Burton's shadows reported that Bernard Miller had emerged from his house by 0900 clasping the same attaché case that he had carried into the house the previous evening.

When he reached the car Miller initially checked that all the car locks were still secure from the night before returning to the driver's door, unlocking it, getting in, switching on the engine, warming the car up – and then setting off north towards Stoke-on-Tern and Prees Green, swiftly losing his two motorcycle tails in the process.

Which had infuriated the Major when he learned of this.

Chapter 35

The static team watching Lawrie Sumner's digs had to wait until 0924 for him to emerge. He walked into the village, bought a newspaper, and returned to his dwellings at 0937. When he entered the shop he had been watched at close quarters by one of his shadows who subsequently confirmed that he only went to the counter to get the newspaper and left with it immediately after purchase, not stopping at any shelves and not talking to anyone, apart from the newsagent when he had handed over his money.

At 1030 Lawrie Sumner was reported to be active once again, this time on foot heading off on the road to Tibberton with a cloth knapsack on his back. His surveillance team were already positioned and only too keen to mobilise and monitor his movements from a distance.

At 1031, back at the theatre, the covert entry team were given the green light to proceed with their orders.

Chapter 36

With no further sign of Bernard Miller in the Crudgington area, according to sentries that the Major had posted on all roads as part of a three-mile intelligence perimeter surrounding the theatre, and with confirmation that Lawrie Sumner was on his way to his lunchtime rendezvous at the pub with John Crawley, Major Burton ordered the covert entry of the erstwhile school buildings.

Two unmarked vans drove close to the buildings, stopped momentarily and then drove away.

Any passer-by would have to have known what to look for to spot anything happening at the old school site. They would not have seen two tradesman vans slowing, but not stopping, to disgorge six armed military personnel in balaclavas all instantly vanishing into the surrounding woodland to take up positions close to the rear of the building.

They also would not have seen hand signals between the soldiers that next meant that they split and stood hard up against the wall either side of the rear entrance. Nor that within 20 seconds they had all completely vanished from sight after opening and entering the building, shutting, and locking the door behind them – leaving the key in the door to prevent anyone else from trying to enter the building from that direction.

The covert entry team was led by the unit's most experienced Sergeant. Static surveillance of the building had suggested that no nightwatchmen were employed by the German spies. However, without a physical sweep of the building this could not be 100% confirmed. Meanwhile the entry team knew that it was unlikely that there would be booby-traps on the ground floor of the building, because their briefing from Major Burton had advised that the theatre's seamstress had her own set of keys and had the run of the ground floor of the old school building with no restrictions placed on her by management on where she could go, apart from up ladders.

This meant that, unless and until they climbed towards the roof, the only thing they were likely to encounter at ground-level would be evidence of tell-tales deployed around the building to alert the Germans that it had been visited while unoccupied. The Major, nevertheless, still wanted to know where the tell-tales were positioned, as mapping their physical locations often helped him to direct search teams more effectively towards the high value items being defended. A command decision had, therefore, been taken that the entry team would first sweep the whole of the ground floor to confirm the building to be unoccupied. Only once this happened would it then move on to securing the radio set. And only after that would a more thorough search of the building for the code books and for other potentially useful intelligence take place.

The Sergeant took the right-hand side of corridor they found themselves in with his Corporal taking the left side. Behind them were two intelligence unit soldiers and two covert entry specialists, one soldier and a locksmith behind the Sergeant and another soldier and a bomb disposal engineer behind the Corporal.

The corridor stretched away to a door at the end which the building plan had shown led into the side of the theatre's auditorium. Off the corridor were a series of offices, the first left-hand door belonging to the seamstress' workroom. A second office on the left-hand side of the corridor was an admin office according to the plan. Three office doors on the right-hand side were between them and the auditorium. The second office belonged to the Theatre Manager, the first office was a kitchen and the third office, closest to the auditorium, belonged to the Technical Manager. When they eventually reached the auditorium and entered it, they would find themselves halfway up it on the left-hand side. A door on the opposite side of the auditorium would lead to three storerooms and to suite of toilets and a washroom. Meanwhile in the main auditorium they would have to check two rooms behind the stage where the actors dressed and waited to go on stage. They would additionally have to check the space under the stage itself and climb up into a small film projector room set into the back wall of the auditorium, opposite the stage.

The Sergeant signalled with his hand for the group to move up the corridor. He could not see any paper tell-tales lying on the ground, though he did note muddy footprints on the floor, all heading in one direction towards the Theatre Manager's office. Moving slowly in silence with their rifles ready to fire, they all moved forward together hugging either side of the corridor. At each doorway, the Sergeant on his side, or the Corporal on his, ducked into each of the rooms in turn to check that they were clear and unoccupied.

It took next to no time for the group to reach the door to the auditorium. On the Sergeant's signal the bomb disposal expert thoroughly inspected all around the door and its hinges for signs of booby-trap trip wires and to look for any tell-tale paper, tape or hairs used by the antagonists to provide them with evidence of unwanted visitors. Nothing was found and so the Sergeant cracked open the door and listened for any sounds of movement in the auditorium or beyond.

After a minute of silence, he signalled to the entry team with his hands to follow him through the door, instructing the Corporal and his two team members to move up the left-hand side of the auditorium while he and his team members went right. They all knew the plan – the Corporal's group would sweep the ground-floor stage area and any spaces under it, while the Sergeant's group would sweep the rear of the auditorium, the projector room and all the ground-floor rooms that lay beyond it.

It took a full ten minutes of cautious, silent, movement for all the school building to be swept and deemed to be clear of any nightwatchman. The entry team then reassembled in the auditorium and gathered by the front row seats, putting their guns down, removing their balaclavas and taking off their rucksacks.

'OK guys, now for the hard bit,' the Sergeant said as he looked up towards the roof above the stage.

He knew from the briefing that one of the antagonists had been seen on a ladder high in the roof, half in and half out of what had been described as a roof void.

He used a small pair of binoculars to look up to the roof past a lighting gantry over the stage and through the rope and pulley system used to raise and lower it. The apex of the roof of the auditorium appeared to run down its length centrally from the rear of the auditorium to the front and beyond to the back of the stage area.

The trouble was he could not see a hatch on the rear wall and could see that the roof of the auditorium was basic wood and knew that it would have the external roof tiles attached to its outer side – with no accommodation for loft storage space.

The Sergeant swore. The entry team all understood the problem, as each of them had twisted their heads towards the roof too to try, in vain, to spot the alleged hatch.

'Right gents, we have a bit of a problem here. We know the intel was explicit ... but we also know it came from a civvie in panic mode. I also remind you that the Major has assured us that the source is genuine and not working for the Germans – before any of you start any malicious rumours!'

'Let's face it, it's not an impossibility, Sarge,' one of the soldiers muttered.

The Sergeant swung his frame around to face the man who had spoken.

'No, it's not an impossibility Private Saunders ... but it's also not our job, especially right now, to have an opinion on that either. Our job is to locate and secure this radio – if it is here. So, I suggest you,' and he looked around the whole entry team, 'you all, do your jobs and let's get this search done. OK?'

The team looked at the floor and everyone quietly mumbled 'Yes, Sarge.'

'First thing first, Corporal I want you and Saunders to get the ladder standing over there on the right-side wall of the stage and place it in the middle of the stage against the back wall. I want to see how high up we can reach with it.'

The two of them did as they had been instructed. Just as they were about to lean the top of the ladder against the wall, the Corporal called over the Sergeant.

'Sarge, can you come up here. I think there are score marks on the back wall where we are about to put the top of the ladder which may suggest this has been done before?'

The Sergeant bounded up the steps at the side of the stage connecting it to the auditorium. He joined his Corporal and inspected the marks on the wall's paintwork being pointed out to him and agreed the height of the ladder matched the marks. He also noticed something else.

'Saunders, you are smeared in white on your front and on your inner arms. What is that?'

Private Saunders had not noticed and looked surprised when it was pointed out to him. 'I dunno Sarge. All I did was grab the ladder with both hands and carry it vertically in front of me and then leaned it against the back wall.' He wiped an index finger over what appeared to be fine powder and tried to smell it. 'Looks like dust or perhaps chalk or sommat to me.'

The Sergeant moved up close to inspect his clothes. 'It looks like fine French chalk or flour to me. How strange ...' he shuffled across to the ladder to inspect it more closely '... which seems to have come from the ladder. There seems to be a layer of chalk dust, or whatever it is, on all the upper sides of the ladder rungs.'

He turned to face his Corporal. 'How high were you able to reach when you were towards the top of the ladder?'

'Only about halfway up the face of the wall Sarge.'

'So high enough to be able to service the light gantry if you turned out to face the front to the stage?'

'Yes, Sarge. You can touch the gantry easily, though the space between the two is very tight because of the boxing on the wall.'

'What do you mean, boxing? What boxing? And boxing what?'

The Corporal led him towards the back wall to get him to see what he was talking about.

'If you look up vertically you can see that about a foot above the top of the ladder the wall comes out towards the gantry as part of some kind of boxing. See, it stands proud of the wall by, what, about six inches? And because of that, the space to be able to service the gantry lights is pretty tight.'

The Sergeant stood in silence from a moment looking up and then moved a little to the left and then right to get a different angle on things. He then walked to the base of the ladder and climbed three rungs.

"Corporal, you see that rope over there secured to the wall? It is the rope for the pulley controlling the height of the lighting gantry. Undo it and raise the gantry as high as it will go and then re-secure the rope.'

The Corporal did as he was instructed, and the lighting gantry rose high in the roof. The Sergeant then climbed another couple of rungs on the ladder and reached out to his right, to the bottom right-hand corner of the boxing on the wall. He then drew back his right arm ... and with it the hinged frontage of the boxing, hinged on its left-hand vertical side. He moved the corner of the boxing that he was clasping over his head, changing his hands and hold on the ladder, until the hinged boxing façade was completely open exposing what was behind it.

As he did so a small paper wrap filled with flour ripped, one side of the wrap secured to the wall and the other side secured to the rear of the opening façade door. Flour dust floated towards the ground over the Sergeant, over the ladder and onto the stage floor.

One of the entry team whistled. 'Bloody 'ell, Sarge, you're not just an ugly face.'

The Sergeant stayed motionless on the ladder for a moment looking down and watching the flour distribute itself. He then clambered back down onto the stage and walked towards the middle of the stage, turning to face the wall and glance down to look at his footprints.

'Now that's a decent tell-tale,' he remarked quietly, nodding, in respectful admiration of the Germans.

Everyone then looked up. Opening the wooden boxing façade had revealed a small wooden hatch not much more than 2 feet square hinged on the left-hand side, secured with a small catch.

The Sergeant looked at the bomb disposal specialist.

'Smudge, over to you. I want to open that small door there. Now. Check it for trips.'

The specialist acknowledged the instruction and opened his rucksack for his torch and kit and then mounted the ladder for a meticulous inspection. He first carefully examined all the edges of the hatch and then used magnified glasses to check the securing catch and hinges in an attempt to identify fine wires that might run elsewhere. After about ten minutes he declared that he thought the hatch was safe to open.

He screwed a hook into the door, close to its small handle, and then unhooked the securing catch. Onto this door hook he attached the end of a ball of string, tossing the ball to one of the team below to catch while ensuring no pull on the door from this action. He created some slack in the string and used some surgical tape to secure the slack arc of string to the side of the ladder and then clambered down. He was given back the ball of string when he reached stage level.

'Sarge, ready when you are. I suggest we retire to the corridor we first entered. I can then pull the string taught and open the hatch – all from the doorway into the auditorium. However, I don't believe there are any trips. I think the door will just swing open.'

Everyone quickly moved back into the corridor with the bomb disposal specialist closest to the auditorium door and every else spread out along the corridor crouching with hands over their ears.

'Pull the cord,' the Sergeant ordered.

Smudge took up the slack on the string to the tape on the ladder and yanked it gently to release the string from the ladder. He then tightened the tautness of the string to take up the remaining slack and pulled sharply on the string. The door swung open.

The Sergeant told everyone to stay in the corridor and muscled his way into the auditorium. He clambered the side steps up onto the stage watching the small hatchway all the time. He then slowly climbed the ladder again and, once able, leaned into the space and shone his torch around.

To begin with he thought it was empty. Then he realised that there was dusty grey blanket covering something under it. Gingerly lifting the blanket off the concealed item, as a groom might peel back the veil of his bride at a wedding, he saw that the blanket in fact concealed a cardboard case under it.

Presuming that it was the Abwehr radio that they were after and taking a calculated risk that there would be no trip switches under the case if its users believed that their storage location was secure, the Sergeant privately appreciated the fact that he had not been detonated into small pieces after leaning into the roof void to prise the case from its hiding place.

It was surprisingly heavy, weighing about 9 lbs. It was roughly 18 inches in length, 12 inches wide and 6 inches deep. The Sergeant called for assistance to manhandle the precious cargo down onto the stage. Quickly there were hands out helping to take the case from him, carefully carrying the case onto the stage floor.

The Sergeant climbed down onto the stage and cleared a space for himself to take a close look at it. He flicked the catches of the case and lifted the lid.

Inside was a metal grey box, the top half of which comprised three further metal grey boxes, one box appearing to be a receiver with a tuning dial and a pair of headphone banana sockets, another box seeming to be a transmitter with antenna sockets, an oscillator tuner and power output dial and a third box apparently being a power terminal box feeding battery power to the transmitter and receiver. The bottom half of case comprised three 90-volt batteries and a fourth 3-volt battery. Inside the case was also a morse key and a set of earphones.

Somebody said 'Bingo.'

The Sergeant looked around the team. 'Well done everyone. Now let's get this kit out of here and give the Major and the rest of the team the run of the building.'

Five minutes later they and their payload were heading out in the unmarked vans.

Seconds later, a fire engine arrived – it spent the next three hours pretending that there had been a fire in the school. The police arrived at the same time and set up perimeter security, putting out a story that a local house had suffered a small fire which was being dampened down.

After the police had secured the site, another unmarked lorry arrived and then departed, depositing another team of six bodies under the command of Major Burton who had himself arrived on site to set about sweeping the building for its code books and any other intelligence of value.

The local roadblocks would stay in place for the rest of the day.

Chapter 37

About an hour later, when Lawrie Sumner was around 30 minutes short of the Sutherland Arms, an unmarked civilian car arrived at his Crudgington lodgings and three people got out, entering the establishment with a police warrant and instructions to take his rooms apart.

Chapter 38

Alice arrived at the Command Building shortly after 8.30 am.

As her staff car had pulled up to the Main Gate a few moments beforehand Private Harris had dipped his head to see who the passenger was.

Seeing Alice, he had burst into laughter and winked at her. 'Well, your boat has definitely come in Miss!'

As the car had passed him, he had saluted smartly, still smirking. Alice had giggled and called out to him through the open window.

'You're a cheeky one Private Harris. Very cheeky indeed.'

As soon as the car had stopped, with the driver clearing her way through the access control positions, Alice entered the Command Building and was immediately ushered into the ladies' toilet by the Group Captain's assistant. She was then given the modified dress that she was to wear for the rendezvous.

It took a bit of adjusting of her underwear both front and back to position the wires, pickups and the bulky combined power and transmitter pack so that it would not be obvious to any casual observer. The RAF commander's assistant, Helen Lockyear, took great care to turn Alice around and around and check her look from different angles. Helen then turned her again to face her, held her shoulders, and kissed her cheeks in the French way.

'You look a million dollars Alice Peters,' she enthused before manoeuvring her charge out of the ladies' room into the main hall. She then linked arms with her, swiftly marching her towards the conference room while, conspiratorially, suggesting that when "all this" was over they deserved a night out on the town "and I'm not talking small town Shrewsbury, I can tell you!".

Alice was deposited by Helen Lockyear at the doorway to the conference room. Helen then vanished.

Not moving her feet Alice craned her neck forward to peep around the door jamb. She could see Ray at the far end of the room in huddled conversation with Jakub. She could see what looked like a senior police officer just putting down his cap and cane on the table. She could see one of Major Burton's army team seated to one side of the room with headphones on listening to mobile radio pack that faced him on a table. She noticed a new, quite old, male face she had not seen before watching her with hawk-like interest. She could see two loudspeakers, each attached to their own cluster of combat green and brown boxes and cables. And, on a side table her old

238

shoulder bag that had been modified to carry the primary microphone and its own power and transmitter unit.

Alice moved into the room and was immediately approached by one of the RAF sergeants she had met the previous afternoon who had been charged with putting the microphone sets together and testing them.

'Good morning, Miss,' he beamed, 'I hope you were able to rest last night.'

'Um, er, yes Flight Sergeant, not too badly thank you.' She lied.

'Before we do anything else could I trouble you for a final test of the two systems?'

'Yes, certainly you can.' Alice replied.

'Are you switched on at the back?' he asked.

'Um, yes, I believe so. I did it just a moment ago.'

The Flight Sergeant then went through a series of tests issuing instructions and reminding Alice how to position her body or how to position the bag microphone. After that he professed himself satisfied and announced to Ray that both systems were fully functional.

Alice was then asked to throw the switch on her power pack to conserve voltage, which she did once she found it groping with her hand behind her back. And a minute or two later all the speakers and receiver equipment had been removed from the conference room.

Ray sauntered up to Alice and sat on the edge of the conference table, silently inviting her to do likewise alongside him. He then shuffled his bottom to close the gap between them until his right hand touched her left hand that was holding on to the table edge. He lifted his little finger and stroked the back of her hand a couple of times with it before wriggling away from her to create space between them.

'You OK?' he enquired.

Alice had momentarily blushed hoping people had not seen them touch.

She looked down at her shoes and swung her legs under the table as a young schoolchild might. 'Yes, Mister Ray.' She mimicked a certain Czech officer and snatched a quick look at Ray. He smiled, though she could see it was a smile tinged with anxiety.

The Group Captain entered the conference room. Everyone stood up for him, so Alice thought she should do so too.

'At ease everyone, please take your seats. This will not take long. I am just checking that everything is going to plan, and everyone is happy.' He nodded towards Alice. 'Miss Peters?'

'Yes, Group Captain, Sir,' Alice blurted, 'I am fully booted and spurred.'

'Good to hear – and thank you again for helping out here. Ray, could you please give us all a quick update?'

'Thank you, Sir.' said Ray standing and moving to the middle of the conference table.

'First thing first, I would like to introduce you all to Major Richardson from Military Intelligence. He is now our Principal Liaison Officer – all intelligence gathered is now being handled and processed through him.'

The officer stood up to identify himself and sat back down without saying anything.

'And also, Chief Inspector Brabham from the Shropshire Constabulary who is assisting us with all kinds of legal and civil jurisdiction matters.'

The policeman also stood and then resumed his seat.

'We currently have Crawley and Sumner visual, both heading for The Sutherland Arms. Miller set off in his car north first thing this morning. Unfortunately, he quickly lost his tails, so we do not currently know his whereabouts. There would be nothing stopping him from turning up at the pub, but we doubt he will do that as we are calculating that Sumner will not want to risk a tenuous relationship going sour by trying to introduce Crawley to too many people before he has established a solid and trusting relationship between himself with Crawley first. He is after technical data – and Miller does not sound to be a technician.'

Alice interjected. 'If Bernard Miller did turn up at the pub that might be a problem for me because I have been in Pearl's workroom with the two of them and he would be bound to recognise me and recall that Pearl had introduced us.'

Ray and the Group Captain exchanged unspoken glances. It was the RAF commander who next spoke.

'I which case Ray, Major Burton's team need to have eyes in their arses as well as in their heads. If his car is seen approaching any of the access roads to The Sutherland, Alice needs to be forewarned and will then have time to excuse herself for the ladies' toilet where she then stays. The primary mic will still be functioning, and her bag will still be in place.'

Ray agreed with the strategy and asked the Major's radio operator to relay the instruction to the Major. The NCO on the radio had been taking notes and nodded his acknowledgement of the order.

Ray continued his briefing.

'There has been a continuous covert watch on the theatre since it was established yesterday. No pieces of equipment have been moved off site – and so we believe we should be able secure the radio when we hit the place. And with Sumner now on the move to the pub the covert entry should be taking place, um,' 'Ray looked at his watch, 'in fact it happened a short time ago.'

Ray turned to the Corporal on the radio set, 'Is there any news from Major Burton yet Corporal?'

The Corporal held his left hand in the air in a stop signal as he noted down a message, as fast as he could write with his other hand, coming in over the radio that very moment.

The whole room waited for him to speak.

The Corporal acknowledged receipt of the message and removed the headphones from his ears. Looking down and reading from his message pad he excitedly announced, 'Message just in from the Major, Sir. The radio set at the theatre has been located and is now safely secured. All diversion activities and roadblocks are now active. End of message, Sir.' He looked up towards Ray, smiling.

Ray beamed. 'Well, that is great news Corporal, thank you for that.'

The Group Captain interjected, directing his intervention at Ray. 'You said Miller lost his tails. Do you think he is onto us? Or was this always a possibility?'

'Unfortunately, Sir, we suspect he is either well-trained in counter surveillance and always conducts manoeuvres to shake off any potential tails, or he was just fortunate that the motorcycles tailing him could not get too close to him on the narrow country lanes that he took when he headed north. Our judgement on this one is that if Miller were suspicious of anything he would have contacted Sumner by now – and Sumner would not now be heading towards the lunchtime rendezvous. Meanwhile we don't consider Miller a threat to the theatre sweep that is currently under way now that the radio had been secured – principally because Chief Inspector Brabham's officers have established that protective cordon around the village mentioned in the radio message that we have just received.'

The Group Captain nodded that he had received a satisfactory reply and nodded his thanks to the Chief Inspector, who nodded back.

'So, to continue.' Ray announced, sounding fractionally exasperated by all the interventions, looking up and down the table from his standing position halfway along it.

'The plan is that Alice will enter the pub and sit down next to the Crawley-Sumner table. Two ladies from Major Burton's team will already be in place occupying two of the tables. Depending upon which table Crawley-Sumner sit at, Alice will take up the table closest to their table, joining whichever one of the Major's team for a female get together drink. The other lady will then quietly depart. And should Crawley and Sumner choose to stand at the bar, the bar manager has had his palm greased to oblige them to sit down.'

Ray stopped his monologue to look straight at Alice. 'Are you happy with the strategy Alice? Is there anything that you are unsure about, or need clarified?'

Alice's cheeks flushed as she realised everyone was looking at her in nervous anticipation of her response.

'I am happy with the plan, Ray. I know what my role is and why we are doing things in this way. Don't worry about me. If I have any worries I will, somehow, find a way to communicate them to Major Burton's team in the room.'

Ray smiled back at her. 'Alright then, thank you.' He then looked around the room to ensure that he had regained the attention of everyone. 'The receivers, speakers and stenographers were all despatched to the pub,' he looked at his watch, 'about five minutes ago. So, they will all be set up out of sight and ready to record and write by the time of the main event.'

'The moment the rendezvous meeting is over, Major Burton will signal for the police to enter the pub to arrest and take both Crawley and Sumner into custody. They will try to do this quietly if they can: but if they cannot, then we shall just have to take the risk of conducting an overt arrest.'

'So that will just leave Bernard Miller to deal with, assuming that he is still on the loose. Until we know when and where he re-appears we cannot decide the best course of action to take against him.'

At this point Major Richardson stood up.

'Group Captain Percival, ladies, and gentlemen, I think I should briefly interject here. We have a great deal to hold against Bernard Miller now – and I suspect much more still to hold against him if what I am starting to hear from my colleagues has legs.' He coughed, more to clear his throat. 'Um, though I am afraid I cannot tell you anything more about that at this precise time.'

He continued.

'The burned battery label remnant found in the dustbin has now been confirmed by our analysts to be from a German Diamon dry cell battery, as I understand Mr Thomas here had previously suggested. We have a sighting of Miller putting papers into the dustbin for burning – along with his trousers and jacket for some unfathomable reason, though thankfully so, as I have been informed that the clothing slowed the burning of the paper below. A number of these papers have now been established to be maps, plus other papers he tried to burn which we have still to evaluate. The maps have led to a grid reference. And to a murder scene. So, we now have a firm evidential link between the theatre, Miller, and the maps – and the maps and a murder. Around the murder site footprints have been found – these are likely to belong to either Miller or

Sumner, or both, if we can match them to shoes belonging to either of them.'

He drew breath, sipped from a glass of water by his side and then continued,

'We also have a triangulation of radio signals that almost certainly will resolve to the Abwehr radio set that was concealed in the rafters of the theatre. Additionally, we have a physical connection between a German military torch and Bernard Miller.'

Alice put up her hand for permission to speak. Everyone looked at her. 'And what about Dougie Newton and his death?' she asked quietly.

The intelligence officer softened his tone. 'I am afraid, Alice, we still don't know what happened there. Likely he came across something that someone didn't want witnessed, but until we have Miller and Sumner in custody we would just be guessing. We are, of course, sorry for the loss of your friend.' Richardson added as an afterthought.

The meeting fell silent, everyone in their own thoughts.

The Group Captain then interceded. 'Well, unfortunately time stops for nobody in the live world. So, if there are no further questions.' There were none. 'Then I suggest to your places. And good luck.'

He stood, took a moment to look everyone, and then swept out of the room.

Chapter 39

Alice waited for Ray to finish his briefing and conversations with everyone in the room. She made sure she was out of earshot of most of it.

While he was talking to the Chief Inspector she wandered over to the far end of the room and idly gazed out of the window that faced onto the hangar apron and watched as a group of flight engineers manoeuvred an aircraft out of the protected hangar cover into the open. She marvelled at the size of the aircraft and remained in awe that it ever got off the ground.

The sun was breaking through. Alice could see new leaves on the trees, blossom, and the presence of burgeoning life – she always loved Spring and the way it invigorated human psyche and human nostrils, teasing out emotion and banishing the gloom of Winter.

Ray sidled up to her. 'Penny for your thoughts?'

She allowed herself to sway into him for a nudge and then resumed their separated positions, both looking out of the window.

'Nothing special or relevant – just watching daily life going on outside of this room.'

They stood together in silence watching the aircraft manoeuvres for another couple of minutes.

'We need to move.'

She turned her head towards him and found him now looking at her. 'OK, let's go now.'

Picking up the bag with the primary microphone in it, she tagged on closely behind Ray as they made their way back out of the Command Building to his parked Wolseley. He opened the passenger door for her and waited until she was settled in her seat and smiled back at him before closing the door. He went around to the driver's side and clambered in.

She watched his every move. His slim, slightly hirsute, hand putting the ignition key into its key slot. Pulling the choke out a small distance – not too much, but not too little either. Tapping the electric ammeter and temperature gauges. Pressing the ignition button. She admired the woodwork in the car and its comfortable leather seats and breathed in the smell of the car, a mixture of fuel, leather and the dried cattle dung stuck to its wheel arches that she had noticed as she got in. She watched his profile and his studied concentration as he reversed and drove the car towards the Main Gate and then away from the air station towards The Sutherland Arms.

Alice then looked at her own hands, which were shaking. She clasped her left and over the right on her lap to control the shakes and conceal what was happening from Ray's eagle eyes. She felt she had just been washed over with adrenalin that had come from nowhere. Her heart rate had palpably increased. She suddenly felt hot and clammy. She was conscious that her breathing rate had also become faster.

She rationalised to herself that it must be the sudden realisation that what she was about to do was for real and possibly dangerous – and that nothing in her life had trained or prepared her for being at least six miles separated from all that she traditionally considered familiar and comfortable.

Meanwhile, she was adamant that she should not say anything to Ray, let alone tell him anything of the sudden onset of physiological sensations that she was experiencing.

For sure she didn't want to panic, anger, or let him down by suggesting, particularly at such a late operational hour, that she couldn't after all step up to the plate when asked.

But then it struck her that this wasn't the genuine reason for concealing her raised physiological state from him. The real reason was far more deeply rooted: she absolutely refused to allow anyone ever again, other than Alice herself, to decide what she was capable of or couldn't do. And with that seminal recognition of self, she suddenly felt at peace and her body quickly returned to a normal pulse rate and temperature.

For the next thirty seconds or so Alice watched Ray out of the corner of her eye, watching his body language, expecting him to have noticed her temporary physiological excursion. But he said nothing and gave every impression that he simply hadn't noticed anything, other than the road and his driving.

It was a couple of minutes later when he raised his voice slightly to be heard above the road and engine noise that she knew that she had got away with it. 'We have to take a circuitous route to the rendezvous, as we mustn't drive past Crawley or Sumner on the way there.'

Alice was hugely relieved. 'No problem,' she replied, 'I am enjoying being chauffeured again. Twice in one day is something that a girl could get used to!'

Ray snatched a quick look across at her and just rolled his eyes.

She replied with a giggle.

For most of the rest of the journey they continued in contented silence, neither wanting nor needing to breach the quiet. She enjoyed the views in his company while he enjoyed driving with Alice by his side. Just occasionally one or other of them would make a humorous remark about something they saw, and they would then fall back into silence, with smiles on both their faces.

At 11.50 they passed a man mending a puncture.

'Shouldn't we offer to help him, Ray? This is the middle of nowhere.'

He chuckled and then found the next gated field entrance to pull into and switched off the car engine. 'What and suffer Major Burton's wrath?' he laughed.

Alice dropped her head and covered her head with her hands 'Oh God, how stupid am I? One of the Major's sentinels, of course!' Ray continued to chuckle.

'We are half a mile short of the pub now. We can be there in a minute or two. We need to wait here for our signal for me to drop you off around the corner from the entrance. And then it's game on.'

He stroked her hair with his left hand. She grasped it and then placed it in her lap holding it and stroking it with both hands.

'You still OK?' he asked sensitively.

She nodded and blinked at him. 'Yes, I am fine, really. Thank you for asking. It is just a bit different from what I normally do and so feels a bit surreal. But weirdly it doesn't feel uncomfortable.'

Ray was quiet for a moment before speaking again. 'We need a conversation when this is over.'

'What do you mean?'

'Let's just concentrate on the job in hand right now,' Ray instructed, 'and then steal some privacy afterwards.'

Alice let go of his hand, as he placed it back on the steering wheel. '

I would like that,' she purred.

That moment, a car passed them coming from the direction of the pub. It flashed its headlamps once as it passed.

'Right here we go – both Crawley and Sumner are now in the pub.' said Ray pressing the ignition button to start the Wolseley.

Within a couple of minutes Alice was getting out of the car and opening the pub door just as she fumbled behind her back under her coat and

251

flicked the switch to power up her body-worn cockpit microphone. She then dipped her hand into her bag to do the same to the power pack for the primary microphone, and then laid a string bag of carrots back on top of the equipment as she entered the building.

The pub was already reasonably busy with a cluster of farmworkers hugging the immediate bar area. Alice was not sure, but she thought she recognised a couple of their faces from the cycling she had done around the locality over the months since arriving in Kynnersley.

Looking ahead she spotted Sumner wedged in the group at the bar waiting to be served. She then glanced right and could see that Crawley was seated, holding a satchel, waiting for Sumner to settle in front of him with drinks. He had chosen a table that was under a window adjacent to the wall, one table back from the main entrance.

One of the Major's girls was seated at the wall table immediately behind Crawley, with a doorway to an adjoining function room immediately behind her.

The other Intelligence Unit girl had been seated on the opposite side of the pub in an alcove table, far too far away to be of any practical value, though, Alice could see, had Crawley sat at any other table then she would have been perfectly positioned. However, just as she had noted her location in the pub, she saw the woman stand and then watched her unobtrusively switch tables, causally sauntering over with drink and bag in hand to sit down at the empty wall table located between the main entrance and Crawley's table. Meanwhile, much to Alice's disconsternation, the ideal inner table, adjacent and alongside to Crawley's position, was occupied with people who were clearly normal pub clients and who were oblivious to what was going on.

This turn of events clearly posed a problem.

With only three sides of Sumner's table now accessible for monitoring and only two sides available, neither of them good, Alice realised that capturing the German's conversation using the either microphone was going to be a tall order. It was going to be impossible for her to slide her shoulder bag along the wall on the floor to get it both unnoticed and close enough to the two men for its pick-up to detect their conversation. Meanwhile, if she placed the shoulder bag on either seat closest to the back of either Sumner or Crawley, she risked the team not hearing what the person facing away from the microphone with their back to it was saying and for any reply being muffled or lost because of their companion's body being in the way, pick-up sensitivity or because of the background noise levels in the pub being high. Alice also knew that the microphone sewn inside her dress would be useless if she was unable to get herself physically closer to the men.

She realised she had little or no time to act. So she quickly chose one of the two available tables and propelled herself to Major Burton's watcher seated on the far side of a table positioned immediately behind Crawley alongside the wall, close to the back door of the pub.

Alice made a great deal of noise hugging and kissing her before sitting in the seat immediately behind the engineer, her back to his back, all for his benefit. 'Rachel, gosh, how long has it been, I mean it must be at least six months now?' she gushed.

Within half a heartbeat the girl she had just called Rachel was in character, was professing her delight in seeing Alice and talking about university friends they both apparently knew. As she was doing this, Alice snatched a glance to check on Sumner's progress at the bar

She suddenly hit upon a plan of action. Ensuring that Crawley could not fail to hear their conversation, Alice asked Rachel if she wanted to change tables, while catching Rachel's eye and shaking her head in silent communication. Rachel played along and declined, announcing loudly that she was happy where she was and with the heat from the fire at their end of the room was not too hot.

Alice then stole the cue that she had just been given, 'OK, but I am quite warm and need to take my coat off.' She then suddenly stood up and deliberately bumped into Crawley's chair a couple of times.

'Oh, I am so sorry. I am just undressing. You can't swing a cat here! These tables are far too close together!'

She then made a play of putting her coat on the back of her wooden chair and theatrically pondered what next to do with her bag and a hat and gloves that she had quietly slipped out of the bag.

Crawley half turned not looking at her and said it was not a problem and agreed that the tables were "quite chummy".

Alice then quickly grabbed her next chance.

'Oh, I say,' she exclaimed, 'I have just noticed you have a rather empty windowsill by you. I don't suppose I could prevail on you by dumping my bag and hat and gloves there – we are in a bit of a thoroughfare here through to the privy and I wouldn't want anyone with light fingers to try his luck with my carrots!'

Crawley chuckled and turned, again without looking at Alice, as any acutely shy man does, and said he was sure it would not be a problem. He stood and laid his satchel on his table before reaching out and taking hold of Alice's bag, hat and gloves and proceeding carefully to lay out everything on the windowsill by the side of his table.

Alice's heart was in her mouth. She prayed that the microphone did not poke out from behind the vegetables.

She was just resuming her seat as Sumner arrived back at Crawley's table with their tray of drinks. He patiently waited for Crawley to finish unhanding the items on the windowsill then sit down and then pick up his satchel and place it on his lap again. After this Sumner set their drinks down on their table and sat down himself, placing the tray he had used to his right on the floor against the wall.

Alice asked the woman she called Rachel to regale her the latest gossip she had heard about a fictitious friend Stan, which was a trigger the

Major's girl attacked with theatrical and raucous relish.

While she was doing that Alice could see one of the RAF NCOs who had set up the pickups and power packs approaching their table on his way to the toilet. A minute of two later he passed by again saying, 'Oooh, that's better Miss,' which had been the message Alice needed to know if the microphones were both picking up sound.

And then, suddenly, out of a group of loud and inebriated men who were clustered around the bar, reeled Private Harris lurching unsteadily towards Alice's table. Rachel kicked Alice's foot to forewarn her of an impending problem heading their way and nodded in Harris' direction to direct her gaze. She swivelled in her seat to look where bid and was horrified to see that the young serviceman was extremely drunk – and he clearly had her in his cross hairs.

'I thought it was you Miss. Has your bicycle broken Miss, or don't we do bikes any more now we have got used to cars? Whassat joke Miss, 'ow do women get minks? The same ways that minks get minks! Ha, ha. ha.' He stood about three feet away from their table, swaying and chuckling at his toilet humour.

Except nobody else in the pub was laughing.

In fact, Alice noticed, the whole pub had momentarily gone completely silent. Then she started to hear murmurings and exclamations from around the room such as "I say, that's out of order!" and "What a revolting man!" and "Did you hear what that bloke just said to that girl?" starting to be uttered.

256

She stole a quick glance behind her, ridiculously and forlornly hoping that neither Sumner nor Crawley had noticed the incident, which of course they had, both now looking straight at her and acting like they were frozen in time in a bizarre tableau.

Alice flushed self-consciously desperately hoping that their attention had not caused them to study her figure and clothing closely enough to notice the slight protrusion on her right shoulder caused by the positioning of the cockpit microphone and its cabling. She knew she had to act quickly.

'Private Harris, I am sure I do not know what you mean!'

'Yeah, sure, Miss, I am sure you don't,' he persisted, leering at her, and swaying more.

On realising that he was not going to let the matter drop, she decided to counter-attack by embarrassing him in public before the conversation became even more awkward and compromising and people started moving about to help her and deal with the inebriated serviceman.

'Private Harris. You have drunk too much – and are completely out of order. If you do not want me to report you to your superiors, I suggest you leave this establishment right now. You know that I have a disability: one on my legs is shorter than the other. You have even rudely commented on that previously – and to date I have not challenged your behaviour. Well, not before today. I now do. Fortunately for you, unlike me, you do not suffer the same affliction. I was in hospital overnight undergoing painful treatment and cannot ride a bike today as I am recuperating. Do you begrudge me car transport to get to work?'

Instantaneously Private Harris did not know where to look or what to do. His leer had been wiped from his face and he looked a crushed man. All he could do was open and shut his mouth in an attempt to speak or perhaps to apologise, like a goldfish – again. No
, but no sounds emerged from his lips.

He then silently turned to his right and as carefully as his balance allowed him, he inched his way to the pub door and left. One person on the far side of the pub started to clap. The rest of the pub's guests started talking again, initially in hushed murmurs.

Rachel looked at Alice, eyebrows raised in shock and surprise, 'Well that told him! What a toad!'

Alice snatched another look over her shoulder at Sumner and Crawley. "Sorry about that," she mouthed in a whisper to them.

Crawley had screwed himself around in his seat to watch the encounter. He shyly smiled back at her. "It's not your fault, Miss, that he is smashed". He then swivelled back to face Sumner and took a sip of his beer.

Just as Alice herself was turning back to face Rachel, she caught Sumner's eye. His stare was intense, devoid of emotion. It felt to her like he was drilling into her core to map and measure her soul. She realised that, at the very least, she was now marked. She could not turn back fast enough to face Rachel across their table again.

For the next twenty minutes Alice and Rachel resumed their fictitious dialogue about imaginary work, friends and boyfriends and recent films they had each allegedly seen.

Rachel kept a laser sight on the two men seated on the table ahead of her behind Alice – and then on the table adjacent to them when it suddenly became vacant. Nodding to Alice the moment it was vacated, Alice grabbed her coat and moved onto one of the empty seats adjacent to Sumner while Rachel took the seat adjacent to Crawley, both women hanging their coats on the back of their new chairs.

The two women clinked glasses agreeing loudly, entirely for the benefit of Crawley and Sumner, that the new table was less of a railway carriage and far cooler away from the heat of the fire.

Crawley immediately noticed the two women changing tables and started to raise himself up to give Alice back her belongings from the windowsill. Alice immediately reacted to save the situation by touching his arm and thanking, telling him not to worry as they would only fall on the floor, so were better to leave well alone until they left. Neither man appeared concerned with her riposte, though Sumner took a long hard look at Alice's mismatched legs before, again, looking intensely at her face. Somehow, she managed neither to catch his eye, nor flush with self-consciousness.

The two men carried on talking, although their body language was starting to suggest to Alice that Crawley seemed increasingly ill at ease and was possibly even looking to find an excuse to leave. She wondered whether he would have been quite so attentive to her table change had he been engrossed and enjoying his conversation with Sumner.

Now that she herself was the closest she could be to Crawley and Sumner's table she tried to position the right side of her body so that the cockpit pickup pinned and sewn under the material on her right shoulder could pick up their conversation. Alice assumed that, if the primary bag microphone had failed, she and Rachel would have received another message that would have then made them all rely upon her body-worn equipment. As they had not, she, therefore, presumed the stenography and recordings were still all working fine.

All Alice could discern from trying to listen in to the men's conversation – in between trying to have a coherent conversation with Rachel – was that Crawley was getting increasingly agitated, constantly shifting in his seat, glancing around the pub for familiar faces, repeatedly picking up and putting down his satchel on the floor between his legs and tapping his right foot constantly.

'Oh, no, I am sure I couldn't,' she heard him say as he shook his head in response to a question Sumner had asked him, '... 'No, I have rules to follow ...' and later '... no that would not be possible at all.'

And then all of a sudden, he just rocked to his feet, looked at Sumner with anger in his voice, and said 'No!' emphatically, so loudly that two or three people seated at other tables turned their heads to see what the commotion was all about.

Crawley bent down and picked up his satchel from the floor and then, without saying another word, headed for the pub door and stomped out. Sumner stayed seated looking at the empty seat. He then raised his beer glass and took a gulp, clearly about to finish its contents and leave the pub himself.

Alice got up and played looking sheepish, 'Excuse me, sorry, but can I possibly just get my shopping ...' her voice trailed off. Sumner glared at her and did not offer to assist as she stretched to reach across his table in front of his nose and then scrabble to recover her bag from the windowsill without the microphone falling out.

She sat down again at her own table and leaned into Rachel quietly mouthing the word 'Oops' and raising her eyebrows, which caused Rachel to laugh and then realise to her horror that an angry Sumner was still staring at her. Quick as a flash she grasped for a fictitious punchline of a fictitious joke that she had not just been telling Alice and both women burst into genuine laughter. Sumner resumed looking at Crawley's empty seat and took another draw on his pint of beer in clear, simmering, anger.

Crawley had only been gone seconds when Alice became aware from the cool air filling the pub of someone entering the room from outside and immediately greeting Major Burton's agent who was still seated at table closest to the main entrance between Sumner and the doorway.

She overheard the woman shriek with laughter and ask her companion 'Gerald, she's wonderful, but what on earth am I going to do with *that*?!'

As she twisted to look over her right shoulder to see what the Major's agent was talking about, she caught Rachel's eye, who was looking at the new arrival, grinning and just shaking her head with disbelief. Alice took note that Sumner too took a quick furtive glance over his shoulder to see what the ruckus was all about before he turned back to resume his vigil of Crawley's empty seat, while he finished his beer in deep contemplation.

The noise had all been caused by a large man, whose back was to Alice, holding a cat basket in which was an angry Burmese cat hissing and scratching to get out. Alice could see that the man was holding the cat basket with two hands and was trying to walk backwards and manoeuvre up the aisle between Sumner's and Alice's tables towards the rear pub door.

Just as the back of the man's thighs and his coat started to press onto and tip over Alice and Rachel's table, he heaved the basket up and leaned over Sumner's table and unceremoniously – with absolutely no warning – shoved it onto the now vacant windowsill inches from Sumner's face, catching him on the chin in the process.

Sumner, surprised as much as Alice with the sudden movement and being hit on the chin, stifled a swear word and grabbed his pint glass to stop it from falling over. Alice and Rachel also stabilised their own table and glasses. Alice snatched a glance over in Sumner's direction to watch his response. From his body language the man with the cat appeared to be apologising to Sumner for the sudden intrusion, but from what Alice heard with her ears, she was not entirely sure because they did not appear to be speaking words that she understood.

The man with the cat spoke first.

'Wodajće prošu!' as he rammed the cat basket hard onto the windowsill. *(Excuse me.)*

Sumner had looked up, completely taken by surprise. He had then reactively and instinctively replied, involuntarily '... Njerozumju.' *(I do not understand.)*

'Oh, Rěčiće Wy serbsce?' the cat owner had asked. *(Oh, do you speak Upper Sorbian?)*

Sumner looked utterly confused 'Um, haj, tróšku, er, um,' He then checked himself and what he was saying, '... njerozumju,' *(Yes, a little ... but I do not understand.)*

However, it was clear from the blood that had drained from Sumner's face that he had just realised the enormity of what had just taken place.

Sumner was just contemplating his escape options when, seconds later, three uniformed police crashed in through the pub's main entrance and two more appeared at the rear door by its toilets, blocking the exit.

Sumner suddenly found his arms being yanked behind him and could feel himself being handcuffed. He was then turned and frog-marched outside by two of the policemen where, after his clothes were searched, he was shoved into the rear of a second police van that had just pulled up.

What Sumner did not know was that in the first police van that had arrived at the pub a few minutes beforehand sat, also handcuffed, a very disorientated John Crawley. The moment he had emerged from the pub – furious, incredulous, and exceptionally uncomfortable that Sumner appeared to have been trying to groom him for a homosexual relationship – he had been seized and pushed face-first against a wall, handcuffed bundled into a police vehicle, where he now sat. He thought he had heard a plain clothes police inspector tell him that he was being arrested under suspicion of something about treachery, though he was not entirely sure what that meant. He was certain that, whatever the misunderstanding was, it would all be quickly sorted out at the Police Station as he was not aware that he had done anything wrong.

Surely, he questioned himself in his head as he sat in the van, it had nothing to do with his just having had a drink with Sumner? He fretted that he must have given off the wrong signals to the man – which was ridiculous because he was just not wired that way. He had only got chatting to Sumner because he and the air station's Chaplain had happened to sit at adjacent tables in the Canteen a few days previously. They had struck up conversation after it had transpired that he was an engineer and knew about amplifiers and other topics in an electronics magazine that Crawley had been reading while he had been quietly eating his lunch. It had emerged that Sumner worked for the local theatre – and happened to mention in passing that the theatre had a problem with an unserviceable stage microphone. Crawley had been extremely happy to offer help to fix the kit, as he fancied the idea of volunteering in the local theatre, if nothing else to force himself to get off the base and develop local interests and a life off the air station, away from direction-finding equipment. In the event there had not been that much wrong with the microphone – more loose connections and low impedance wiring than anything fundamentally wrong with the device.

Meanwhile, back in the pub, the large man with the cat bent down and picked up and raised Sumner's beer to him through the window.

'K strowosći! Hač do bórze' he called out after him. *(Cheers! See you soon.)*

Only then did Alice recognise Jakub Novák.

He put the glass down, turned to face Alice with a beaming smile, patted her shoulder twice and winked at her. He then walked out of the pub, leaving the still hissing cat behind.

Alice leaned forward in her seat so she could manipulate the power switch on her pickup set. Rachel and Alice then sat still waiting for instructions. Sure enough, a few moments later the RAF NCO they had seen earlier walked past their table again and this time told them to leave the pub via the toilets. They both got up and picking up their bags and coats and headed for the rear door.

Chapter 40

Outside Ray was seated in the Wolseley with the engine running and the passenger door open.

Rachel was met by Major Burton who patted her on the back and led her to his car. His other agent was already seated inside it. Rachel stopped as she was about to get in her car and looked across the car park towards Alice who was about to get into Ray's Wolseley.

Alice looked up at that moment too. Alice mouthed a thank you and in return received thanks back and a big smile.

'So ...?' Ray asked the moment the door slammed shut, 'Harris didn't help did he?' He laughed.

'God, I wanted the ground to swallow me up. What a silly man. He really isn't like that normally, Ray, really, he's not. We have good banter normally. It was just the drink talking today. But I am going to have to have a word with him.'

'Well, he very nearly fucked everything up. I am quite sure someone we know will be talking to

266

him as soon as he is sober, so you can save yourself the effort.' Alice detected definite terseness in Ray's voice.

But she was not bothered about the young soldier – rather, she was still buzzing from what she had just gone through.

'Private Harris is really not important,' she pronounced. Ray agreed with a nod.

'So, tell me, did it all work? Oh God Ray, they sat against the wall of all places! It was impossible to reach them! I am so sorry. I just couldn't get any closer because those drinkers had taken the table that we should have had. Why didn't the Major and his people secure that table first, although we did get it in the end? My microphone will have been useless! Oh, what a fandango! Fiddlesticks. Pooh. Oh Goodness, I have let you and the Group Captain and everyone down! I cannot believe what a hash it all was. But that was Jakub a moment ago, wasn't it? And what a nasty cat! Where on earth did he find it? And more importantly how did he irritate it so? And -'

Ray still had not set off. He leaned over and with his right hand and pressed his index finger hard on Alice's lips to stop her speaking any more.

'Shhh, shut up Alice-from-the Canteen.' he whispered in her ear. 'It was a total success or as close to one as we could have expected. You thought on your feet brilliantly and ended up perfectly positioning the primary pick up between the two of them. We heard most of their conversation. The main microphone battery in the bag died before the end, but your cockpit pickup and amp worked fine throughout, and so we caught everything that Jakub said to Sumner and everything he said back. Between the two transcripts and the recording we have an almost complete record of their conversation and oversight of the relationship between Crawley and Sumner, with the added bonus of proof of Sumner's unique linguistics skills.'

'Oh,' said Alice, 'I thought I had messed up'

'On the contrary, you saved the day principally because of your ability to improvise and because you have balls. You're a natural Alice-from-the-Canteen.'

'Ray Thomas!' she chided him for using such language, but was soon pensive again.

'And so had these Germans successfully groomed and recruited Crawley?'

Ray held Alice's hands in his, resting his hands on her lap. 'They were *trying* to groom him, but he was clearly having none of it. In fact, in the pub, Sumner tried to reel him in with the offer of a homosexual encounter back at the theatre later today – presumably to compromise him before then moving to extort technical information. Sadly, Crawley is like many engineers – someone who loves solving technical problems and adores their subject, but who is, dare I suggest, not as worldly astute as others and can be taken advantage of. Crawley came across as very loyal to the King and did not give away anything about his secret work – but he clearly did give enough of himself away to become a light source that attracted moths. When Sumner pushed harder to find out what he did, he resisted and seemed to realise that he was getting out of his comfort zone. The sexual offer was the final straw it seems. In the end Crawley panicked and left as fast as he could.'

Alice agreed. 'Yes, I could sense that from the snippets of the conversation that we overheard, and from looking at Crawley's body language. I actually felt quite sorry for him – or, rather, I would have done, if I had known at that point that he was innocent.'

'But the truth is he wasn't totally innocent, darling.' Ray explained, 'He shared far too much information about himself and his technical knowledge, so in some respects you cannot be surprised an antagonist flushed him out and showed an interest in him.'

'What will happen to him?'

'He will be interviewed at length, dusted down and then set back to work, much wiser and all the more cautious for your interventions!'

'And what did Jakub talk to Sumner about? I know enough from my school lessons to know that that wasn't German that they were speaking.'

Ray smiled. 'I seem to recall, amusingly, Jakub first apologising for intruding. These Czechs have learned so much about English etiquette since being at the air station!' He grinned, liking his dry humour, as Alice showed she also did, with her big smile.

'He then asked Sumner if he spoke Upper Sorbian, to which, amazingly and still shocked, Sumner admitted that he did ... though he professed himself a bit confused by the whole incident. Ha! I am not surprised! Meanwhile that nasty bloody cat will now go down in the annals of Czech Air Force history as the savour of their country!'

They both chuckled.

'What the hell is Upper Sorbian when it's at home?'

'It's a bit complicated to explain. It's an old Slavic dialect spoken in a small part of eastern Germany, and which is only understood in parts of Germany and by Czechs and Poles. Jakub's Mess Steward first raised suspicions of Sumner's language knowledge and shared his concerns with Jakub who, in turn, shared them with me earlier this week.'

'So, you already *knew* that Sumner was suspect? And you didn't tell me?!'

'Our judgment, I am afraid, was that it was better that we allowed the intelligence picture build of its own volition, rather than make assumptions and miss potential corroborative evidence that might confirm or clarify information that we had already partially gathered.'

Ray then looked a bit sheepish.

'But yes Alice, I am sorry that we didn't tell you what we were planning. And we needed the closing incident to be a surprise for Sumner, which meant we also needed to keep you in the dark as well, so that your actions and reactions were natural.'

Alice pretended to adjust an imaginary pair of glasses and scold him.

'And us Ray, what about us now?'

'Well, we have a conversation still to have about that ... but in the meantime, it is not all over yet. We need to lock up Bernard Miller when he resurfaces.'

'Dare I ask how the raid on the theatre went? Did you find the radio you were looking for?'

'Yes, we did, so this has been a good day. Relax now, please.'

'Ray?'

'Yes?'

'I am so tired, quite suddenly.'

Ray put his left hand on her hands and squeezed them.

'You've been way out of your comfort zone. The pressure is now off you. Right now I am going to drive us both up onto the top of the Long Mynd for some time out and views. When you have woken up and feel fresher, we will then drive back to the air station and find out what is happening. Meanwhile everything regarding Miller is in the hands of Chief Inspector Brabham and Major Burton and their colleagues.'

Alice did not hear any of Ray's comfort or assurance – she had already fallen asleep.

Ray started the car and set off for the hills.

Chapter 41

By 11 am Bernd Müller had parked up and had his binoculars out surveying the groundworks and activity going on in the Montford Bridge vicinity. His initial impression was that there was certainly a great deal of time and money being invested in the area and he could see military roadblocks preventing access to an area of ground a little further to the west.

He got back in his car and made some annotations and notes on his map.

When he had set off from Sambrook earlier that morning, his primary aim for the day had been to force some private thinking time because there was no doubt that having to kill the gamekeeper posed an existential threat to his unit's purpose and its ongoing value to the Führer. He had decided that needed time and space to think through how to stabilise the ship and so decided that he could buy private thinking time by going for a drive to look at things that he heard of over the previous few days which sounded operationally interesting.

He also knew, in the light of receiving the encoded signal that the Deputy Führer was missing in Britain and had to be located, that he needed to think carefully through his plan for tennis in a couple of day's time with the Duke of Sutherland at Lilleshall House. He also knew he needed to work out how to handle dinner with the CO of RAF High Ercall and his wife a couple of days after that.

Things were moving so fast around him. Everything was demanding on his time that he knew he needed time out to get order back into his life: otherwise he risked either burning out ... or being burnt.

Indeed, the reason he was where he was at that moment was because he had heard rumours of new military activity planned for the Montford Bridge, Maesbrook, and Ford area to the west of the region and wanted to take a look. A chance overheard conversation in the greengrocer had revealed that there were major railway works going there at the behest of the War Office and that rail crews from the Shropshire and Montgomeryshire Light Railway had been commandeered by the military for some reason.

He picked up his binoculars to look towards the rail works again. 'You need to return here Herr Müller ... in a week or two I think should do it.'

He had also wanted to get a better idea of what was going on in the west, north-west and north of the region, because he had heard from PoWs who had broken out of camps near Oswestry that there were rumours of plans for the construction of a new airfield close by that would be designated for the RAF's Bomber Command and for 'special operations' whatever they meant. On hearing this Müller had mused that if Bomber Command was arriving in the area, then so too would be a need for armament depots or rail resupply routes, which the Luftwaffe would certainly need to know about. He had also heard rumours, again through the Oswestry PoWs, of huge radio masts starting to be constructed on the eastern side of the River Severn somewhere between Oswestry and Welshpool and was curious to flush them out at some point too.

Müller put the map down on the passenger side seat and sighed. He gazed out of the car again looking into the distance. 'You can't be everywhere all the time Bernd my friend. You must ration yourself. You must build the picture gradually,' he told himself.

But his mind, once more, came back to the murder.

It annoyed him intensely that he had allowed himself to stand so close to the gamekeeper so that, when his throat was cut, the blood spurt was of sufficient force that his face, jacket, trousers, and shoes had all been struck. He was irked that he had had to burn his nice clothes. He was frustrated too that the last few months of careful development of the PoW repatriation network was now likely going to have to be suspended beyond the short-term – and might even have to stop completely if he could not work out a solution. Whichever way he looked at it, it was no longer a viable proposition to continue supplying clothes to escaped PoWs at pre-arranged local rendezvous or dead letter drop locations.

The death – and his, or was it their, error in failing to take the body to a separate deposition site far away from Ercall Heath – had forced his hand now to start the process of looking for alternative hand-over points outside the immediate local area for that moment when they might be able to resume normal services.

He also conceded that they would also now have to devise different arrangements for monitoring Abwehr radio broadcasts and sending their intelligence reports back to Berlin, as the gamekeeper's death now robbed him of his preferred reception location on the heath.

Bernd Müller gazed out of the car and idly wondered how Lorenz Sommer would get on at his lunchtime meeting with the engineer he had met on his RAF High Ercall follow up visit earlier in the week. Sommer was convinced the engineer was not a general aircraft engineer as he understood quite complex physics and electronics and so he wanted to try to get close to him to discover more. As far as Müller himself was concerned Sommer was the engineering expert of the two of them and so he was very agreeable for the two technicians to try to forge a close relationship. And as far as he was also concerned the more tendrils they spread the more likely they would pick up high value intelligence to relay back to the Abwehr.

Bernd Müller looked back at his map. It had not taken him too long to reach Montford Bridge, so he decided next to head north-east towards

Whitchurch which he estimated was about an hour and a half away given all the farm traffic on the road at that time of year.

He had just reached Prees Green and was only a few miles short of Whitchurch when two large military trucks, one a fuel tanker and the other a canvass-topped truck, came up fast behind him and flashed to overtake his car. He pulled over and allowed them to pass and then noticed that the rear canvass-topped one lorry contained soldiers. Almost immediately after overtaking him, the trucks indicted right and turned into a small road heading towards Lower Heath and Sandford.

He was intrigued as to why such large trucks were using such small roads, so he decided to follow them at a safe distance. Because they stood proud of the hedgerows it was easy for Bernard to track the movements of the pair of lorries. When they reached Sandford, they turned east towards Tern Hill, as Bernard himself did shortly after, though far enough back for any soldiers in the lorry not to suspect that they were being tailed.

And when the trucks reached the Tern Hill junction, they both thundered off north-east towards Market Drayton.

Müller took his time to reach the crossroads and turned left towards Market Drayton too. But he was then confronted with something he had not expected to see. Only about a mile from the previous junction the two lorries were now indicating a turn to the right into a farm.

As Müller drove on past the same spot, he slowed his car a little and stole a surreptitious look to his right. The vehicles had been stopped by a heavily guarded military control point. He looked around for notices or names to identify the location but all he saw was barbed wire fencing and someone in military uniform patrolling the inner perimeter of whatever was beyond it with an Alsatian attack dog. The was no signage to indicate anything.

Müller carried on driving looking in his mirror to see if he could see anything else. He then found a turning point, marked a question mark on his map in the correct location and then drove back along the road, straining to look left as he passed the site. By this time, some metal gates had been closed and all that was visible from the road were the unmarked gates and the wire fencing, which you would not notice if you were just driving along the road into or out of Market Drayton. It looked like just another farm to all intents and purposes. Müller vowed to return to this spot, wondering what needed a fuel tanker and armed protection.

He then set course back to Sambrook.

Half an hour later he pulled into the car park of the lodgings and sat in the car for a minute thinking.

He was tired. It was the weekend. He had been on the road for around 6 hours, and it had been a busy week with too many pre-dawn PoW rendezvous starts during the week. Part of him wanted to go out again on Sunday – to check out what was going on in the middle of RAF High

Ercall for himself and drive over to the River Severn in the west to look for the aerials that he had heard about – but he knew that, following the death of the gamekeeper, the priority had to be to do a proper weed of anything potentially connected to the repatriation network that might still laying around in the theatre, even though he thought he had probably incinerated everything already.

Plus, he knew he needed to know how the lunchtime meeting had gone with the air engineer so that he could draft the content of his next Abwehr radio transmission. He decided, therefore, that the River Severn visit could wait for another outing – and that he could drive around the periphery of the air station the next time he set out.

Müller got out of the car and locked the door, separately checking that the boot was also locked.

He cussed under his breath that during the day he had still not thrown the bloody shoes away that were still in the boot. He had intended to but had allowed himself to become distracted by Montford Bridge and that interesting Tern Hill junction farm site. He vowed to deal with them first thing in the morning.

Müller walked in through the front door and shut it behind him. He turned in the hall to head towards his room and the bathroom and was met by three uniformed constables and a uniformed Chief Inspector.

'Mr Bernard Miller?' Chief Inspector Brabham asked.

'Um, yes Inspector?' Müller replied.

'Chief Inspector Brabham of the Shropshire Constabulary to you, Sir.'

Müller suddenly felt his master intelligence map inside his jacket burning a hole in his very soul.

'Under the Treachery Act 1940 I am arresting you under suspicion of being a spy ...'

The same van that had taken Lawrie Sumner away a few hours earlier now swung into the drive of the lodgings.

Realising that the game was up Bernd Müller's heart rate rocketed and he suddenly felt giddy with shock, his mind racing to try to understand how the British had identified and exposed an undercover operation that had been so carefully planned.

Müller's eyes rapidly scanned his surroundings trying to identify an escape route. Meanwhile, instinctively, he attempted to make a grab for a small, concealed, gun that he always carried in his inside jacket pocket.

The moment that his hand started to lift from his sides both of his hands were unceremoniously grabbed from behind and his arms were yanked behind him into a lock position. An instant later he was handcuffed, and a black hood was thrown over his head, causing his world to cascade into darkness. Müller was then frisked, and his sock knife discovered and removed. His shoes were taken off him and his belt was removed.

For a bizarre moment Müller allowed himself to be impressed by the swiftness and thoroughness of his disarmament. Seconds later he was led outside into a waiting van and driven away with an armed security escort vehicle following it.

Chapter 42

Three weeks later. June 1941

Alice got to Newport Station in good time for her early morning London departure. It was going to be a long day.

She thought that the station was surprisingly busy for 6.30 am, but soon rationalised that it was probably quite normal for a time of day where everyone and everything passing through it had purpose, direction, and a sense of urgency. Fleetingly, she wondered what had happened to the man she had seen in Shrewsbury wearing Pearl's naval uniform. She wondered if he had been found out and his identity and intentions discovered. She did not hold much hope for him – he had seemed to be entirely exposed, as if a spotlight would be on him wherever he went.

She reached the barrier to her platform. Her ticket was clipped by a bored elderly official who had not the will or energy to look his customers in the eye. Alice stifled a smile thinking how different it would be if Private Harris were manning the platform barrier. Not a man to lose even half a heartbeat where chatting up lines or long-distance vision were required. She hoped he had been disciplined for his drunken antics back in The Sutherland Arms – but, at the same time, she hoped that he had not been too harshly penalised.

Alice had mulled taking an overnight bag with her and staying in London with her schoolfriend Catriona, of Ministry of Information fame, but was in the end persuaded by her parents to visit the capital only for the day. The horrors of the intense blitz of London in the late Autumn 1940 were still very raw and indelibly stamped on everyone.

Yes, the Luftwaffe had eventually been pushed back by the incredible achievements of the RAF and everyone working to support the country's airborne defences, but Alice knew only too well from the sorties over the past fortnight of the various squadrons from her own air station in their air defence role, that the threat – and risk – was by no means past and clear. So, she had bought a return ticket for the same day.

Well, in all honesty, she herself had not bought it. She had handed over a Government Warrant to the station ticket office clerk who had exchanged it for a First-Class return ticket. Alice had never ridden in a First-Class carriage before.

She gathered her coat around her when she found her carriage and mounted the steps. She then worked her way along the corridor unto she found an empty 6-berth compartment and sat next to the window to secure the seat before anyone else came in. She looked around the compartment. And then changed window seats to the one opposite so that she was facing the direction of travel and would have a more pleasurable view of the countryside once the train got going.

The compartment was sumptuous. Each of the six seats, three of each side, had a linen cover for the headrests. Above both sets of seats were sturdy wooden and metal luggage racks. On one compartment side was a large mirror and on the other a painting of a rural scene. The seats themselves all had their own arm rests and where luxuriously covered in a classic William Morris Strawberry Thief design.

Alice rubbed the glass to see what she could see through the misted-up window. On the opposite platform people, all dressed in greys and browns with not a hint of colour anywhere, stood motionless and cold waiting for their fire eating beasts to huff and puff their way past them pulling their loads.

She glanced briefly at her own clothing – her own coat was brown too, as were her skirt, jacket, shoes, gloves, and fedora. Except for her hat, which was her indulgent pride and joy, all her clothing looked as if it had seen better days. Meanwhile, Alice's nod to Spring – and signalling difference – involved sporting a yellow silk scarf over the top of a crisply-ironed white blouse. She hoped that she looked presentable for her interview.

The journey to London was comfortable and pleasant. Alice's compartment only half-filled and, apart from a mother and daughter having an ongoing argument about school commitment, stayed largely quiet, although people entered and left the compartment throughout the ride.

Alice herself stayed seated and warm, sometimes idly watching fields and villages rush past and at other times drifting off into light sleep, hearing everything going on around her but allowing her mind to mash all kinds of images and stories together into a dynamic pot-pourri of utterly illogical thought.

As the train approached Kings Cross Station and its Victorian magnificence, Alice finally woke from her madcap reveries and contemplated the next stage of her journey. She dismounted the carriage and headed for the exit.

As she passed the barrier Major Richardson stepped in front of her and held out his hand in greeting.

Alice shook it warmly.

'Hello Major, it's lovely to see you again. Thank you so much for kindly meeting me from the train. It has been such a long time since I have been to London that I would have been sure to have got lost – and I am also certain that London doesn't look anything like I recall it at the moment either.' Alice pointed to the presence of sandbags and soldiers guarding all the access points to the station.

He smiled. 'Yes, you are right there Alice. When you work here you forget that most people in the country do not have any comprehension of how the city must organise itself in these grim times. But at least we don't have to concern ourselves with its minutiae today – my car is waiting just outside here, to the right.'

He indicated the direction that Alice should move. 'Was your journey OK? And no problem with the rail warrant your end?'

'Thank you Major, all was fine and the railway carriage extremely comfortable, thank you.'

The two of them arrived at the Major's car. His driver was a woman in army uniform who looked to be a remarkably similar age to Alice herself. She opened the rear passenger door for Alice and beckoned her to get in the vehicle. As Alice settled in her rear seat the door opened opposite and the Major slid into the other back seat.

In fact the car journey only took about ten minutes, with their route taking them past University College into Tottenham Court Road, finally stopping outside a nondescript and unmarked red brick fronted building close to the entrance to Goodge Street Underground Station. They had exchanged only small talk during trip.

Major Richardson got out and went around the rear of the car to open Alice's door for her. As he told her to follow him, his head and eyes were looking up and down the street scanning people. The moment she was on the pavement he slammed the car door shut and tapped its roof once. It then sped off. The Major set off at a pace up eight steps that bridged a void that gave partial light to a series of basement windows below. Alice worked her way up the steps as fast and as best she could but was forced to hold onto the railing on her right side for stability and to allow her purchase to lift her shorter leg with its stacked soles to the next higher step.

The Major, realising that Alice had not kept up with him, had stopped in the foyer and had turned to watch her come into the building.

'Sorry, I forgot. You carry yourself so well it is, unfortunately, easy to forget. At least we have lifts in this building.'

Alice mixed a grimace and a smile 'Don't worry about me. I always get there in the end, even if it is slightly more slowly than others,' She straightened herself up and puffed out her cheeks theatrically to signify that effort had just been exerted. She looked around her. The foyer was lined with sandbags. Three Army guards watched her, two on one side and one of the other of the entrance, guns ready for use. To the left was a booth with an official dressed in a black suit.

'Could you please sign in and permit these gentlemen to check your bag?'

Alice consented and soon she and the Major had got into a metal-grilled lift and were speeding up to the third floor. The Major first opened the inner grill and then pushed open the heavy metal door that gave them access to the floor. He beckoned her to exit the lift first and then followed her onto the landing, shutting the grill then the door behind them.

Asking her to let him know if he was walking to fast, he opened a wooden and glass door into a wood-panelled corridor passing numerous closed doors on either side of the passageway as they moved forward. Eventually they arrived at a door that the Major unlocked and entered, switching on the overhead room light as he entered.

'Can I take your coat Alice? Tea perhaps?' He walked over to a bookcase to check it. 'Or something stronger if you would prefer?' He had grabbed a bottle of whisky and was waggling it in her direction questioningly.

'Oh no goodness, no, tea would be wonderful. It's a bit early in my day for the hard stuff.'

He looked at the bottle and screwed up his face and replaced the bottle in the bookcase. 'Yes, you're probably right!'

The Major picked up his phone and pressed a button. After a couple of rings that Alice could just make out, a voice answered. The Major requested a pot of tea and some biscuits. After putting the phone down, he hung Alice's coat on a coat stand located in the corner of the room and invited her to sit and make herself comfortable on a large chair that was positioned on the opposite side of his large wooden desk.

Alice snatched a look around his office, which was quite large. On the far side of the office was a conference table with seven chairs around it. Behind it along the full length of the wall was an enormous cork pin board, but with nothing pinned onto to it. Alice sat facing the Major's large glass-topped director's desk with a window behind his seat. Between his desk and the conference table on the floor was a large potted plant. To the right of his desk was a large, padlocked metal post box next to a smaller open waste bin. And along the wall to Alice's right were two large, padlocked filing cupboards, then the bookcase with the whisky on it. Behind Alice along the wall opposite the window and just along from the door into his office were two large padlocked six-foot high, double-fronted, metal cupboards. The room was two-tone, magnolia on the wall up to the picture rail and then white up to the ceiling and on the ceiling itself. A solitary picture of the King hung from the picture rail above the pair of filing cupboards.

A moment later a lady in Canteen uniform smock, so familiar to Alice, knocked and wheeled a trolley into the room placing the tea and biscuits and the cup, saucer and plates on the Major's table before turning to leave, shutting the door behind her. The Major served Alice first and offered her a biscuit. She held up her hand to decline. He then served himself and sat back in his seat with his cup and saucer in hand surveying Alice.

'Well first I must thank you Alice for coming here today to meet me. I am sorry that I haven't been able to get back up your way since the arrest of the two Germans but, as I am sure you can imagine, they jointly revealed things which, shall we say, required rather urgent attention.'

Alice nodded her acknowledgement but elected to let the Major continue, which he did.

'I can tell you that because of everything that happened three weeks ago, we now have early indications of movements of money from known Abwehr-controlled accounts into British bank accounts – going as far back as in early 1939, many months before Germany invaded Poland in the September.'

'In consequence we here in London now believe that the theatre company was set up as a deep cover propaganda unit and intelligence conduit – and much else besides that we have still to ascertain. This suggests that the German intelligence activity was by no means opportunist in design. This, in turn, begs many more questions … which … um, shall we say, those well above my grade must now gravely consider.'

He went momentarily quiet, appearing to wish to choose his words carefully.

'Early checks into the backgrounds of both Miller and Sumner now indicate that we are actually dealing with a Herr Bernd Müller and a Herr Lorenz Sommer, the former an army Major brought up on the Rhine near Mannheim, and the latter a native of the Oberlausitz region of Germany – which, if you do not know, is south east of Dresden and awfully close to the Czech border.'

Alice exhaled in amazement. 'Gosh. Incredible. Calculated. And right under everyone's noses in plain sight.'

The Major sipped his tea noisily and put his cup and saucer down on his desk, watching Alice closely. 'Quite.' He agreed. 'Right under everyone's noses … in plain sight,'

He allowed his words to be absorbed. Then, when he felt they had been processed fully by her, he continued.

'And this neatly leads on to why I was keen for us to have a chat, um, shall we say, with no obligations.'

'Right …' Alice said warily.

'Let me please speak straight to you Alice.' He moved his teacup and saucer to one side and leaned forward to face her, resting his body weight on his forearms, clasping his hands together as if in prayer.

'Many people who have become cognisant of the events in Shropshire over these past few weeks have remarked upon your personal role in helping to close this German intelligence cell down. It is of irrefutable fact that had you not been thoughtful, aware, and resourceful, then we might still be unaware of the severity of what we faced, and we would, in all honesty, still be trying to triangulate a threat using our limited technical resources.'

'Meanwhile, putting no too finer point on things, shall we say, without your interventions our air defence capability may have been entirely compromised and our ability to stand up to Jerry may have been decimated from more accurate and better directed Luftwaffe targeting of numerous military assets in the Shropshire region.'

'Alice, I can assure you that it is as big as that, notwithstanding the severe risk of the government inadvertently funding the Fourth Reich, a network of deep cover German propagandists trained and skilled in destabilising military or political alliances and acting in a manner to undermine our very history and national culture.'

'That's some speech Major,' Alice suggested.

'It's not a speech Alice. It's fact. Your unassuming leadership on the ground; your ability to socialise and engage coherently and effectively with a wide mix of people; your ability to slip into character when required while remaining a part of a team; and all that on top of your self-evident intellectual depth and breadth means that we must ask if you might do us the honour and consider joining the organisation that I represent.'

'Military intelligence? Me? But I know nothing about military intelligence Major. I work in a Canteen on an air station. I like films. I have a physical disability. I have always been a country girl and have no knowledge or experience of international diplomacy or military tactics or anything like that.'

Major Richardson looked long and hard at her 'But you didn't say no.'

Alice looked back at him and chose not to speak.

'Look, Alice, the clue is in the name – military *intelligence*. Yes, you have a *slight* physical constraint.'

'It is not slight,' Alice harrumphed. 'Furthermore, many organisations say my polio and physical disability trumps everything and that without being fully able bodied they could not consider me. I know Major, I have applied for enough positions and been rejected enough bloody times to know this as fact, let us say.'

Alice knew she was parroting the Major and risked incurring his wrath, but she felt that if he was talking straight then it was time that she did too.

The Major held up a hand and indicated that she should stop talking.

'I was going to qualify myself, but you interrupted. And I can assure you that I am not offended. In fact, I would not have expected a lesser response from you. But please hear me out. I said that you have a *slight* physical constraint. Alice, it is because you yourself do not allow your disability to get in the way of what you want to do, by virtue of this your disability becomes *slighter*. I am not saying that it is not a serious physically limiting disability, but I am saying that you Alice Bridgette Peters do not allow your disability to define you, nor do you allow your disability to impede your innate intelligence, which is what we in *this* government department want. Nay, need.'

'We can train you in military affairs and we can mould you in a way that serves our operational purposes. That is the easy bit. What we cannot teach, or train, is innate intelligence – but we can benefit from it, if you allow us to do so.'

'I am speaking bluntly here Alice. We need analysts like you – yes, you are already a field-proven analyst – who can apply reasoning and thought to events, facts, or evidence. We need someone like you who has already shown an ability to make sound decisions having made delicately balanced judgements. We need people like you with the clear ability to evaluate and make sense of situations that have built over time in either a partial or sporadic way and within which there lurks a threat that only occasionally reveals its presence. And we need people of your proven ability to draw inferences and understand the spatial relationships between concepts, things, or people.'

'Look, we are setting up a counter-espionage unit Alice. The objective of this unit is to flush out more people like Herr Müller and Herr Sommer and any other bad actors operating against Britain that we can identify. We do not know how many more Müllers or Sommers there are out there, nor do we yet know the extent or depth of the Abwehr's pre-war investment strategy. And there are many other domestic intelligence matters that we must get to the bottom of. What we're asking – what I am asking – is would you please consider joining us?'

Alice allowed silence to fall on the room before answering.

'You are asking a lot of a mere Canteen Assistant, Major. Whatever I might be minded doing, I must factor in the needs of others too, such as my family. So, I cannot decide here and now.'

'But you still have not said no,' he again proffered.

'That is quite correct, Major Richardson. I have not said no, and, um ... I am humbled that you have approached and invited me in the manner you have.'

Major Richardson's body visibly relaxed and he leaned by into his seat.

'Well then, I quite understand your desire to talk things through with your family ... or significant others. I did not for a moment anticipate that you would give me a reply today.

All I would ask is that you are circumspect with what you discuss about all this – and with whom. Please do not discuss any details of our work with anyone not cleared to do so. I suggest to most people you just say that a War Office position has arisen that a friend has put you forward for and that you are considering it – if that is what you would like to do.'

'Understood Major.' Then Alice plucked up courage. 'May I be permitted to discuss the details of our conversation with Ray, um, Ray Thomas?'

The Major smiled. 'I think that would be strictly forbidden Alice … but only if we knew about it.'

Alice smiled back. 'How long do I have to get back to you with my decision?'

'Let's say a week?'

'Thank you Major.'

Major Richardson stood up and held out his hand, which she shook. 'Thank you for everything over the past few weeks – and for giving me time for this chat.'

The Major picked up his phone, '3.19 here. Can I please have an escort for one down to the staff car booked for KX. Thank you.'

After replacing the receiver, he addressed Alice. 'In a couple of minutes, someone will take you down to the car which will drive you back to King's Cross.'

Almost immediately there was a knock on his door and a young secretary opened it and stood waiting smiling while Alice was given her coat back and gathered her things ready to leave.

Alice held her hand out to the Major again. She looked at him earnestly, 'À bientôt Major. And thank you ... in more ways than you could ever imagine.'

He smiled back at her, holding her hand and her gaze, 'Don't thank me Alice, you have more than earned your spurs.'

He held his office door open for her to pass. 'By the way,' he impishly tossed into the air, 'I have always preferred the phrase à bientôt over au revoir, haven't you?'

Alice had started to walk down the corridor away from his office. She flicked him a smile and giggled. 'Good try Major!'

Major Richardson chuckled.

But they both knew they would meet again.

Alice-from-the Canteen was escorted back down to the ground floor in the lift. The secretary led her to the front door which she opened for her. She then moved past her as Alice crossed the basement void carefully navigating the steps and stood with the car door open.

Alice thanked her and manoeuvred herself into the rear driver side seat. The secretary then said goodbye and shut the car door.

She was suddenly aware of not being alone in the back seat and turned in total shock to see Ray seated beside her, grinning.

'I got the London train after yours this morning ... and by weird twist of fate, goodness know how, I have just discovered that we have the same train back.'

Alice slapped his shoulder playfully.

Author's Notes

General activities in the locality

Between 1940 and 1945 and within approximately 10 miles of Shrewsbury, there were at least 16 Royal Observer Corps watch stations, 8 RAF air stations, 5 US air stations, 10 German PoW camps, 8 Italian PoW camps, 3 major armament depots, a major allied fuel pumping station, a major HF, LF and VLF radio transmitter and radio intercept station and an Army listening station.

This might have been a target-rich environment for intelligence gathering, or attack by the Luftwaffe, had Germany known what was going on in the vicinity at the time.

RAF activities

From early on in the war air stations in the region provided a range of differing activities, such as supplying basic flying training, delivering operational and conversion training, hosting operational squadrons, establishing special operations training facilities (e.g. for Horsa special operations glider training), serving aircraft storage and maintenance requirements, and providing relief and standby airfield runway capacity should airfields elsewhere become unserviceable or be needed for additional launch capabilities.

Training aircrews, from basic flying training to preparing young pilots for operational squadrons and giving them basic navigation, cross-country navigation, bombing and radio training skills, was principally carried out by RAF Shawbury.

Meanwhile Operational Training Unit squadrons involving varying aircraft type were established at different airfields, provided the space and time for crews to hone their flight and tactical skills for their aircraft types. 61 OTU was based at RAF Rednal and involved Spitfire training and, later in the war, Mustang III training. RAF Ternhill provided flying training for No 93 Group Bomber Command. RAF Tilstock was not an operational airfield until August 1942, but for most of the rest of the war served the operational training needs of Whitley and Wellington bomber crews and later hosted a Heavy Conversion Unit for crews converting to Sterling and Halifax aircraft.

RAF Atcham was No 9 Group Section Station for controlling No.74 Squadron, No.131 Squadron, No.232 Squadron and No.350 Squadron, all Spitfire squadrons.

- RAF High Ercall was very much an operational air station and hosted No.68

Squadron which comprised Bristol Blenheims (and later, by May 1941, Beaufighters) that delivered a vital night-time air defence role using the RDF-2A airborne radar system. The airfield was also used by No.255 Squadron (Beaufighters) and No.257 Squadron (Typhoons) and by 1456 Flight (Bostons, Havocs) in the same operational capacity:

- From July 1941 No.68 Squadron had a strong Czechoslovak aircrew in exile element.
- At least eight crews were made up entirely of Czechs.

Radar developments

In 1939 Britain had a rudimentary radar system functioning called RDF (Range and Direction Finding). By 1940 the RAF had fully integrated RDF as part of the national air defence.

- Although Britain knew where the inbound Luftwaffe were using RDF, the Germans had realised that unless air defence fighters made visual contact, they could still operate effectively at night and in poor meteorological visibility.
- In direct consequence a miniature RDF system was developed and by 1939 an AI radar (Airborne Interception Radar) was deployed on Bristol Blenheim aircraft (and later, on Bristol Beaufighters). The first

version was designated RDF-1 and the later AI version was designated RDF-2A.

- The introduction of the AI system increased Luftwaffe losses. This was achieved not only by enabling the airborne platform to locate and prosecute its own targets, but also by, in collaborative escort of a flight of night fighters, to illuminate the enemy bombers with a searchlight, enabling the fighters then to attack the illuminated aircraft (e.g. as commonly performed by Douglas Havocs and Bostons).

- In time RDF systems were installed on several fighter aircraft, eventually negating the need for escorted sorties to illuminate targets.

- During the war Britain established the Telecommunications Research Establishment in south Dorset near to Worth Maltravers:

- In later post-war years it relocated to Malvern and became the most significant part of the Defence Research Agency (DRA).

- Prime Minister Sir John Major sold off the DRA. Many commentators consider it to have been seriously undersold and that highly valuable UK defence-related intellectual property was gifted to the US government via a rushed privatisation deal involving the US private equity firm Carlyle Group, which had deep US defence and security interests.

- Shortly afterwards, after leaving Parliament, Sir John Major became Carlyle Group's first UK Chairman.
- The erstwhile DRA currently trades as QinetQ plc.

Theatres and picture houses

During the war, the government funded theatres and companies on the home front through its Council for Encouragement of Music and the Arts (CEMA). *(For the record, government funding for ENSA -Entertainments National Services Association- was entirely separate and was directed towards entertaining the armed forces only)*

- CEMA, established in January 1940, was perceived to have a vital role in delivering education and propaganda.
- The government recognised how important it was to foster and maintain national culture as a vital constituent of the national soul when times were dark and foreboding.
- At the outbreak of hostilities in September 1939 theatres had temporarily been closed as a safety precaution, but, over time, the situation had reverted, not just because the government wanted something distract people from the constant burden of war, but because it knew that the war itself was an ideological battle as much as a physical fight for territory – and that

300

Britain needed to fight for its cultural heritage too and be uplifted, educated and bonded by a sense of pitting its history and civilisation against that of Nazi barbarism. Consequently, theatres were perceived as a means of distracting a public weary of the war effort and were used to imprint British ideologies on audiences and contrast them with everything to do with Nazi Germany

- Such was the interest of the government in the value of arts funding as a propaganda tool that by March 1942 the government had even secured direct state intervention in the arts by signing into defence regulations a provision that permitted the Home Secretary to *prohibit or restrict* performances if they were detrimental to the war effort.

- CEMA funding supported amateur and professional companies and helped to bring classical music (e.g. chamber music or symphonies), opera, ballet, and drama (especially Shakespeare, as the very definition of national heritage and given that his plays provided useful tools for pressing home desired political messaging) to urban and rural areas alike, from theatres to works canteens.

- Professional companies like Sadlers Wells Ballet, Ballet Rambert and the Old Vic frequently toured the country. Through CEMA, the government sought to fund the professional companies and associate itself with the cult of celebrity, actively supporting artists (notably from Ministry of Information propaganda budgets) who were supporting the war effort without any personal financial gain.

- Gang Shows emanated from the establishment of the Department of Air Force Welfare. Under the supervisions of Ralph Reader, who had established the 1930s Boy Scout Gang Shows, the shows were intended to boost morale and provide RAF High Command with feedback on the morale of the service. The objective was to run many touring shows and recruit men from the lower ranks who were not aircrew and who did not have an engineering expertise or other skills vital to the war effort.

The Abwehr and Abwehrstelle operations

- The Abwehr started life as a department within the armed forces but in 1938 was reorganised to become significantly more independent.
- The Abwehr was responsible for collecting foreign intelligence, sabotage, and counter-intelligence.
- Throughout his tenure as head of the Abwehr, commencing in 1935, Admiral Wilhelm Canaris fought a battle with Heinrich Himmler of the SS and Reinhard Heydrich of the SD, both of whom who sought control of all German intelligence organisations. Admiral Canaris was very

wary of the Nazi Party and in fact, throughout the war, secretly worked against Hitler and impeded the expansionist and political aspirations of his regime. Admiral Canaris was eventually executed, but not before he had successfully stalled or prevented many plans from becoming realities.

- Instructions from Berlin tasking covert Abwehr cells relied upon encrypted radio transmission broadcasts if agents could not be physically passed written face-to-face instructions.

- One catch was that field agents needed to be listening for the broadcasts at predesignated times of day, either to catch the original transmission or its cycled repeat if they had been unable to energise their radio sets earlier on. But doing so risked them being discovered using their covert radio equipment and inexplicably being absent from general life whenever they operated the equipment.

- Another catch was that field agents had to transmit their encrypted messages in as much detail, but in as short a time as possible, to avoid counter-detection.

- One of the biggest problems for the Abwehr was that, while some field operators were effective foreign agents, there simply were just not enough of them to cover the ground and give the German leadership the real-time intelligence insights that it needed.

Rudolf Hess

- Rudolf Walter Richard Hess was the appointed Deputy Führer in 1933.
- On Saturday 19th May 1941 Hess flew solo to Eaglesham in Scotland where his Messerschmitt crash landed.
- Hess few over to visit the Duke of Sutherland, allegedly, to attempt to broker a peace treaty that would give Europe to the Germans in exchange, to the British, for territories held by Germany elsewhere in the world.
- In May 1941 when Hess arrived, Douglas Douglas-Hamilton, the Duke of Sutherland, was an RAF Wing Commander (shortly to be promoted to Group Captain) and was responsible for the aerial defence of Southern Scotland and Northern England.
- As soon as Hess came into the Duke's custody it is reported that he handed him in and then flew south to brief Prime Minister Winston Churchill in person.
- Three days after Hess crash landed, on Tuesday 13th May 1941, it was announced to the public on the BBC that Rudolf Hess was in custody in the UK.
- Rudolf Hess was then held in custody for the rest of his life, eventually dying in Spandau Prison in 1987 (as its only prisoner) following a hanging incident.
- While this fictional story hints that Hess was rendered south via a high security bunker at RAF High Ercall, there is no

truth in this. It is also pure fiction that the Abwehr ever signalled their British *Abwehrstelles* to try to locate and repatriate Hess. If any signal had been sent for them to locate him, they would more than likely have included an assassination order (unless he had flown to negotiate peace with Hitler's blessing – something both men took to their graves).

Nazi sleeper cells

MI5 files released in 2011 suggested that the Nazis had planned a 'Fourth Reich' in post-war Europe with the aim of funding sleep cells with which to destabilise governments:

- In April 1945, a French Collaborator had allegedly attended a Munich conference describing how funds had already been deposited in Argentina to finance the sleeper cells in the future.
- The conference claimed that so-called "bankers", responsible for the distribution of the money, had been embedded in Spain and Switzerland and would provide funds to national movements that would create unrest and civil war. The aim was to cause problems to the Allies and to give the Nazi party time to rebuild and reappear and build a fourth Reich. It was envisaged that the funds would support planning, strategy, and propaganda work.

- This German collaborator was French and was paid monthly cash by the German Abwehr.
- He was a former architect who designed warehouses and then worked for a company specialising in theatre acoustics.
- It was stated that he also had contact with nationalist movements in Ireland, Cornwall, Wales, and Scotland.

Pertrix

Pertrix 679L was one of a series of portable torches manufactured by the Pertrix Company for the Wehrmacht:

- The torches underwent design evolution over time from a basic light and coloured filter in the 1930s to coloured filters and stealth sliders by the mid-1940s.
- Battery production was a major wartime activity for Pertrix e.g. it made igniter batteries for the Luftwaffe.
- It also made dry cell batteries (e.g. the Diamon brand).
- The Diamon 4.5-volt battery carried a Morse Code '*morsetafel*' decoder on the back when it was not displaying the German eagle.
- It is alleged that during the war Pertrix employed forced labour ranging from Berlin Jews to prisoner of war, internees and concentration camp prisoners from Eastern Europe and Poland.

- As of January 2021 the company still exists and is currently a subsidiary of the Quandt Group Company AFA, owners of BMW and much else besides.

Local armament depots

The Shropshire and Montgomeryshire Light Railway was commandeered by the War Office in 1941 to create the Central Ammunition Depot at Nesscliffe. Royal Engineers built additional service tracks along a nine-mile length between Maesbrook and Crossgate on the River Severn.

There were three major armament depots in the area CAD Nesscliffe, COD Donnington and RNAD Ditton Priors:

Central Ammunition Depot Nesscliffe comprised four sub-site sites capable of storing 55,000 tons of shells. Incendiary and chemical weapons were also stored locally at Loton Park.

Ordnance from Woolwich Arsenal, which was at risk from aerial bombing over London, was moved to Central Ordnance Depot Donnington

Royal Naval Armament Depot Ditton Priors was established in 1939, storing naval mines and other maritime ordnance supplies.

Transmission/Reception/Intercept/Direction -Finding radio stations

The Criggion Radio Station was principally established to provide Britain with an (HF) High

Frequency (3MHz – 30MHz), (LF) Low Frequency (30kHz – 300MHz) and (VLF) Very Low Frequency (3Hz – 30kHz) radio transmission capability to ground stations, submarines, surface ships and aircraft:

- The first HF transmitter was commissioned into operation in 1942 with more HF transmitters following during the war years. This frequency was vital for communicating with naval military forces (surface ships and submarines operating at shallow depth or in surface transit) and with merchant fleets, convoys, and aircraft.
- By early 1943 a new VLF transmitter was installed and was being tested to provide a standby transmission capability should Britain's primary site at Rugby suffer damage from Luftwaffe raids on Coventry and Birmingham.
- Criggion's VLF transmitter function continued for decades after the war.

It is believed that Criggion also had a role intercepting foreign wireless signals being transmitted primarily in the HF spectrum. Intercepts were then passed on to Bletchley Park for decoding and analysis.

This would have included intercepts of voice, morse and data transmissions being transmitted by land-based stations, submarines, surface ships and aircraft.

- The Abwehr covert agent network typically transmitted at or close to the 3MHz – 8 MHz frequency spectrum (e.g. SE

98/3 radio set) using encrypted Morse Code.

- Although the radio sets employed by the covert agent network were low-powered (the SE 98/3 covert radio set delivered only 3 Watts of power compared to fixed transmitters stations like Criggion that transmitted using far higher 40kW power outputs), with sensitive receivers and known transmission frequencies and known broadcast times, receiving stations (and intercept stations) were able to capture the transmissions of some of the weakest radio signals.

In the north of the region, in Whitchurch, there was an HF Direction-Finding Y-Service listening station run by the Foreign Office.

This station comprised one of 50 UK-based Y-Stations that channelled information to Station X, Bletchley Park.

Worldwide there were roughly 600 Y-stations, both ashore and afloat variously operated by the Foreign Office, Navy, Army, RAF, General Post Office, and the Marconi Company.

PLUTO Pipeline Under the Ocean

A Pipeline Under the Ocean (PLUTO) pumping station was located just outside Market Drayton, less than a mile from the Tern Hill junction (mentioned in the story):

- The PLUTO oil pipeline played a vital role in the liberation of Europe in 1944. It ran from the Ellesmere Port oil refinery on the Mersey River to Fawley, near Southampton in Hampshire, then on to Shanklin on the Isle of Wight and then finally across The Channel to Cherbourg in France.

- The pipeline was constructed to deliver fuel to Allied Forces after D-Day.
- The pumping station at Fordhall Farm, close to Market Drayton, provided a vital link in the PLUTO system, and without which liberation of Europe could have been seriously compromised if there had been a need to move fuel to Allied Forces in different ways.

PoW camps

During WW2, either across the whole period or at some point during the war Shropshire had 18 PoW or internment camps in it.

The camps typically accommodated German or Italian prisoners.

Escapes from the PoW camps were not unusual.

Sorbian language

Sorbian is a minority language in the Lausitz area of eastern Germany in Lausatia, south-east of Dresden, bordering the Czech and Polish borders.

The West Slavic language used to be more widely spoken in Germany and was spoken as far north as Berlin and across Saxony and Brandenburg, but over many generations the number of bilingual people has shrunk. In the 21st Century today, only 1% of Lausatian inhabitants still speak the language.

It is understood by Poles and Czechs but is not understood by many Germans.

About the Author

Now semi-retired, Guy initially served in the Royal Navy for a decade, before moving into industry for a time. For the next thirty years he worked in the investment and risk analysis sector. He has spent the last four years devising and delivering self-employment training for offenders transitioning out of the criminal justice system.

Although he has written other stories - and is currently in the process of writing new tales - *Transients* is his first novel to be published.

https://www.qtankpress.co.uk/

Printed in Dunstable, United Kingdom